𝕭eowulf

In Parallel Texts

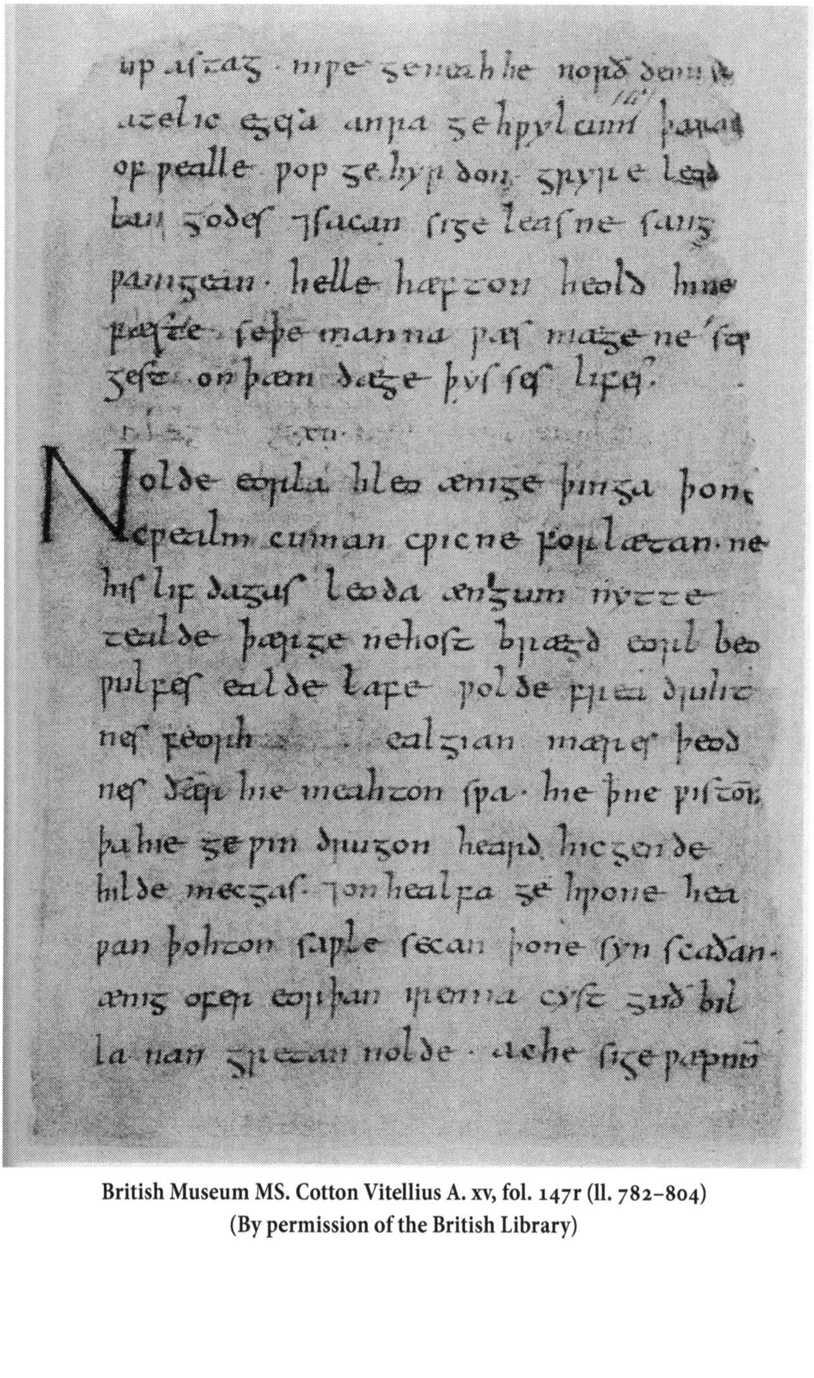

Beowulf

In Parallel Texts

Translated with Textual
and Explanatory Notes by

Sung-Il Lee

With a Foreword by
Robert D. Stevick

 CASCADE *Books* · Eugene, Oregon

BEOWULF IN PARALLEL TEXTS
Translated, with Textual and Explanatory Notes

Cascade Books
An Imprint of Wipf and Stock Publishers
199 W. 8th Ave., Suite 3
Eugene, OR 97401

www.wipfandstock.com

PAPERBACK ISBN: 978-1-5326-1017-2
HARDCOVER ISBN: 978-1-5326-1019-6
EBOOK ISBN: 978-1-5326-1018-9

Cataloguing-in-Publication data:

Names: Lee, Sung-Il. | foreword by Stevick, Robert D. (Robert David), 1928–

Title: Beowulf in parallel texts : translated, with textual and explanatory notes / Sung-Il Lee, with a foreword by Robert D. Stevick.

Description: Eugene, OR: Cascade Books, 2017 | Includes bibliographical references and index.

Identifiers: ISBN 978-1-5326-1017-2 | ISBN 978-1-5326-1019-6 (hardcover) | ISBN 978-1-5326-1018-9 (ebook)

Subjects: LCSH: Beowulf | Monsters—Poetry | Dragons—Poetry | English poetry—Old English, ca. 450–1100 | Grendel (Monster)—Poetry | Epic poetry, English (Old)—History and criticism.

Classification: PR1585 L36 2017 (print) | PR1585 (ebook)

Manufactured in the U.S.A.   JULY 19, 2017

In memory of my father,
Professor Insoo Lee
(1916–50),
who read *Beowulf* at UCL

Contents

Foreword

Why read this translation of *Beowulf*? Because there isn't a better one to be found. Here are the reasons I say this:

It reads so well aloud. The text did so in its oldest form, and it must do so in any translation worth reading. This translation from Old English is oral composition, first heard, and then written down to be heard again. Nothing gets in the way of oral performance of an account of heroic actions, in heroic times, shaped and tempered by wisdom of the world and reflections upon the upshot of human endeavors. It is that performance that is the poem, and it is that which the translation manages so well to give us anew, in Modern English verse.

Nothing gets in the way. The commonest impediments to successful translation have been theories of this and that, High Principles to be upheld, or just romantic notions about "olde tyme" English poetry. Sometimes it is a choice to imitate the general sound of the original text—two half-lines separated by syntax but linked by alliteration. The one successful instance came many, many years ago from Charles W. Kennedy, but even this text tends to accelerate unfittingly as the rhythm continues unrelenting. Sometimes it is a decision to imitate the blank verse of the Renaissance. Sometimes it may be choice of a verse-form such as nine-syllable lines defended by reasoning rather than readability. Sung-Il Lee's translation is not trammeled in any ways like these. The syllable-count is unpredictable: it is instead the phrasings that embody the verse rhythms.

It is not merely the metrical basis of the translation that has to be right. The syntax must be right at the same time. This means simply: the flow of phrase by phrase within the clauses and sentences must move steadily and never stumble, never create a tangle that a reader has to pause and undo. Such is hard enough to manage under any circumstances, but it is often

neglected—or despaired of—in translating Old English verse, chiefly be-
cause of the prominence of "variation," "the very soul of the Old English
poetical style," as Frederick Klaeber expressed it. When a sentence-part gets
re-expressed, and sometimes re-expressed again, and sometimes yet again,
a sentence may move haltingly once it leaves the metrics of Old English
style: "I wish to announce to the son of Halfdane, the glorious prince, my
business here, to thy lord" (344–46a) is a piecemeal translation patterned
on the original text. Translating verse-by-verse, half-line-by-half-line when
possible, can't keep the sentences going aright in Modern English. Sung-Il
Lee's resolution of these problems is successful consistently: the variations are
not discarded, but re-folded into patterns that keep the text moving forward.
Typically at least one of them is delayed—just as the *Beowulf*-poet always
does—so that with its occurrence the syntax requires a hearer to loop back
(mentally) to the syntactic slot of a prior variant, to a tacit experience yet
again of the accumulated syntactic structure. It's a marvelous device for regu-
lating the pace of the narrative, the reading, the telling, to keep it ruminative
rather than fit only for a pell-mell tale of adventure and monster bashing.

There is something similar, though it is actually an innovation, in the
repetition of a small sentence part, after a delay, which triggers reflective
replay of the related portion of a sentence. It, too, controls the pace of the
poem. In 930–31 it is simply "may," or in 2158–59 "had"; in 2124–25 it is
merely "could not."

Also regarding pace and continuity—cohesion, in fact—of the mix
of a "main" narrative, reflections, "episodes," and "digressions": in reading
this translation I had a sense of the sweep and cohesion of the source text
that I have not found in other translations. The way in which the section
divisions come and go is also impressive (and incidentally highlights the
independence of section divisions from "natural" divisions of the poem).
Similarly, in local passages, say, 1292–1311, the pace is never compromised
as the topics shift here and there within the large memory that the whole
poem embodies.

The meter and the syntax—the flow of sounds and the flow of sen-
tence-parts—can be right, and there is still the matter of the words we hear,
in the translation. Imitation of the original text by trying to mimic it is a
temptation to many, but always leads to inferior translations. Without an
exception a compound noun or adjective in the original text is right and
powerful, but enigmatic or awkward if rendered piecemeal in the lexicon
of Modern English. Here is where a translator's tact—not theory—has to be

active, and his word-sense entirely in tune with the poetic texture. Unferth is going to challenge the hero in front of everyone; he *onband beadu-rūne* (501), which says he "unbound" his "battle-rune," according to glossing conventions, obscure enough that Klaeber paraphrases it as "commenced fight." Lee's rendering: he spoke, "Revealing his revulsion." A group of warriors who *hrēa-wīc hēoldon* (1214), "held a place of corpses" in the basic glossary reading, reads "Kept the place filled with bodies," conveying the sense exactly without the opacity of glossary-transplants. At 2999–3000 there is a stack of compounds in variation which would be grotesque in word-by-word translation; so we get "That is the malevolence and the mutual malice, /The deadly hate between men . . . ." The most affective word choice perhaps is one of the simplest and most obvious: "the old (one)"—for *þām gomelan* (2817) and *se gomela* (2851)—is accurate, but empty of both force and feeling. When it is read out as "the old man" (and not just once) for Beowulf in his defeat and death from his fight with and defeat of the fire-dragon, it is evocative of the grief of Beowulf's lifelong companions, and of the listeners to this poem: "The old man."

These right renderings of the text are found at every turn: *heortan wylmas* (2507) becomes "his pulsating heart"; *līce gelenge* (2732) makes good sense as "with fleshly legacy"; *mæl-gesceafta* (2737) is caught just right with "the dictum of destiny." A notoriously dense and complex passage of kennings and variations describing the funeral-fire for the hero is rendered faithfully and most effectively this way:

> Wood-smoke arose,
> Black over the fire; the roaring flame bellowed,
> Mingling with the weeping—the twirling wind died out—
> Till it had burnt down the bone-wrapping body-flesh,
> Hot in its heart. With their souls soaked in sadness,
> They mourned the death of their lord, deep in their hearts.
>
> (3144b–3149)

The choice of words is always true to the text being translated, and always belongs to the active literary language of Modern English. There just aren't any convenient calques, bland approximations, or mere glossary insertions. From the past four-hundred years of language of literature in English it draws extensively, but without any sign (or smell) of "olde tyme" diction. The words are chosen from a heritage of current English. And each one seems (and smells) like a careful choice by a connoisseur of English literary composition. Any number of times I reached for my Modern English dictionaries, both British and American, to check on the semantic range and the etymology of various words in the translation, and never found a flaw with an unexpected choice: "turbid" for *gedrēfed* (1417), for example, or "woven link by link by hand" for *hondum gebrōden* (1443), or "palanquin" for *bær* (3105).

Having said these things about the ways of translating, a brief observation should be made about the competence of the translator. Any translator must face choices among the possible meanings of any part of the source text, in light of the debates and arguments among scholars and, ultimately, his own sense of the text itself. (Never mind that two of the very popular "translations" in the past forty-some years were versifications of translations done initially by others.) It is clear that Dr. Lee has read extensively in the editorial discussions, and his text shows a successful series of choices among the ambiguities and cruces, let alone the obscurities of the original text of *Beowulf*—the blow-by-blow action of the Beowulf-Grendel wrestling match (745–61), for example; or the theft from the dragon's hoard (2216–31).

Forty-five years since I began leading others through the labyrinth of diction, variation, narrative embellishments of *Beowulf*, and reading their translation examinations, and reading most of the published translations; and forty years since I began scrutiny of the spellings and graphotactics system of the sole manuscript text. When I carefully read this new translation line by line, making notes on the many surprising but always interesting locutions, the movement forward was felt all the way through, with even the episodes and digressions (as they are usually regarded) seeming to be at first unproblematic, and then appearing, as they should, as beautiful assets to the action-narrative and its affectivity. In brief, the translation by Dr. Sung-Il Lee succeeded better for an old reader (that I am) than earlier ones have done, and my sense is that it will succeed very well for readers with any degree of less familiarity with the earliest known text. If we still offered seminars on The Art of Translation, this would be a good centerpiece. An old poem here, unimpaired in translation. It is the best we have among the remnants of Anglo-Saxon culture, and in its newer voice.

Robert D. Stevick
University of Washington

Prefatory Note

This volume is meant to serve dual purposes: sharing with the general readers—who may not have been exposed to the old language in which *Beowulf* was composed—the pleasure I have had over the years while reading it, *and* providing the serious students of English language and literature with a translation for them to refer to while they tackle the Old English text.

My memory goes back to my youthful days when I struggled with Frederick Klaeber's *Beowulf* text for the first time, verifying what I could gather from looking up word after word in his Glossary, by referring to E. Talbot Donaldson's prose translation and Edwin Morgan's verse translation. It was an excruciatingly arduous journey of groping over an apparently never-ending misty path. Yet each time I found what I had managed to construe with the help of Klaeber's Glossary to concur with Donaldson's translation or Morgan's, the joy was compensation enough for my toil, which then seemed almost Sisyphean. I hope this volume will turn out, for the students of Old English, comparable to what the translations by Donaldson and Morgan were to me in my youthful days.

No less weighty is the sense of mission I feel toward myself as well as the students of Old English and the general readers. Providing a Modern English verse translation of *Beowulf* that can touch the heartstrings of the readers has ever been a dream of mine. Not for a vainglorious motive. English is an acquired language to me; and I have been a student of English language and literature all my life. Walking out onto the stage to show all I have come to claim as my own is a scary occasion that will tell whether my lifelong dedication has been a worthwhile one. If my lines can please the ears of the English-speaking people and receive an approving nod of the *Beowulf*-scholars, I shall be happy.

Any of the authoritative texts, edited by such scholars as Frederick Klaeber, Elliott Van Kirk Dobbie, and A. J. Wyatt (later revised by R. W. Chambers), can be chosen to be the anchor for translating the epic. But I did not stick to any of the three editions of the *Beowulf* text. Whenever I found any textual discrepancy between them, I turned to Julius Zupitza's transliteration of the Cotton Vitellius Manuscript, in hopes of arriving at a reading that would strike the right note for me as a translator. I must confess that my reading of the original poem, insofar as the textual variants are concerned, has been eclectic.

This volume consists of what common sense asks for in preparing a book of this kind: an Introduction, in which I state what I had in mind in translating the first epic to appear in English literature, my Modern English verse rendition of the poem, and Textual and Explanatory Notes, which I hope will help the students of Old English as they read the work in its original text.

The sole extant manuscript of the poem bears Roman numerals indicating the allocation of *fitts*. Although Elliott Van Kirk Dobbie eliminated these Roman numerals in his edition, I restored them in the text of the original poem as well as in my translation.

Whenever I thought that the reader might need a note, I put an asterisk after a word, a phrase, or a passage in the original text and my translation, so that the reader may refer to the relevant entry in the Textual and Explanatory Notes with the line number or numbers preceding it. I decided to have all the notes put together after the poem—for fear that the sight of a note appearing at the bottom of each page might interrupt the reader's enjoyment of the lines running in an epic sweep.

I am grateful to Professor Robert D. Stevick, a lifelong *Beowulf*-scholar, who read my translation carefully and decided to enrich this volume with his Foreword. I only fear that my work may not quite measure up to the commendatory words his Foreword contains. Grateful acknowledgment is due also to Professor Derek Pearsall, whose comments on particular lines and words in my translation have made me turn my eyes to several parts that needed stylistic improvement. I thank Dr. Robin Parry for reading my typescript carefully and providing a number of helpful suggestions in the final stage of editing. Finally, I wish to express my heartfelt gratitude to Professor J. Harold Ellens, who has given me strong support on the project and recommended this work to Wipf and Stock Publishers to let it have the honor of being on the list of the Cascade Books.

Introduction

Reading *Beowulf* aloud always proves a unique experience: it allows the reader to relive the moments of listening to a minstrel's recitation of the epic and participating in the poetic situation of oral delivery and aural reception. The lapse of ten centuries since the time when the poem was composed and recited is no hindrance to our reliving the moments of the mutual transaction between the vocal performer and the auditor. This realization consolidates our belief that the *Beowulf*-poet must have envisioned the "theatricality" of the poetic situation that the lines he was composing would create while being recited—an awareness of the poem in the making. Every single line reflects the poet's keen awareness of the impact that its sound quality will have on the auditors' imagination. Narration at any given moment thus mandated the poet's full exertion of his verbal power for a maximum effect of striking the right notes in conveying the poetic messages.

The major task of a translator of the poem is thus to make the sound quality of the original lines felt all along in translation—to transfigure it in a modern tongue all the way through. In order to attain that goal, neither providing a word-to-word lexical rendition nor creating new verse for the sake of comfortable reading in a modern tongue will do. Within the confinement set by the verbal rhythm and the sound quality of the original poem, a translator must produce verses acceptable to the ears of the speakers of a modern tongue.

Here are some of the principles that I have tentatively set up in translating *Beowulf*:

i. Since the original text is heavily loaded with alliteration, the translation should reflect its sound quality by containing as much alliteration as possible;

ii. The verse rhythm maintained in the original text, each verse containing on-verse and off-verse, should be reflected in the translation with verses containing *caesurae*;

iii. The translation should be in a colloquial language with idiomatic expressions; it should be in a *live* language—easy to follow, both in aural perception and oral delivery;

iv. The translation should evoke the sense of remoteness both in time and place, but it should be attained through the use of familiar language;

v. The word order and the sentence structure in the original text should be honored; but the text of a translation should sound natural. In other words, the original lines should reverberate in the translation.

Rather than prolonging a discussion on the theory and practice in the translation of *Beowulf* with critical jargon, I will go directly to what I have done, sampling a few passages in my translation, in hopes of having the readers' reception of them attuned to mine.

Beowulf's first adventure is, of course, his encounter with Grendel. The appearance of Grendel in Heorot after Beowulf's arrival at the Danish court, therefore, has to be narrated with a lot of dramatic tension, for it is the first encounter with the monster—not only for the hero of the epic, but for the audience or the reader:

> Com on wanre niht
>
> scriðan sceadugenga.   Sceotend swæfon,
>
> þa þæt hornreced   healdan scoldon,
>
> ealle buton anum.   Þæt wæs yldum cuþ,   705
>
> þæt hie ne moste,   þa Metod nolde,
>
> se scynscaþa under   sceadu bregdan;—
>
> ac he wæccende   wraþum on andan
>
> bad bolgenmod   beadwa geþinges.
>
> Ða com of more   under misthleoþum   710

Grendel gongan,   Godes yrre bær;

mynte se manscaða   manna cynnes

sumne besyrwan   in sele þam hean.

Wod under wolcnum   to þæs þe he winreced,

goldsele gumena   gearwost wisse   715

fættum fahne.   Ne wæs þæt forma sið,

þæt he Hroþgares   ham gesohte;

næfre he on aldordagum   ær ne siþðan

heardran hæle,   healðegnas fand!

Com þa to recede   rinc siðian   720

dreamum bedæled.   Duru sona onarn

fyrbendum fæst,   syþðan he hire folmum æthran;

onbræd þa bealohydig,   ða he gebolgen wæs,

recedes muþan.   Raþe æfter þon

on fagne flor   feond treddode,   725

eode yrremod;   him of eagum stod

ligge gelicost   leoht unfæger.

Geseah he in recede   rinca manige,

swefan sibbegedriht   samod ætgædere,

magorinca heap.   Þa his mod ahlog;   730

mynte þæt he gedælde,   ær þon dæg cwome,

atol aglæca   anra gehwylces

lif wið lice,   þa him alumpen wæs

wistfylle wen.   (ll. 702b–34a)

It is a cliché that there should be correspondence between sound and
sense in poetic lines. This principle of poetic composition is fully actualized
in the above passage. Apart from the fact that the lines are heavily charged
with alliteration, there is a certain sound quality that we can hardly miss.
The resonance of the lingering sound [om], [un], and [um], for instance,
helps to build up a certain atmosphere of ominous eeriness. The repeated
use of the sibilant [s], along with the [sh] sound—

scriðan sceadugenga.   Sceotend swæfon, (line 703);

se scynscaþa   under sceadu bregdan;— (line 707);

mynte se   manscaða manna cynnes

sumne besyrwan   in sele þam hean. (ll. 712–13)—

creates the illusion of hearing the sound of serpentine gliding, or of sens-
ing the gradual approach of foggy mist, though we cannot clearly envi-
sion Grendel with any definite physical shape. The gradual approach of the
monster to Heorot, his tearing the door open in fury, stepping onto the hall
floor, and casting his eyes glaringly on the thanes fast asleep—all this is
narrated in one sweep of breath in the couple of dozen lines (ll. 710–34a)
quoted above. My effort to make my translation reflect what I read in the
above passage has led me to the following rendition:

> Striding in the dark night,
>
> The shadowy stroller came. The warriors were sleeping—
>
> Those who should guard the gabled building—
>
> All of them, except one. It was well known to men 705
>
> That, when the Lord willed it not, the devilish foe
>
> May not draw them beneath the dark shadows.
>
> But watching out for the wretch in wrath,
>
> He waited for the outcome of the fight in fury.
>
> Then from the moor under the misty slopes came 710
>
> Grendel, gradually approaching, bearing God's ire.
>
> The direful destroyer of mankind intended
>
> To take one in his grip in that lofty dwelling.
>
> He advanced beneath the clouds to the wine-hall,
>
> Till he most clearly discerned the golden hall 715
>
> Gleaming with gold plates. Nor was it the first time
>
> For him to seek the home of Hrothgar.
>
> Never in his days of life, neither before nor since,
>
> He found the hall-thanes a harder lot to bear.

Then to the hall the marauder made his way,   720

A stranger to life's joy. The door sprang open,

When his hands gripped the fast-forged bar.

He pulled it open to break the hall-door,

Wrapped up in anger. Then quickly

On the flowery floor the fiend stepped,   725

And walked in, full of anger. In his eyes

Gleamed a flame shooting out an ugly beam.

He saw in the hall many a man of strength,

A band of kinsmen, sleeping together,

A troop of young retainers. Then he exulted   730

At the thought of tearing, before dawn broke,

Each one's life from his body, as the horrid fiend

Intended, his mouth watering in anticipation

Of a lavish feast.

One of the most chilling and startling passages in *Beowulf* appears when Hrothgar depicts the marshland where Grendel and his mother dwell. In retaliation for Beowulf's physical victory in his first encounter with Grendel, the defeated monster's mother makes an assault on Heorot, and Æschere becomes a victim of her vengeful attack of Hrothgar's palace. Grief-stricken by the loss of his beloved thane, Hrothgar asks Beowulf to venture to visit the underwater dwelling of Grendel and his mother in order to eliminate the root of all the evil that has devastated his land.

Hie dygel lond

warigeað wulfheloþu,   windige næssas,

frecne fengelad,   ðær fyrgenstream

under næssa genipu   niþer gewiteð,   1360

flod under foldan.   Nis þæt feor heonon

milgemearces,   þæt se mere standeð;

ofer þæm hongiað   hrinde bearwas,

wudu wyrtum fæst   wæter oferhelmað.

Þær mæg nihta gehwæm   niðwundor seon,   1365

fyr on flode.   Nō þæs frod leofað

gumena bearna,   þæt þone grund wite.

Ðeah þe hæðstapa   hundum geswenced,

heorot hornum trum   holtwudu sece,

feorran geflymed,   ær he feorh seleð,   1370

aldor on ofre,   ær he in wille,

hafelan [hydan];   nis þæt heoru stow!

Þonon yðgeblond   up astigeð

won to wolcnum,   þonne wind styreþ

lað gewidru,   oð þæt lyft drysmaþ,   1375

roderas reotað. (ll. 1357b–76a)

Hrothgar's description of the moorland where Grendel and his mother dwell is a chilling narration that makes any reader of *Beowulf* shudder: the dreadful landscape that the lines invoke is unmatched by any passage that has ever been written to depict a nightmarish scene the human imagination is capable of envisioning. Here is my Modern English rendition of the above passage:

> They inhabit a hidden land—
> Wolf-infested slopes, windy headlands, and
> A perilous fen-path, where the mountain-stream
> Falls down in the mist from the headlands   1360
> And flows beneath the earth. Not far from here,
> A few miles away, stands the mere,
> Over which droop trees covered with frost.
> The wood darkens the water with entangled roots.
> There every night a fearful wonder is seen—   1365
> Fire flaring on the water. None alive among men,
> No matter how wise, knows how deep it is.

Fleeing from far off, chased by hounds, a stag

May seek a holt-wood to hide his strong horns;

Yet he will rather give up his life, lingering   1370

On the bank, than plunge his head into the pool

To save his life; that is not a pleasant place!

From there surging waves rise up,

Darkening the clouds, while the wind swirls,

Threatening storms, till the air turns choking   1375

And the sky howls.

Any student of Old English poetry will face the exhilarating and painful moment of reading the last passage of *Beowulf*. The excruciatingly arduous journey is about to reach its end; and the memory of turning the leaves of the glossary provided by that literary giant, Fr. Klaeber, is about to recede into the past. It is a moment of tremendous relief—entailing a sense of wistfulness and regret over not having to cope with the lines—not for some time, at least. The *Beowulf*-poet must have felt the same way, as he was reaching the end of his epic, the composition of which must have exhausted him, both emotionally and physically. All this is reflected in the lines that conclude the epic. Beowulf, our hero, is no more; and those who have survived him, whether his thanes, or the listeners of the heroic saga, must mourn the passing of the warrior-king into the realm of the remote past and oblivion.

Þa ymbe hlæw riodan   hildedeore,

æþelinga bearn,   ealra twelfe,   3170

woldon care cwiðan,   [ond] kyning mænan,

wordgyd wrecan   ond ymb wer sprecan;

eahtodan eorlscipe   ond his ellenweorc

duguðum demdon,—   swa hit gedefe bið,

þæt mon his winedryhten   wordum herge,   3175

ferhðum frēoge,   þonne he forð scile

of lichaman   læded weorðan.

Swa begnornodon   Geata leode

hlafordes hryre,   heorðgeneatas;

cwædon þæt he wære   wyruldcyninga   3180

manna mildust   ond monðwærust,

leodum liðost   ond lofgeornost. (ll. 3169–82)

When a student of literature encounters lines like these, he or she should feel that the notes one could ever hope to hear at the end of a work have finally hit the eardrums. Here we find the convergence of what we have wished to hear and what we hear—the complete fusion of what the text has been brewing in our hearts and what we finally have attained after reading so many lines! It is a moment of catharsis; and the lines of *Beowulf* are finally loosening their grip on our heartstrings:

Then the battle-brave ones rode round the mound—

Inheritors of noble blood, twelve all told—   3170

Uttering words of grief over loss of their lord

In a mournful dirge to commemorate their king.

They lauded his manliness, and spoke highly of

His brave deeds—as it befits a man

To praise his dear lord in words,   3175

While longing springs in his heart, when he

Is finally freed from the confinement of flesh.

So the people of Geatland mourned the death

Of their lord, recalling the warmth of his hearth.

They said that, of all earthly kings, he was   3180

The gentlest of men, the most warm-hearted,

Kindest to his people, and most eager for fame.

When I was reading the very last passage of *Beowulf,* the above was roughly what I heard in my mind's ear. I would not call it a translation; the above is only an echo of what dug into my heart while I was reading the concluding lines of the epic. Though falling short of the emotional elevation attained by the lines in the original text, the above was the outcome of my desperate attempt to revive in a modern tongue the most magnificent passage literature has ever produced.

Poetry means condensation of verbal expressions of human thoughts and emotions; and it demands not only succinctness but also accuracy in hitting the right notes that capture all the feelings that have to be expressed. When the *Beowulf*-poet wrote that the Geatish warriors had built a monument holding the ashes of their lord on a promontory, so that the sailors could see it from afar, it was an indirect way of expressing the poet's wish that his work would be read and remembered by his posterity for a long time. Here is the convergence of what the actual lines of a poem say and what the creator of the work really wanted to say. As the last lines of the epic fade away with the last twang of the minstrel's harp, both our hero of the epic *Beowulf* and the poet who composed the more-than-three-thousand lines recede into the past—along with the fading out of the minstrel's voice. The last couplet contains a series of superlatives:

manna mildust   ond monðwærust,

leodum liðost   ond lofgeornost. (ll. 3181–82)

The emphatic use of the superlatives notwithstanding, the repeatedly heard sound [st] somehow leaves the lingering note of wistfulness over the poem that has reached its end. The epic opened with the powerful and fully inflated ejaculation, "Hwæt!" Now the very last lines create the feeling that the air is being released from an inflated ball. With the four adjectives in the superlative, carrying with them the tired minstrel's hoarse voice, the poet himself steps back into the past, as does the hero of the epic.

Translation means reliving the moments when the poet was composing the lines. It is not a later-age person's attempt to record what he or she has understood while reading the original lines for the readers. As a translator's pen glides on a blank sheet, it should be a moment that resurrects the agony that the poet embraced, while groping for the right words, line after line.

Beowulf

In Parallel Texts

Hwæt! We Gar-dena   in gear-dagum,
þeodcyninga,   þrym gefrunon,
hu ða æþelingas   ellen fremedon.

   Oft Scyld Scefing   sceaþena þreatum,
monegum mægþum   meodosetla ofteah,   5
egsode eorlas.   Syððan ærest weartð
feasceaft funden,   he þæs frofre gebad,
weox under wolcnum,   weorðmyndum þah,
oð þæt him æghwylc   þara ymbsittendra
ofer hronrade   hyran scolde,   10
gomban gyldan.   Þæt wæs god cyning!
Ðæm eafera wæs   æfter cenned
geong in geardum,   þone God sende
folce to frofre;   fyrenðearfe ongeat,
þe* hie ær drugon   aldorlease   15
lange hwile;   him þæs Liffrea,
wuldres Wealdend,   worold-are forgeaf;
Beowulf* wæs breme   —blæd wide sprang—
Scyldes eafera   Scedelandum in.
Swa sceal geong guma   gode gewyrcean,   20
fromum feohgiftum   on fæder bearme,
þæt hine on ylde   eft gewunigen
wilgesiþas,   þonne wig cume,
leode gelæsten;   lofdædum sceal
in mægþa gehwære   man geþeon.   25

   Him ða Scyld gewat   to gescæphwile
felahror feran   on Frean wære.
Hi hyne þa ætbæron   to brimes faroðe,

What! We have heard of the glory
Of the Spear-Danes' kings in olden days—
How those princes performed deeds of valor.

    Not a few times Scyld Scefing seized
The seats of banquet from many a tribe,   5
Mighty opponents, and terrified the earls.
Since the time when he was found a deserted infant,
He grew up in tender care, soared to the sky,*
And prospered with unparalleled honor, till
All neighboring nations over the sea came   10
To obey and pay tribute to him: a good king he was!
To him a son was born later—a toddler
In his large dwelling, whom God sent
To comfort the nation. He saw the dire distress
Of those who had long suffered without a lord   15
To rule them; in that cause, the Lord of life,
The Ruler of glory granted him worldly honor.
Beow* attained renown—his name spread wide—
The son of Scyld, all over the land of the Danes.
Such is what a young man, while in his father's protection,   20
Must do, through manly acts and bounteous bestowing,
To secure the blessing in old age of having
Close kinsmen and loyal subjects to stay near
In times of war; of whatever clan, a man
Is bound to prosper through praiseworthy deeds.   25

    Then at his destined hour Scyld the strongman departed,
Embarking on a journey to the bosom of the Lord.
Then his dear followers carried him to where

swæse gesiþas,   swa he selfa bæd,

þenden wordum weold   wine Scyldinga;   30

leof landfruma   lange ahte.

Þær æt hyðe stod   hringedstefna,

isig ond utfus,   æþelinges fær;

aledon þa   leofne þeoden,

beaga bryttan   on bearm scipes,   35

mærne be mæste.   Þær wæs madma fela

of feorwegum   frætwa gelæded;

ne hyrde ic cymlicor   ceol gegyrwan

hildewæpnum   ond heaðowædum,

billum ond byrnum;   him on bearme læg   40

madma mænigo,   þa him mid scoldon

on flodes æht   feor gewitan.

Nalæs hi hine læssan   lacum teodan,

þeodgestreonum,   þon þa dydon,

þe hine æt frumsceafte   forð onsendon   45

ænne ofer yðe   umborwesende.

Þa gyt hie him asetton   segen g[yl]denne

heah ofer heafod,   leton holm beran,

geafon on garsecg;   him wæs geomor sefa,

murdnende mod.   Men ne cunnon   50

secgan to soðe,   selerædende,

hæleð under heofenum,   hwa þæm hlæste onfeng.

(I) Ða wæs on burgum   Beowulf Scyldinga,

leof leodcyning   longe þrage

folcum gefræge   —fæder ellor hwearf,   55

aldor of earde—,   oþ þæt him eft onwoc

heah Healfdene;   heold þenden lifde,

gamol ond guðreouw,   glæde Scyldingas.

4

The waves surge, as he himself had bidden,

When the lord of the Danes ruled with his words.   30

He had kept them long as their dear lord.

There at the harbor stood the ring-prowed ship,

The prince's vessel, covered with ice and ready to set out.

Then they laid down their dear lord,

Their renowned ring-giver, in the bosom of the ship,   35

Right by the mast. Many a treasure had been

Brought there, precious things from faraway places.

I have not heard of a ship more grandly adorned

With weapons and battle-gear,

With bills and coats of mail; on his breast lay   40

Many a treasure, which was bound to go

Far with him, drifting on the powerful waves.

They no less lavishly provided him with gifts,

People's treasures, than those who did

At the outset let him float down alone   45

As a child, drifting on the turbulent waves.

To boot, they set up a golden banner for him,

High over his head, let the sea bear it,

Gave it to the ocean; for them sadness welled in hearts,

Grief overflowed the hearts' brim. Men cannot   50

Tell truly—hall-thanes or field-warriors—

Who received the cargo beneath the sky.

(I) Then in the castle Beow of the Danes, dear

Prince of the people, long remained renowned

Among nations—his father and lord having gone elsewhere,   55

Away from his earthly dwelling—till for them again

Rose high Healfdene, who, aged and fierce in battle,

Ruled the glorious Danes while he lived.

Ðæm feower bearn   forð gerimed
in worold wocun, weoroda ræswa[n],   60
Heorogar ond Hroðgar   ond Halga til;
hyrde ic þæt [. . . .]   wæs Onelan cwen,
Heaðo-Scilfingas   healsgebedda.

    Þa wæs Hroðgare   heresped gyfen,
wiges weorðmynd,   þæt him his winemagas   65
georne hyrdon,   oðð þæt seo geogoð geweox,
magodriht micel.   Him on mod bearn,
þæt healreced   hatan wolde,
medoærn micel,   men gewyrcean
þonne yldo bearn   æfre gefrunon,   70
ond þær on innan   eall gedælan
geongum ond ealdum,   swylc him God sealde,
buton folcscare   ond feorum gumena.
Ða ic wide gefrægn   weorc gebannan
manigre mægþe   geond þisne middangeard,   75
folcstede frætwan.   Him on fyrste gelomp,
ædre mid yldum,   þæt hit wearð ealgearo,
healærna mæst;   scop him Heort naman
se þe his wordes geweald   wide hæfde.
He beot ne aleh,   beagas dælde,   80
sinc æt symle.   Sele hlifade
heah ond horngeap;   heaðowylma bad,
laðan liges;   ne wæs hit lenge þa gen,
þæt se ecghete   aþumswerian*
æfter wæl-niðe   wæcnan scolde.   85

    Ða se ellengæst   earfoðlice
þrage geþolode,   se þe in þystrum bad,
þæt he dogora gehwam   dream gehyrde

6

To him four children all told were born
In the world, to the leader of the bands: 60
Heorogar and Hrothgar and good Halga;
I have heard that . . . was Onela's queen,
Dear bed-sharer of the Heatho-Scilfing.*
    Then to Hrothgar was granted success in battles,
Warlike glory, so that his friendly kinsmen obeyed him   65
With all their hearts—till the youth grew to command
A great band of retainers. It came into his mind
That he would give out the order that men build
A pavilion, the greatest mead-hall that
The sons of men had ever heard of,   70
And therein distribute to the young and the old
All the possession that God had given him—
Except public property and people's lives.
Then, I have heard, it was widely bidden
That many a clan throughout the world   75
Partake in building the folk-stead. It came to pass in time,
Forthwith among men, that it became quite ready,
The greatest of halls. He named it Heorot,
He who had the power to make his words widely listened to.
He did not fail to keep his promise to dispense rings,   80
Treasure at feast; the hall towered,
High and wide-gabled: it waited for the hostile flames
Of a dreadful fire; it was by no means time yet
That hostility between a son-in-law and his father-in-law
Came to rise after a deadly feud.*   85
    Then the powerful demon could hardly endure
Distress—he who dwelt in darkness—
That he heard loud merrymaking every day,

hludne in healle; þær wæs hearpan sweg,

swutol sang scopes. Sægde se þe cuþe   90

frumsceaft fira feorran reccan,

cwæð þæt se Ælmihtiga eorðan worh[te],

wlite-beorhtne wang, swa wæter bebugeð,

gesette sigehreþig sunnan ond monan

leoman to leohte landbuendum,   95

ond gefrætwade foldan sceatas

leomum ond leafum, life eac gesceop

cynna gehwylcum þara ðe cwice hwyrfaþ.

Swa ða drihtguman dreamum lifdon

eadiglice, oð ðæt an ongan   100

fyrene fre[m]man feond on helle;

wæs se grimma gæst Grendel haten,

mære mearcstapa, se þe moras heold,

fen ond fæsten; fifelcynnes eard

wonsæli wer weardode hwile,   105

siþðan him Scyppend forscrifen hæfde

in Caines cynne— þone cwealm gewræc

ece Drihten, þæs þe he Abel slog;

ne gefeah he þære fæhðe, ac he hine feor forwræc,

Metod for þy mane, mancynne fram.   110

Þanon untydras ealle onwocon,

eotenas ond ylfe ond orcnêas,

swylce gigantas, þa wið Gode wunnon

lange þrage; he him ðæs lean forgeald.

(II) Gewat ða neosian, syþðan niht becom,   115

hêan huses, hu hit Hring-Dene

æfter beorþege gebun hæfdon.

Fand þa ðær inne æþelinga gedriht

Coming from the hall; there was the sound of a harp,

The minstrel's ringing song. He who could unfold 90

The origin of mankind from far back, asserted

That the Almighty created the earth,

The beautiful plain surrounded by streams,

Established the triumphant sun and moon,

The luminaries to lighten the land-dwellers, 95

And adorned the regions of the earth

With branches and leaves, and also created life

For each of the races, which move about alive.

Thus the retainers lived in mirth,

Happily, till a certain fiend of hell 100

Began to perpetrate an act of atrocity.

The grim demon was called Grendel,

A notorious borderland haunter, he who held the moors

As fen and stronghold. The unhappy creature

Warded the region of the race of monsters awhile, 105

Since the Creator had him condemned

As Cain's kin—then the Eternal Lord

Punished the killing, in which he slew Abel.

Cain did not rejoice at the feud, but the Lord banished him far;

The Lord, for the crime, drove him away from mankind. 110

From him arose all the evil brood,

Giants and elves and evil spirits—

The very giants who contended against God

For a long time; the Lord gave them proper requital for that.

(II) Then Grendel departed to seek out, when night came, 115

The tall house—to see how the Ring-Danes

Had settled in it after their beer drinking.

Then he found therein a band of retainers

swefan æfter symble;   sorge ne cuðon,

wonsceaft wera.   Wiht unhælo,   120

grim ond grædig,   gearo sona wæs,

reoc ond reþe,   ond on ræste genam

þritig þegna;   þanon eft gewat

huðe hremig   to ham faran,

mid þære wælfylle   wica neosan.   125

   Ða wæs on uhtan   mid ærdæge

Grendles guðcræft   gumum undyrne;

þa wæs æfter wiste   wop up ahafen,

micel morgensweg.   Mære þeoden,

æþeling ærgod,   unbliðe sæt,   130

þolode ðryðswyð,   þegnsorge dreah,

syðþan hie þæs laðan   last sceawedon,

wergan gastes;   wæs þæt gewin to strang,

lað ond longsum.   Næs hit lengra fyrst,

ac ymb ane niht   eft gefremede   135

morðbeala mare   ond no mearn fore,

fæhðe ond fyrene;   wæs to fæst on þam.

Þa wæs eaðfynde   þe him elles hwær

gerumlicor   ræste sohte,

bed æfter burum,   ða him gebeacnod wæs,   140

gesægd soðlice   sweotolan tacne

healðegnes hete;   heold hyne syðþan

fyr ond fæstor   se þæm feonde ætwand.

   Swa rixode   ond wið rihte wan,

ana wið eallum,   oð þæt idel stod   145

husa selest.   Wæs seo hwil micel;

twelf wintra tid   torn geþolode

wine Scyldinga,   weana gehwelcne,

Fast asleep after a banquet. They did not know sorrow,

What men could suffer from; the unhallowed creature,   120

Grim and greedy, was more than ready,

Fierce and furious, and from their resting place took

Thirty thanes; thence he departed to go

Back to his home, exulting in his booty—

Content with his fill of slaughter, toward his abode.   125

    Then at dawn with the break of day

Grendel's strength was manifest to men.

Following a feast, weeping rose up,

A great cry in the morning; the renowned lord,

The good prince, sat joyless;   130

The mighty monarch suffered sorrow for the thanes,

When they beheld the track of the hateful one,

The evil monster; that ordeal was too strong,

Loathsome and long lasting! It was not long after,

But on the very next night again he perpetrated   135

A greater grisly deed, feeling no remorse for it,

A hostile and wicked crime; he was intent on them.

Then many a one sought resting place

Elsewhere at more distance for himself,

Bed among outbuildings, when the hostility of   140

The one who had ransacked the hall was shown to him,

Made clear by manifest token; he who had fled from the fiend

Remained farther away, and more secure afterwards.

    So he held sway and strove against right,

One against all, till the best of houses   145

Came to stand empty. It lasted for a great while.

The friendly lord of the Danes suffered affliction

For the length of twelve winters, every woe,

sidra sorga;　forðam [secgum]* wearð,

ylda bearnum,　undyrne cuð,　　　　　　　　　　150

gyddum geomore,　þætte Grendel wan

hwile wið Hroþgar,　heteniðas wæg,

fyrene ond fæhðe　fela missera,

singale sæce,　sibbe ne wolde

wið manna hwone　mægenes Deniga,　　　　　　155

feorhbealo feorran,　fea þingian,

ne þær nænig witena　wenan þorfte

beorhtre bote　to banan folmum;

[ac se]* æglæca　ehtende wæs,

deorc deaþscua,　duguþe ond geogoþe,　　　　　160

seomade ond syrede,　sinnihte heold

mistige moras;　men ne cunnon,

hwyder helrunan　hwyrftum scriþað.

Swa fela fyrena　feond mancynnes,

atol angengea,　oft gefremede,　　　　　　　　165

heardra hynða;　Heorot eardode,

sincfage sel　sweartum nihtum;

no he þone gifstol　gretan moste,

maþðum for Metode,　ne his myne wisse.

Þæt wæs wræc micel　wine Scyldinga,　　　　　170

modes brecða.　Monig oft gesæt

rice to rune;　ræd eahtedon,

hwæt swiðferhðum　selest wære

wið færgryrum　to gefremmanne.

Hwilum hie geheton　æt hærgtrafum　　　　　　175

wigweorþunga,　wordum bædon,

þæt him gastbona　geoce gefremede

wið þeodþreaum.　Swylc wæs þeaw hyra,

Great sorrow. Therefore, it became well known
To men, to the offspring of human kind,   150
Through sadly sung tales, that Grendel had fought
Against Hrothgar for long, borne fierce hatred,
Perpetrated much crime and atrocity for many a year,
Continual conflict: he would not have peace
With anyone of the Danish host of men,   155
Remove his deadly evil, or settle with riches.
Nor there any wise man had good cause to expect
Slackening of the sore from the slayer's hands;
But the fiend, the dark shadow of death, was
Relentless in his grip of the old and the young,   160
Hovered near and ambushed. In darkness he held
The misty moors; men do not know
Where the hellish demons move along, gliding.
In this way the enemy of mankind, the horrid monster,
Often committed a great mass of wicked crimes,   165
Severe injuries: he inhabited Heorot,
The richly decorated hall, in the dark nights;
He was never allowed to approach the gift-seat,
Treasure for God, nor did he know His love.
That was a great distress to the lord of the Danes,   170
Battering of spirit: many powerful often sat down
For consultation; they deliberated on the solution,
What would be the best that the brave ones
Could do to rid themselves of the awful horrors:
Now and again they promised sacrifices   175
At heathen temples, and entreated with words
To the soul-slayer* to bring about remedy
And rid them of distress. (Such was their practice,

hæþenra hyht;   helle gemundon

in modsefan,   Metod hie ne cuþon,   180

dæda Demend,   ne wiston hie Drihten God,

ne hie huru heofena Helm   herian ne cuþon,

wuldres Waldend.   Wa bið þæm ðe sceal

þurh sliðne nið   sawle bescufan

in fyres fæþm,   frofre ne wenan,   185

wihte gewendan;   wel bið þæm þe mot

æfter deaðdæge   Drihten secean,

ond to Fæder fæþmum   freoðo wilnian.

(III) Swa ða mælceare   maga Healfdenes

singala seað;   ne mihte snotor hæleð   190

wean onwendan;   wæs þæt gewin to swyð,

laþ ond longsum,   þe on ða leode becom,

nydwracu niþgrim,   nihtbealwa mæst.

     Þæt fram ham gefrægn   Higelaces þegn,

god mid Geatum,   Grendles dæda;   195

se wæs moncynnes   mægenes strengest

on þæm dæge   þysses lifes,

æþele ond eacen.   Het him yðlidan

godne gegyrwan;   cwæð, he guðcyning

ofer swanrade   secean wolde,   200

mærne þeoden,   þa him wæs manna þearf.

Ðone siðfæt him   snotere ceorlas

lythwon logon,   þeah he him leof wære;

hwetton higerofne,   hæl sceawedon.

Hæfde se goda   Geata leoda   205

cempan gecorone   þara þe he cenoste

findan mihte;   fiftyna sum

sundwudu sohte;   secg wisade,

Hope of the heathens; they thought of hell
In their mind; they did not know God, 180
The Judge of men's doings, nor knew they God the Lord,
Nor indeed they knew how to praise the Protector of heavens,
The Lord of glory; woe is to him who must
Through dangerous hostility push a soul
Into the bosom of fire, not hope for solace, 185
Nor change at all! Blessed is he who may
After the death-day seek the Lord
And ask for peace in the Father's bosom!)
(III) And so Healfdene's son continually brooded over
The care of the time; no wise man could remove 190
The misery; the hardship that had come upon the people
Was too harsh, loathsome, and long lasting.
It was a grim, dire distress, and the greatest nightmare.

    A thane of Hygelac, brave among the Geats,
Then heard at home of Grendel's deeds. 195
He was the strongest in might of all men
In that time of this life, noble and mighty.
He ordered that a strong ship
Be built for him; he said that he would seek
The war-king, the famous prince, over the sea, 200
Now that for him there was need of men.
The prudent men did not find fault with
The adventure, though he was dear to them.
They urged the valiant one, studied omens.
He had the warriors chosen from the courageous 205
Men of the Geats, those he could find
Most brave. He sought the ship with
Fourteen others. The man skilled in seafaring

lagucræftig mon,   landgemyrcu.

Fyrst forð gewat;   flota wæs on yðum,   210

bat under beorge.   Beornas gearwe

on stefn stigon;   streamas wundon,

sund wið sande;   secgas bæron

on bearm nacan   beorhte frætwe,

guðsearo geatolic;   guman ut scufon,   215

weras on wilsið,   wudu bundenne.

Gewat þa ofer wægholm   winde gefysed

flota fami-heals   fugle gelicost,

oð þæt ymb antid   oþres dogores

wundenstefna   gewaden hæfde,   220

þæt ða liðende   land gesawon,

brimclifu blican,   beorgas steape,

side sænæssas;   þa wæs sund liden,

eoletes æt ende.   Þanon up hraðe

Wedera leode   on wang stigon, 225

sæwudu sældon;   syrcan hrysedon,

guðgewædo;   Gode þancedon

þæs þe him yþlade   eaðe wurdon.

   Þa of wealle geseah   weard Scildinga,

se þe holmclifu   healdan scolde,   230

beran ofter bolcan   beorhte randas,

fyrdsearu fuslicu;   hine fyrwyt bræc

modgehygdum,   hwæt þa men wæron.

Gewat him þa to waroðe   wicge ridan

þegn Hroðgares,   þrymmum cwehte   235

mægenwudu mundum,   meþelwordum frægn:

   "Hwæt syndon ge   searohæbbendra,

byrnum werede,   þe þus brontne ceol

Showed them how to reach the shore.

In due time the boat was on the waves,   210

Floating under a promontory. The ready warriors

Went up to the prow; the currents swirled,

Water against the sand; the men bore

Into the bosom of the boat bright weapons,

Splendid armors. The men pushed the ship forward,   215

The tight-braced vessel ready for desired journey.

Then over the sea, impelled by the wind,

The foamy-necked ship launched most like a bird,

Till after due time on the second day

The ship with a curved prow had made advance,   220

So that the seafarers could see the land,

The gleaming sea-cliff, the steep hills,

Large headlands. The sea had been traversed;

The voyage was over. Thence up quickly

The people of Geatland stepped onto the land,   225

And moored the ship. The mail-coats rattled,

The warlike dresses. They thanked God

For their voyage made smooth and easy by His grace.

    Then from the wall saw the Danish sentinel—

He whose charge was to guard the sea-cliff—   230

The bright bosses of shields borne on the gangway,

Ready war-gear; he was gripped by a desire to learn

What on earth these men were, in his thoughts.

Then the thane of Hrothgar rode his horse

Down to the shore, brandishing a mighty spear   235

Forcefully in both hands, and asked in formal words:

    "What sort of fighting men are you,

Protected by coats of mail, who thus have come,

ofer lagustræte   lædan cwomon,
hider ofer holmas?   [Hwæt, ic hwi]le wæs   240
endesæta,   ægwearde heold,
þe on land Dena   laðra nænig
mid scipherge   sceðþan ne meahte.
No her cuðlicor   cuman ongunnon
lindhæbbende;   ne ge leafnesword   245
guðfremmendra   gearwe ne wisson,
maga gemedu.   Næfre ic maran geseah
eorla ofer eorþan,   ðonne is eower sum,
secg on searwum;   nis þæt seldguma,
wæpnum geweorðad,   næfne him his wlite leoge,   250
ænlic ansyn.   Nu ic eower sceal
frumcyn witan,   ær ge fyr heonan,
leassceaweras,   on land Dena
furþur feran.   Nu ge feorbuend,
mereliðende,   minne gehyrað   255
anfealdne geþoht;   ofost is selest
to gecyðanne,   hwanan eowre cyme syndon."
(IV) Him se yldesta   ondswarode,
werodes wisa,   wordhord onleac:
    "We synt gumcynnes   Geata leode   260
ond Higelaces   heorðgeneatas.
Wæs min fæder   folcum gecyþed,
æþele ordfruma,   Ecgþeow haten;
gebad wintra worn,   ær he on weg hwurfe,
gamol of geardum;   hine gearwe geman   265
witena welhwylc   wide geond eorþan.
We þurh holdne hige   hlaford þinne,
sunu Healfdenes,   secean cwomon,

Bringing a tall ship over the watery road,

Hither crossing the waves? What, while I have been   240

A coast-guard, holding watch by the sea,

None hostile to the Danish people could

Inflict any injury on this soil with a ship-army.

No shield-bearers undertook to come here

More openly, nor have you acquired   245

Word of leave from my commanders,

Consent of my kinsmen. Never have I seen one,

Among men on earth, mightier than one of you—

Yon man wearing war-gear. That is not a mere retainer,

Bedecked with weapons, unless his appearance belies him—   250

A peerless sight! Now I must have full knowledge

Of your origin before you go any farther hence,

Deceitful observers on the land of the Danes,

Not one step further. Now you far-dwellers,

Seafaring men, hear and learn my   255

One-fold thought. It is best to be in a hurry

To make clear whence you are coming."

(IV) The chief answered him, the leader

Of the band, unlocking a hoard of words:

"We are men of the Geatish stock,   260

And Hygelac's hearth-companions;

My father was well known to the peoples,

A noble chieftain, whose name was Ecgtheow.

He lived through many winters before he went away,

An ancient man, from his dwelling: every wise man   265

Well remembers him, far and wide throughout the world.

We have come to seek Healfdene's son, your lord,

The protector of people, with well-disposed intention;

leodgebyrgean;   wes þu us larena god.

Habbað we to þæm mæran   micel ærende   270

Deniga frêan;   ne sceal þær dyrne sum

wesan, þæs ic wene.   Þu wast, gif hit is

swa we soþlice   secgan hyrdon,

þæt mid Scyldingum   sceaðona ic nat hwylc,

deogol dædhata,   deorcum nihtum   275

eaweð þurh egsan   uncuðne nið,

hynðu ond hrafyl.   Ic þæs Hroðgar mæg

þurh rumne sefan   ræd gelæran,

hu he frod ond god   feond oferswyðeþ,

gyf him edwendan   æfre scolde   280

bealuwa bisigu,   bot eft cuman,

ond þa cearwylmas   colran wurðaþ;

oððe a syþðan   earfoðþrage,

þreanyd þolað,   þenden þær wunað

on heahstede   husa selest."   285

     Weard maþelode,   ðær on wicge sæt,

ombeht unforht: "Æghwæþres sceal

scearp scyldwiga   gescad witan,

worda ond worca,   se þe wel þenceð.

Ic þæt gehyre,   þæt þis is hold weorod   290

frean Scyldinga.   Gewitaþ forð beran

wæpen ond gewædu,   ic eow wisige;

swylce ic maguþegnas   mine hate

wið feonda gehwone   flotan eowerne,

niwtyrwydne   nacan on sande   295

arum healdan,   oþ ðæt eft byreð

ofer lagustreamas   leofne mannan

wudu wundenhals   to Wedermearce,

Be good to us with words of your counsel!
We have a grand mission to fulfill for the renowned   270
Lord of the Danes; there shall not be anything
Hidden, of which I think. You know—if it is
Indeed so as we have heard—that with the Danes
A ravager, of what sort I do not know,
An unknown evil-doer in the dark nights,   275
Manifests in a terrible manner strange hostility,
Injury, and slaughter; about this I can offer
Advice to Hrothgar in all good intention
On how he, wise and good, can overcome the fiend,
If reversal, relief from the distress of the afflictions,   280
Should ever come for him again,
And the boiling of care may become cooler;
Or ever after he will have to endure tribulation
And distress, so long as stands there
On the lofty place even the best of all halls."   285
        The watchman spoke, seated on his horse,
A dauntless officer: "A sharp shield-bearer
Shall be a judge of each of the two,
Words and deeds, if he can think well.
I hear that this is a band of men well-disposed   290
To the lord of the Danes. Go forth, bearing
Your arms and armors. I will lead you;
Also I will order my young retainers to guard
Your ship against any of the enemies—
Your fresh-tarred boat on the shore—   295
Upon their honor, till again it will bear
Over the sea-streams its dear man—
The ship with a curved prow—to the land of the Geats.

godfremmendra   swylcum gifeþe bið
þæt þone hilderæs   hal gedigeð."   300
  Gewiton him þa feran.   Flota stille bad,
seomode on sale   sidfæþmed scip,
on ancre fæst.   Eoforlic scionon
ofer hleorber[g]an   gehroden golde,
fah ond fyrheard;   ferhwearde heold   305
guþmod grimmon.*   Guman onetton,
sigon ætsomne,   oþ þæt hy sæl timbred,
geatolic ond goldfah,   ongyton mihton;
þæt wæs foremærost   foldbuendum
receda under roderum,   on þæm se rica bad;   310
lixte se leoma   ofer landa fela.
Him þa hildedeor   hof modigra
torht getæhte,   þæt hie him to mihton
gegnum gangan;   guðbeorna sum
wicg gewende,   word æfter cwæð: 315
"Mæl is me to feran;   Fæder alwalda
mid ar-stafum   eowic gehealde
siða gesunde!   Ic to sæ wille
wið wrað werod   wearde healdan."
(V) Stræt wæs stanfah,   stig wisode   320
gumum ætgædere.   Guðbyrne scan
heard hondlocen,   hringiren scir
song in searwum,   þa hie to sele furðum
in hyra gryregeatwum   gangan cwomon.
Setton sæmeþe   side scyldas,   325
rondas regnhearde,   wið þæs recedes weal,
bugon þa to bence;   byrnan hringdon,
guðsearo gumena;   garas stodon,

Be it granted to such of those acting bravely

That he pass through a battle-storm, unharmed."   300

      Then they set out. The ship stayed still;

The wide-floored ship remained attached to a rope,

Fastened on anchor. The boar-figures shone

Over the cheek-guards decorated with gold,

Glittering and fire-hardened: the warlike emblem held   305

Guard over life for the grim fighters. Men hastened,

Marched together, till they could see

A timbered hall stately and gold-adorned.

That was the hall most renowned under the sky

Among earth-dwellers, in which the mighty one dwelled;   310

Its beam shone over many a land.

Then the battle-brave one pointed out for them

The bright dwelling of the brave, so that they might

Go straight to it. A worthy warrior as he was,

He turned his horse, and spoke thus: 315

"Time for me to turn back. The Almighty Father

May guard you with His favors,

Safe in your ventures! I will to the sea,

And return to my task of guarding against any foes."

(V) The road was paved with stones, the path led   320

The men marching together. The mail-coats glittered,

Tightly linked by hand; the bright chain-mail

Clanged in the armors, as they first approached

The hall in their fearsome battle-gear.

Sea-weary, they set down their broad shields,   325

The strong shield-bosses against the wall;

Then they sat on benches. Their mail-coats rang,

The warriors' battle-wear did. Spears stood,

sæmanna searo,   samod ætgædere,

æscholt ufan græg;   wæs se irenþreat   330

wæpnum gewurþad.   Þa ðær wlonc hæleð

oretmecgas   æfter æþelum frægn:

"Hwanon ferigeað ge   fætte scyldas,

græge syrcan   ond grimhelmas,

heresceafta heap?   Ic eom Hroðgares   335

ar ond ombiht.   Ne seah ic elþeodige

þus manige men   modiglicran.

Wen ic þæt ge for wlenco,   nalles for wræcsiðum,

ac for higeþrymmum   Hroðgar sohton."

        Him þa ellenrof   andswarode,   340

wlanc Wedera leod,   word æfter spræc,

heard under helme: "We synt Higelaces

beodgeneatas;   Beowulf is min nama.

Wille ic asecgan   sunu Healfdenes,

mærum þeodne,   min ærende,   345

aldre þinum,   gif he us geunnan wile,

þæt we hine swa godne   gretan moton."

        Wulfgar maðelode   —þæt wæs Wendla leod;

wæs his modsefa   manegum gecyðed,

wig ond wisdom—:   "Ic þæs wine Deniga,   350

frean Scildinga,   frinan wille,

beaga bryttan,   swa þu bena eart,

þeoden mærne,   ymb þinne sið,

ond þe þa ondsware   ædre gecyðan,

ðe me se goda   agifan þenceð."   355

Hwearf þa hrædlice   þær Hroðgar sæt

eald ond anhar   mid his eorla gedriht;

eode ellenrof,   þæt he for eaxlum gestod

24

The seamen's arms put together—
The ash-spears gray from above: the armed troop   330
Was worthy of their weapons. Then a proud warrior there
Asked the men-at-arms about their lineage:
"Wherefrom do you bring your ornamented shields,
Gray mail-shirts and masked helmets,
And so many spears? I am Hrothgar's   335
Messenger and officer. I have not yet seen
A band of foreign men looking more warlike.
I think that you have sought Hrothgar
For a daring and high purpose, not in exile."
    Then to him answered the brave strong man,   340
The proud Weather-Geat spoke the words,
Hardy under his helmet: "We are Hygelac's
Table-sharers; Beowulf is my name.
I wish to tell the son of Healfdene
My mission to the renowned prince,   345
Your lord, if he will grant us
That we be allowed to greet his good grace."
    Wulfgar spoke, a man of the Wendlas,*
Whose spirit was well known to many—
A man of valor and wisdom—: "I will ask on this   350
The friend of the Danes, Lord of the Scyldings,
Our ring-giver, our renowned prince,
As you have requested, about your undertaking,
And speedily make the answer known to you,
That the good man thinks fit to give me."   355
He then quickly went to where Hrothgar sat,
Old and gray-haired, with his retinue of earls;
The bold man stepped to stand before the shoulders

Deniga frêan;   cuþe he duguðe þeaw.

Wulfgar maðelode   to his winedrihtne: 360
"Her syndon geferede,   feorran cumene
ofer geofenes begang   Geata leode;
þone yldestan   oretmecgas
Beowulf nemnað.   Hy benan synt,
þæt hie, þeoden min,   wið þe moton   365
wordum wrixlan;   no ðu him wearne geteoh
ðinra gegncwida,   glædman Hroðgar.
Hy on wiggetawum   wyrðe þinceað
eorla geæhtlan;   huru se aldor deah,
se þæm heaðorincum   hider wisade."   370
(VI) Hroðgar maþelode,   helm Scyldinga:
"Ic hine cuðe   cnihtwesende;
wæs his eald fæder   Ecgþeo haten,
ðæm to ham forgeaf   Hreþel Geata
angan dohtor;   is his eafora nu   375
heard her cumen,   sohte holdne wine.
Ðonne sægdon þæt   sæliþende,
þa ðe gifsceattas   Geata fyredon
þyder to þance,   þæt he þritiges
manna mægencræft   on his mundgripe   380
heaþorof hæbbe.   Hine halig God
for arstafum   us onsende,
to West-Denum,   þæs ic wen hæbbe,
wið Grendles gryre.   Ic þæm godan sceal
for his modþræce   madmas beodan.   385
Beo ðu on ofeste,   hat in gân
seon sibbegedriht   samod ætgædere;
gesaga him eac wordum,   þæt hie sint wilcuman

Of the lord of the Danes; he knew the retainers' custom.

    Wulfgar spoke to his friendly lord: 360

"Here are brought, coming from afar

Over the expanse of the sea, the people of Geatland;

The men-at-arms call their chieftain

Beowulf. They are in earnest petition

That they might with you, my Prince,   365

Exchange words. Do not refuse to grant their wish

In your answer, gracious Hrothgar;

Judged from their battle-gear, they appear worthy

Of the esteem of warriors; indeed, their leader is strong,

He, who has led the fighting men here."   370

(VI) Hrothgar spoke, the protector of the Scyldings:

"I knew him when he was a youngster;

His deceased father's name was Ecgtheow,

To whom Hrethel of the Geats gave for home

His only daughter;* his son is now   375

Pressingly come here, has sought a glad friend.

Then I have heard that the seafarers say—

Those who carried gifts of the Geats

There for their pleasure—that he has

Strength of thirty men in his hand-grip,   380

Brave in battle. Him God the Holy

Has sent to bestow His grace upon us,

To the West-Danes, as I do hope,

Against the terror of Grendel. I must

Offer him treasures for his brave daring.   385

Be you in haste, bid them to come in

To see my band of kinsmen together;

Tell them also clearly that they are welcome

Deniga leodum."

[Þa to dura eode
widcuð hæleð,]*   word inne abead: 390
"Eow het secgan   sigedrihten min,
aldor East-Dena,   þæt he eower æþelu can,
ond ge him syndon   ofer sæwylmas
heardhicgende   hider wilcuman.

Nu ge moton gangan   in eowrum guðgeatawum,   395
under heregriman   Hroðgar geseon;
lætað hildebord   her onbidan,
wudu, wælsceaftas,   worda geþinges."

    Aras þa se rica,   ymb hine rinc manig,
þryðlic þegna heap;   sume þær bidon,   400
heaðoreaf heoldon,   swa him se hearda bebead.

Snyredon ætsomne,   þa secg wisode,
under Heorotes hrof;   [heaþorinc eode,]*
heard under helme,   þæt he on heo[r]ðe gestod.

Beowulf maðelode   —on him byrne scan,   405
searonet seowed   smiþes orþancum—:

    "Wæs þu, Hroðgar, hal!   Ic eom Higelaces
mæg ond magoðegn;   hæbbe ic mærða fela
ongunnen on geogoþe.   Me wearð Grendles þing
on minre eþeltyrf   undyrne cuð;   410
secgað sæliðend,   þæt þæs sele stande,
reced selesta,   rinca gehwylcum
idel ond unnyt,   siððan æfenleoht
under heofenes hador   beholen weorþeð.

Þa me þæt gelærdon   leode mine,   415
þa selestan,   snotere ceorlas,
þeoden Hroðgar,   þæt ic þe sohte,

To the Danish people."

                        [Then to the door went

The well-known man,]* told the message from within: 390

"My dread lord, victorious ever, Chieftain of the East-Danes,

Has commanded me to tell you that he knows your lineage,

And you are welcome here to him,

Having bravely sailed over the surging waves.

Now you may go in your battle-shirts,   395

Wearing your helmets, to meet Hrothgar;

Let your battle-shields wait out here,

The wooden lances also, for the outcome of the talk."

    Then rose up the strong man, many a warrior around him,

The band of mighty thanes; some remained there,   400

Kept guard over the battle-gear, as their chief bade them to.

They hastened together as the man led

Under the roof of Heorot; [the warrior went,]*

Resolute under his helmet, so that he reached the hearth.

Beowulf spoke—on him shone his armor,   405

The mail-coat a smith wrought with all his skills—:

    "All hail, Hrothgar! I am Hygelac's

Kinsman and retainer. I have undertaken in youth

Many a worthwhile task. The issue of Grendel

Has come to be known to me in my homeland;   410

Seafaring men say that this hall, the grandest

Of buildings, stands idle and useless

For every warrior, once the evening-light

Becomes hidden under the heaven's vault.

Then my people advised me,   415

The best of them, the wisest men,

That I should visit you, Prince Hrothgar,

forþan hie mægenes cræft   minne cuþon;

selfe ofersawon,   ða ic of searwum cwom,

fah from feondum,   þær ic fife geband,   420

yðde eotena cyn,   ond on yðum slog

niceras nihtes,   nearoþearfe dreah,

wræc Wedera nið   —wean ahsodon—,

forgrand gramum;   ond nu wið Grendel sceal,

wið þam aglæcan,   ana gehegan   425

ðing wið þyrse.   Ic þe nu ða,

brego Beorht-Dena,   biddan wille,

eodor Scyldinga,   anre bene,

þæt ðu me ne forwyrne,   wigendra hleo,

freowine folca,   nu ic þus feorran com,   430

þæt ic mote ana   [ond] minra eorla gedryht,

þes hearda heap,   Heorot fælsian.

Hæbbe ice eac geahsod,   þæt se æglæca

for his wonhydum   wæpna ne recceð;

ic þæt þonne forhicge,   swa me Higelac sie,   435

min mondrihten,   modes bliðe,

þæt ic sweord bere   oþðe sidne scyld,

geolorand to guþe,   ac ic mid grape sceal

fon wið feonde   ond ymb feorh sacan,

lað wið laþum;   ðær gelyfan sceal   440

Dryhtnes dome   se þe hine deað nimeð.   (Lord's doom.)

Wen ic þæt he wille,   gif he wealdan mot,

in þæm guðsele   Geotena leode

etan unforhte,   swa he oft dyde,

mægen Hreðmanna.   Na þu minne þearft   445

hafalan hydan,   ac he me habban wile

dreore fahne,   gif mec deað nimeð;

30

For they knew what strength I have;
They saw when I from battles returned,
All bloody from my foes, where I had bound five, 420
Destroyed the giants' clan, and on the waves slain
Water-fiends of night, endured dire distress,
Avenged the pain of the Geats—they had sought trouble—
Crushed the enemies; and now with Grendel,
With the fierce demon, I alone shall have encounter, 425
Confront this fiend. Now I wish,
Lord of the Bright-Danes, Protector of the Scyldings,
Guard for fighting men, generous friend of good folks,
To entreat you not to deny me one boon—
Now that I have come thus from afar— 430
That I alone, [and] the band of my troopers,
This pack of hardy men, may be allowed to cleanse Heorot.
I have also heard that the fiend,
For his unwariness, scorns use of weapons.
I take it lightly—so my lord Hygelac 435
May be pleased with me in his mind—
That I bear a sword, or a broad shield—
That brown stuff—to battle, but with my grip I shall have
A grueling duel with the fiend and give or take life,
As foes hateful to each other; there he who will be 440
In death's grip shall trust the verdict of the Lord.
I expect that, if he is allowed to attain victory,
In the battle-hall he will, undeterred by fear,
Gorge himself on the Geats, as he has often done,
The choicest of men; there won't be any need 445
For you to bury me, for he will have me,
All besmeared in blood, if death takes me.

byreð blodig wæl,   byrgean þenceð,

eteð angenga   unmurnlice,

mearcað morhopu;   no ðu ymb mines ne þearft   450

lices feorme   leng sorgian.

Onsend Higelace,   gif mec hild nime,

beaduscruda betst,   þæt mine breost wereð,

hrægla selest;   þæt is Hrædlan laf,

Welandes geweorc.   Gæð a wyrd swa hio scel."   455

(VII) Hroðgar maþelode,   helm Scyldinga:

"For gewyrhtum þu,   wine min Beowulf,

ond for arstafum   usic sohtest.

Gesloh þin fæder   fæhðe mæste;

wearþ he Heaþolafe   to handbonan   460

mid Wlfingum;   ða hine Wedera cyn

for herebrogan   habban ne mihte.

Þanon he gesohte   Suð-Dena folc

ofer yða gewealc,   Ar-Scyldinga;

ða ic furþum weold   folce Deniga   465

ond on geogoðe heold   ginne rice,*

hordburh hæleþa;   ða wæs Heregar dead,

min yldra mæg   unlifigende,

bearn Healfdenes;   se wæs betera ðonne ic.

Siððan þa fæhðe   feo þingode;   470

sende ic Wylfingum   ofer wæteres hrycg

ealde madmas;   he me aþas swor.

Sorh is me to secganne   on sefan minum

gumena ængum,   hwæt me Grendel hafað

hynðo on Heorote   mid his heteþancum,   475

færniða gefremed;   is min fletwerod,

wigheap gewanod;   hie wyrd forsweop

He will bear my bloody body, thinking to taste it,
And the lone one who goes away will eat ravenously,
Staining his moor-stead; no longer will you need   450
Worry about taking care of my body.
Send to Hygelac, if the battle seizes me,
The best of battle-gear that guards my breast,
The peerless garb that Hrethel once wore,
The work of Weland.* Fate always goes as it must!"   455
(VII) Hrothgar spoke, Protector of the Scyldings:
"For what's been done in the past and for the favors,
You have sought us, Beowulf, my friend.
Your father incurred the worst feud with fighting:
He happened to slay Heatholaf with his own hands   460
Among the Wylfings;* then the clan of the Geats
Could not keep him, for he was a threat to peace.
From there he sought the folk of the South-Danes—
The Honor-Scyldings—over the swelling sea-waves,
When I had begun to rule the Danish people,   465
And in youth held a wide kingdom,*
A strong fortress of warriors: Heorogar, Healfdene's son,
My elder kinsman, was then dead,
No longer alive; he was a man better than I.
Since then I settled the feud with money: 470
I sent to the Wylfings, over the surge of the waves,
Old treasures; he* swore oaths to me.
Sorrow swells in my soul to say
To anyone what Grendel has brought about—
Humiliations in Heorot and sudden assaults—   475
With his hostility; my hall-troop,
My daring band has dwindled; doom has swept them

on Grendles gryre.   God eaþe mæg

þone dolsceaðan   dæda getwæfan.

Ful oft gebeotedon   beore druncne   480

ofer ealowæge   oretmecgas,

þæt hie in beorsele   bidan woldon

Grendles guþe   mid gryrum ecga.

Ðonne wæs þeos medoheal   on morgentid,

drihtsele dreorfah,   þonne dæg lixte,   485

eal bencþelu   blode bestymed,

heall heorudreore;   ahte ic holdra þy læs,

deorre duguðe,   þe þa deað fornam.

Site nu to symle   ond onsæl meoto,

sigehreð secgum,   swa þin sefa hwette."   490

    Þa wæs Geatmæcgum   geador ætsomne

on beorsele   benc gerymed;

þær swiðferhþe   sittan eodon,

þryðum dealle.   Þegn nytte beheold,

se þe on handa bær   hroden ealowæge,   495

scencte scir wered.   Scop hwilum sang

hador on Heorote.   Þær wæs hæleða dream,

duguð unlytel   Dena ond Wedera.

(VIII) Unferð maþelode,   Ecglafes bearn,

þe æt fotum sæt   frean Scyldinga,   500

onband beadu-rune   —wæs him Beowulfes sið,

modges merefaran,   micel æfþunca,

forþon þe he ne uþe,   þæt ænig oðer man

æfre mærða þon ma   middangeardes

gehedde under heofenum   þonne he sylfa—:   505

"Eart þu se Beowulf,   se þe wið Brecan wunne,

on sidne sæ   ymb sund flite,

Away into Grendel's horror. God may with ease
Deter the devilish ravager from his deeds.
Full often my valiant fighters have vowed 480
Over ale-cups, drunk with beer,
That they in the mead-hall would remain to meet
The assault of Grendel with grim-edged swords;
Then in the morning when daylight shone forth,
This drinking hall had become drenched all over, 485
All the bench-boards bedewed with blood,
A hall for horrible gore; I had less men loyal to me,
My dear daring men, for death had taken them.
Sit down now for a banquet, and untie your thoughts
And the past triumphs to men, as your heart urges." 490
     Then for the men of the Geats to sit together
A bench was cleared in the beer-hall.
There the strong-willed men went to sit,
Sure of their strength. A thane tended the task,
Who bore in his hands an embellished cup for beer, 495
Let them share shining bubbles; a minstrel sang meanwhile,
To be heard in Heorot. There was mirth for the men,
Not a small band of the Danes and the Weather-Geats.
(VIII) Unferth spoke, son of Ecglaf,
Who sat near the feet of the lord of the Scyldings, 500
Revealing his revulsion—for him the plan of Beowulf,
A daring seafarer, was cause enough for displeasure,
Because he would not allow that any other man
Should ever dare attain more glory on earth
Than he himself under the heavens would: 505
"Are you that Beowulf, the one who contended with Breca,*
Competed in swimming across the wide waves?

ðær git for wlence   wada cunnedon

ond for dolgilþe   on deop wæter

aldrum neþdon?   Ne inc ænig mon,   510

ne leof ne lað,   belean mihte

sorhfullne sið,   þa git on sund rêon;

þær git eagorstream   earmum þehton,

mæton merestræta,   mundum brugdon,

glidon ofer garsecg;   geofon yþum weol,   515

wintrys wylmum.*   Git on wæteres æht

seofon niht swuncon;   he þe æt sunde oferflat,

hæfde mare mægen.   Þa hine on morgentid

on Heaþo-Ræmas   holm up ætbær;

ðonon he gesohte   swæsne eþel,   520

leof his leodum,   lond Brondinga,

freoðoburh fægere,   þær he folc ahte,

burh ond beagas.   Beot eal wið þe

sunu Beanstanes   soðe gelæste.

Ðonne wene ic to þe   wyrsan geþingea,   525

ðeah þu heaðoræsa   gehwær dohte,

grimre guðe,   gif þu Grendles dearst

nihtlongne fyrst   nêan bidan."

Beowulf maþelode, bearn Ecgþeowes:

"Hwæt, þu worn fela,   wine min Unferð,   530

beore druncen   ymb Brecan spræce,

sægdest from his siðe.   Soð ic talige,

þæt ic merestrengo   maran ahte,

earfeþo on yðum,   ðonne ænig oþer man.

Wit þæt gecwædon   cnihtwesende   535

ond gebeotedon   —wæron begen þa git

on geogoðfeore—   þæt wit on gar-secg ut

36

There you two for vanity ventured the depths,

And for your dotard-like boast in the deep water

Risked your lives; no one, friend or foe, 510

Could keep the two of you from

Plunging into peril, when you dared into the deep.

There you two covered the sea-current in your arms,

Waded through the waves, hastened your hands,

Slid over the surge; the sea swelled with waves, 515

Winter's welling. You two in water's domain

Seven nights strove. He who overpowered in swimming

Was the one with more strength. Then in the morning

The sea bore him up where the Heatho-Ræmas* live;

From there he sought his sweet homeland, 520

Dear to his people, the land of the Brondings,*

The fair fortress where he had his folk,

Town, and treasures. All vow made against you

The son of Beanstan* faithfully fulfilled.

Then I expect an outcome worse for you— 525

Though you may have won in all war-storms,

In bloody battles—if you dare wait near

For Grendel in a vigil of nightlong watch."

Beowulf spoke, son of Ecgtheow:

"What, my friend Unferth, drunk with beer, 530

You have said a bit too much about Breca,

Gabbled on about his feats! I maintain the truth,

That I have had more sea-faring strength,

Suffering on the sea-waves, than any other man:

We two agreed and avowed together 535

In our boyish boast—we were both then yet

In unripe years—that we two would risk our lives

aldrum neððon, ond þæt geæfndon swa.

Hæfdon swurd nacod, þa wit on sund rêon,

heard on handa; wit unc wið hronfixas 540

werian þohton. No he wiht fram me

flodyþum feor fleotan meahte,

hraþor on holme; no ic fram him wolde.

Ða wit ætsomne on sæ wæron

fif nihta fyrst, oþ þæt unc flod todraf, 545

wado weallende, wedera cealdost,

nipende niht, ond norþanwind

heaðogrim ondhwearf; hreo wæron yþa.

Wæs merefixa mod onhrered;

þær me wið laðum licsyrce min, 550

heard hondlocen, helpe gefremede,

beadohrægl broden on breostum læg

golde gegyrwed. Me to grunde teah

fah feondscaða, fæste hæfde

grim on grape; hwæþre me gyfeþe wearð, 555

þæt ic aglæcan orde geræhte,

hildebille; heaþoræs fornam

mihtig meredeor þurh mine hand.

(IX) Swa mec gelome laðgeteonan

þreatedon þearle. Ic him þenode 560

deoran sweorde, swa hit gedefe wæs.

Næs hie ðære fylle gefean hæfdon,

manfordædlan, þæt hie me þegon,

symbel ymbsæton sægrunde neah;

ac on mergenne mecum wunde 565

be yðlafe uppe lægon,

sweordum aswefede, þæt syðþan na

Out on the sea-waves, and we carried it out so.
When we swam into the sea, we had naked swords,
Hard in our hands: we thought to defend ourselves 540
Against the whales. Not at all far ahead of me
Could he float faster on the foamy waves,
Nor would I slack off to fall behind him far.
So we two together were on the sea
For five nights, till dashing flood drove us apart, 545
The surging sea-waves, the coldest of weathers,
Darkening night and the north wind
Battle-grim blew on us; fierce were the waves.
Anger was aroused in the sea creatures.
There my mail-shirt, hard-locked by hand, 550
Performed protection of me against the predators:
The woven war-wear, embellished with gold,
Lay on my breast. A fiendish foe full of hatred
Fiercely pulled me to the floor of the sea,
Grim in its grip; however, it happened to be granted me 555
That I attacked the atrocious demon with my dagger,
My battle-sword; the blast of a bloody duel destroyed
The mighty monster of the deep, thanks to my hand.
(IX) So often loathsome creatures perpetrated
Persecution on me pressingly. I paid back to them 560
With my fine sword, insomuch as fit it was.
They by no means had the pleasure of feasting,
These rapacious ravagers, of ravenously devouring me,
Sitting around a round table, near the seafloor.
But in the morning, wounded by my mace, 565
They floated up along the foamy shore,
Slaughtered by my sword, that since then never

ymb brontne ford   brimliðende

lade ne letton.   Leoht eastan com,

beorht beacen Godes;   brimu swaþredon,   570

þæt ic sænæssas   geseon mihte,

windige weallas.   Wyrd oft nereð

unfægne eorl,   þonne his ellen deah.

Hwæþere me gesælde,   þæt ic mid sweorde ofsloh

niceras nigene.   No ic on niht gefrægn   575

under heofones hwealf   heardran feohtan,

ne on egstreamum   earmran mannon;

hwaþere ic fara feng   feore gedigde,

siþes werig.   Ða mec sæ oþbær,

flod æfter faroðe   on Finna land,   580

wadu weallendu.   No ic wiht fram þe

swylcra searoniða   secgan hyrde,

billa brogan.   Breca næfre git

æt heaðolace,   ne gehwæþer incer,

swa deorlice   dæd gefremede   585

fagum sweordum   —no ic þæs [fela]* gylpe—,

þeah ðu þinum broðrum   to banan wurde,

heafodmægum;   þæs þu in helle scealt

werhðo dreogan,   þeah þin wit duge.

Secge ic þe to soðe,   sunu Ecglafes,   590

þæt næfre Grendel swa fela   gryra gefremede,

atol æglæca,   ealdre þinum,

hynðo on Heorote,   gif þin hige wære,

sefa swa searogrim,   swa þu self talast;

ac he hafað onfunden,   þæt he þa fæhðe ne þearf,   595

atole ecgþræce   eower leode

swiðe onsittan,   Sige-Scyldinga;

They prevented the sea-faring men from their passage
Over the soaring sea-waves. Light came from the east,
God's bright beacon; the surging waves subsided,   570
That I could see the headlands with
The wind-blown walls. Fate often spares a man
Not yet doomed to die, when his daring deserves it!
Anyhow it was my lot that with my sword I slew
Nine nether-water monsters; I have not heard of   575
A fiercer fight at night beneath the heaven's vault,
Nor of a man put in more miserable state in the sea.
However, I delivered myself from the demons' grip,
Weary of war. Then the sea carried me off,
The flood with its flow onto the land of the Finns,   580
The surging swells did. No such thing about you
Have I heard say of, so severe sword-slashing,
Such brutal butchering; Breca never yet
In the games of battle, nor either of the two of you,
Has done so daring a deed with shining swords—   585
Nor do I boast of it much—
Though you became the killer of your own brothers,
Your close kinsmen; for that you will in hell
Endure damnation, though your brain may be bright.
I tell you truly, son of Ecglaf,   590
That Grendel, that fearful ferocious foe, would never
Have inflicted so many infamous injuries on your lord,
Humiliation on Heorot, had your heart,
Your fervor, been as fierce as you deign to declare.
But he has found out that he need not much fear   595
Any angry retaliation, repercussion of swishing swords,
From your people, the Scyldings destined for victory.

nymeð nydbade,   nænegum ara ð
leode Deniga,   ac he lust wigeð,
swefeð ond sendeþ,   secce ne weneþ   600
to Gar-Denum.   Ac ic him Geata sceal
eafoð ond ellen   ungeara nu,
guþe gebeodan.   Gæþ eft se þe mot
to medo modig,   siþþan morgenleoht
ofer ylda bearn   oþres dogores,   605
sunne sweglwered   suþan scineð."
    Þa wæs on salum   sinces brytta,
gamolfeax ond guðrof;   geoce gelyfde
brego Beorht-Dena,   gehyrde on Beowulfe
folces hyrde   fæstrædne geþoht.   610
    Ðær wæs hæleþa hleahtor,   hlyn swynsode,
word wæron wynsume.   Eode Wealhþeow forð,
cwen Hroðgares,   cynna gemyndig,
grette goldhroden   guman on healle,
ond þa freolic wif   ful gesealde   615
ærest East-Dena   eþelwearde,
bæd hine bliðne   æt þære beorþege,
leodum leofne;   he on lust geþeah
symbel ond seleful,   sigerof kyning.
Ymbeode þa   ides Helminga   620
duguþe ond geogoþe   dæl æghwylcne,
sincfato sealde,   oþ þæt sæl alamp,
þæt hio Beowulfe,   beaghroden cwen
mode geþungen,   medoful ætbær;
grette Geata leod,   Gode þancode   625
wisfæst wordum   þæs ðe hire se willa gelamp,
þæt heo on ænigne   eorl gelyfde

He takes toll by force, reserving mercy for no man
Of the Danish stock, but he takes delight,
Destroys and dispatches, expects no deterrence   600
By the Spear-Danes; but I shall show to him
The strength and spirit of the Geats soon now,
How we fight. He who may will walk again
Toward mead in good mood, when the morning light
Of another day, the sun dressed in dazzling rays,   605
Throws beams from the south over the sons of men!"

    Then glad was the giver of treasure, gray-haired
And brave in battle; the guardian of the Bright-Danes
Could hope for help: the herd of the folk
Had heard from Beowulf a firm and fixed resolution.   610

    There was men's laughter; din made delightful sound,
Words were pleasant. Wealhtheow walked forward,
Queen of Hrothgar, caring of courtesy,
The gold-adorned one greeted the men in the hall,
And the noble lady proffered to pass a cup,   615
First to the guardian of the land of the East-Danes,
And bade him to be blithe at his beer-drinking,
Beloved of his people. He partook of the pleasure,
The triumphant king did, of the feast and the hall-cup.
Then the woman of the Helmings* went round   620
To each group of men, well-tried warriors and youthful ones,
Offering them the valued vessel, till it came to pass
That she, the gold-adorned queen, the good gracious one,
Brought along the bowl for mead to Beowulf.
She greeted the man of the Geats, thanked God,   625
Wise in the use of words, since her pleasure had come to pass,
That she might put her trust in one man, who would

fyrena frofre.   He þæt ful geþeah,
wælreow wiga,   æt Wealhþêon,
ond þa gyddode   guþe gefysed;   630
Beowulf maþelode,   bearn Ecgþeowes:
"Ic þæt hogode,   þa ic on holm gestah,
sæbat gesæt   mid minra secga gedriht,
þæt ic anunga   eowra leoda
willan geworhte,   oþðe on wæl crunge   635
feondgrapum fæst.   Ic gefremman sceal
eorlic ellen,   oþðe endedæg
on þisse meoduhealle   minne gebidan."
Ðam wife þa word   wel licodon,
gilpcwide Geates;   eode goldhroden   640
freolicu folccwen   to hire frean sittan.
      Þa wæs eft swa ær   inne on healle
þryðword sprecen,   ðeod on sælum,
sigefolca sweg,   oþ þæt semninga
sunu Healfdenes   secean wolde   645
æfenræste;   wiste þæm ahlæcan
to þæm heahsele   hilde geþinged,
siððan hie sunnan leoht   geseon ne meahton,
oþðe nipende   niht ofer ealle,
scaduhelma gesceapu   scriðan cwoman,   650
wan under wolcnum.   Werod eall aras.
      Gegrette þa   guma oþerne,
Hroðgar Beowulf,   ond him hæl abead,
winærnes geweald,   ond þæt word acwæð:
"Næfre ic ænegum men   ær alyfde,   655
siþðan ic hond ond rond   hebban mihte,
ðryþærn Dena   buton þe nu ða.

Help hinder the heinous butchery. He received that bowl,

The ferocious fighter, from the hand of Wealhtheow,

And then, resolved to fight the fiend, uttered thus— 630

Beowulf spoke, son of Ecgtheow:

"I made up my mind, when I set out on the sea,

Sat in the sea-boat with the troop of my men,

That I would by all means fulfill the wish

Of your folk, or die in the deadly fight, 635

Fast in the fiend's grip. I shall fulfill

A deed worthy of a man; or, let me breathe

My last breath right here in this mead-hall!"

These words well pleased the woman,

Coming from the Geat full of stomach; gold-adorned, 640

The good queen of folk went to sit beside her sire.

Then were again as before within the hall

Spirited words spoken, people in jollity,

Boisterous sound of boastful folk, till soon afterwards

The son of Healfdene wanted to retire 645

To bed for the night's rest. He knew of the battle

Appointed by the hateful demon in the high hall,

From the time when they could see the light of the sun

Till night deepening in the dark over all,

The shapes of shadows came, gliding, 650

Wan under the clouds. The whole host arose.

Then the men greeted one another,

And Hrothgar bade Beowulf the best of luck,

Wielding of the wine-hall, and uttered thus:

"Never before have I yielded to any man, 655

Since I could lift my hand and a shield,

Rule of the mighty Danish hall, but to you now.

Hafa nu ond geheald   husa selest,

gemyne mærþo,   mægenellen cyð,

waca wið wraþum.   Ne bið þe wilna gad,   660

gif þu þæt ellenweorc   aldre gedigest."

(X) Ða him Hroþgar gewat   mid his hæleþa gedryht,

eodur Scyldinga,   ut of healle;

wolde wigfruma   Wealhþeo secan,

cwen to gebeddan.   Hæfde Kyningwuldor   665

Grendle togeanes,   swa guman gefrungon,

seleweard aseted;   sundornytte beheold

ymb aldor Dena,   eotonweard abead.

Huru Geata leod   georne truwode

modgan mægnes,   Metodes hyldo.   670

    Ða he him of dyde   isernbyrnan,

helm of hafelan,   sealde his hyrsted sweord,

irena cyst,   ombihtþegne,

ond gehealdan het   hildegeatwe.

Gespræc þa se goda   gylpworda sum,   675

Beowulf Geata,   ær he on bed stige:

"No ic me an herewæsmun   hnagran talige

guþgeweorca,   þonne Grendel hine;

forþan ic hine sweorde   swebban nelle,

aldre beneotan,   þeah ic eal mæge.   680

Nat he þara goda,   þæt he me ongean slêa,

rand geheawe,   þeah ðe he rof siê

niþgeweorca;   ac wit on niht sculon

secge ofersittan,   gif he gesecean dear

wig ofer wæpen,   ond siþðan witig God   685

on swa hwæþere hond,   halig Dryhten,

mærðo deme,   swa him gemet þince."

46

Have now and hold the best of all houses,

Bear in mind the glory, make mighty valor known,

Be wary against the wretch! There will be no want of rewards,   660

If you succeed in the valorous venture and stay alive."

(X) Then Hrothgar left with his band of retainers,

Prince of the Scyldings did, out of the hall.

The warlord wanted to seek Wealhtheow,

His queen, for his bedfellow: the King of Glory had   665

Appointed a hall-guardian, as men came to know,

To deal with Grendel; he attended to a special task

Near the lord of the Danes, offered watch against the monster.

Indeed, the man of the Geats had a firm faith

In his spirited strength, and in God's grace.   670

    Then he took off his iron corselet,

The helmet off his head, and handed his adorned sword,

The best of all swords, to his attendant;

And he ordered him to keep guard of the battle-gears.

Then the brave one spoke some boasting words,   675

Beowulf of the Geats, before he went to bed:

"I do not consider myself poorer in martial prowess

For warlike works, than Grendel himself;

Therefore, I will not put him to sleep with sword,

Deprive him of his life, though quite I may.   680

He has no recourse that he may better strike me,

Shatter my shield, though he may be strong enough

For his heinous deeds; but we two shall at night

Deal without a sword, if he dares seek

War without weapon; and so may the wise God,   685

The holy Lord, assign victory on whichever hand,

The way it may seem to be proper to Him."

Hylde hine þa heaþodeor,   hleorbolster onfeng

eorles andwlitan,   ond hine ymb monig

snellic særinc   selereste gebeah.   690

Nænig heora þohte,   þæt he þanon scolde

eft eardlufan   æfre gesecean,

folc oþðe freoburh,   þær he afeded wæs;

ac hie hæfdon gefrunen,   þæt hie ær to fela micles

in þæm winsele   wældeað fornam,   695

Denigea leode.   Ac him Dryhten forgeaf

wigspeda gewiofu,   Wedera leodum,

frofor ond fultum,   þæt hie feond heora

ðurh anes cræft   ealle ofercomon,

selfes mihtum. ⌈Soð is gecyþed,   700

þæt mihtig God   manna cynnes

weold wideferhð.⌉

　　　　　　　Com on wanre niht

scriðan sceadugenga.   Sceotend swæfon,   *shadow - stalker .*

þa þæt hornreced   healdan scoldon,

ealle buton anum.   Þæt wæs yldum cuþ,   *all except one* 705

þæt hie ne moste,   þa Metod nolde,

se scynscaþa   under sceadu bregdan;

ac he wæccende   wraþum on andan

bad bolgenmod   beadwa geþinges.

(XI) Ða com of more   under misthleoþum   710

Grendel gongan,   godes yrre bær;

mynte se manscaða   manna cynnes

sumne besyrwan   in sele þam hean.

Wod under wolcnum   to þæs þe he winreced,

gold-sele gumena,   gearwost wisse,   715

fættum fahne.   Ne wæs þæt forma sið,

Then the battle-brave one lay down, a pillow propped
The earl's head, and around him lay down
On the hall floor many a sea-borne brave warrior.   690
None of them thought that he should from there
Ever seek his dear homeland again—either his folk,
Or fair town where he had been brought up.
But they had heard that cruel death had carried off
Far too many of the Danish people in the mead-hall, 695
Up till now. But the Lord granted them,
The people of the Weather-Geats, the fortune of
Victory, solace, and support, so that they suppressed
Their foe entirely through one man's strength
And power. The truth has been made known,   700
That the mighty God has ruled the human race
Always, and ever will.
      Striding in the dark night,
The shadowy stroller came. The warriors were sleeping—
Those who should guard the gabled building—
All of them, except one. It was well known to men 705
That, when the Lord willed it not, the devilish foe
May not draw them beneath the dark shadows.
But watching out for the wretch in wrath,
He waited for the outcome of the fight in fury.
(XI) Then from the moor under the misty slopes came 710
Grendel, gradually approaching, bearing God's ire.
The direful destroyer of mankind intended
To take one in his grip in that lofty dwelling.
He advanced beneath the clouds to the wine-hall,
Till he most clearly discerned the golden hall 715
Gleaming with gold plates. Nor was it the first time

þæt he Hroþgares   ham gesohte;

næfre he on aldordagum   ær ne siþðan

heardran hæle,   healðegnas fand.

Com þa to recede   rinc siðian   720

dreamum bedæled.   Duru sona onarn,

fyrbendum fæst,   syþðan he hire folmum [æthr]an;

onbræd þa bealohydig,   ða *he* [ge]bolgen wæs,

recedes muþan.   Raþe æfter þon

on fagne flor   feond treddode, *paced / stepped / trod*   725

eode yrremod;   him of eagum stod

ligge gelicost   leoht unfæger.

Geseah he in recede   rinca manige,

swefan sibbegedriht   samod ætgædere,

magorinca heap.   Þa his mod ahlog;   730

mynte þæt he gedælde,   ær þon dæg cwome,

atol aglæca,   anra gehwylces

lif wið lice,   þa him alumpen wæs

wistfylle wen.   Ne wæs þæt wyrd þa gen,

þæt he ma moste   manna cynnes   735

ðicgean ofer þa niht.   Þryðswyð beheold

mæg Higelaces,   hu se manscaða

under færgripum   gefaran wolde.

Ne þæt se aglæca   yldan þohte,

ac he gefeng hraðe   forman siðe   740

slæpendne rinc,   slat unwearnum,

bat banlocan,   blod edrum dranc,

synsnædum swealh;   sona hæfde

unlyfigendes   eal gefeormod,

fet ond folma.   Forð near ætstop,   745

nam þa mid handa   higeþihtigne

For him to seek the home of Hrothgar.
Never in his days of life, neither before nor since,
Had he found the hall-thanes a harder lot to bear.*
Then to the hall the marauder made his way, 720
A stranger to life's joy. The door sprang open,
When his hands gripped the fast-forged bar.
He pulled it open to break the hall-door,
Wrapped up in anger. Then quickly
On the shining floor the fiend stepped, 725
And walked in, full of anger. In his eyes
Gleamed a flame shooting out an ugly beam.
He saw in the hall many a man of strength,
A band of kinsmen, sleeping together,
A troop of young retainers. Then he exulted 730
At the thought of tearing, before dawn broke,
Each one's life from his body, as the horrid fiend
Intended, his mouth watering in anticipation
Of a lavish feast. Fate was not so ordained
That he would be allowed to take more of mankind, 735
When that night was over. The mighty kinsman of Hygelac
Watched out to see how the wicked ravager would
Proceed by attempting a sudden swirl of attack.
The atrocious one did not mean to give any reprieve,
But he promptly took in his grip first 740
A warrior sound asleep, rent him ravenously,
Bit his bone-locking joints, drank blood pouring out,
Swallowed flesh in sumptuous chunks. He soon had
Gulped down the entire body of the dead man—
Not leaving feet and hands. He stepped forth nearer, 745
Then seized with his hands the strong-hearted warrior,

rinc on ræste,   ræhte ongean*
feond mid folme;   he onfeng hraþe
inwitþancum   ond wið earm gesæt.

    Sona þæt onfunde   fyrena hyrde,   750
þæt he ne mette   middangeardes,
eorþan sceata,   on elran men
mundgripe maran;   he on mode wearð
forht on ferhðe;   no þy ær fram meahte.

Hyge wæs him hinfus,   wolde on heolster fleon,   755
secan deofla gedræg;   ne wæs his drohtoð þær
swylce he on ealderdagum   ær gemette.

Gemunde þa se goda,*   mæg Higelaces,
æfenspræce,   uplang astod
ond him fæste wiðfeng;   fingras burston;   760
eoten wæs utweard;   eorl furþur stop.

Mynte se mæra,   [þ]ær he meahte swa,
widre gewindan   ond on weg þanon
fleon on fenhopu;   wiste his fingra geweald
on grames grapum.   Þæt wæs geocor sið,   765
þæt se hearmscaþa   to Heorute ateah.

    Dryhtsele dynede;   Denum eallum wearð,
ceasterbuendum,   cenra gehwylcum,
eorlum ealuscerwen.   Yrre wæron begen,
reþe renweardas.   Reced hlynsode.   770
Þa wæs wundor micel,   þæt se winsele
wiðhæfde heaþodeorum,   þæt he on hrusan ne feol,
fæger foldbold;   ac he þæs fæste wæs
innan ond utan   irenbendum
searoþoncum besmiþod.   Þær fram sylle abeag   775
medubenc monig,   mine gefræge,

Who was reposing. The fiend reached out his hand
Toward Beowulf, who quickly took it in his grip
In undaunted hostility, and sat up, supported by an arm.

    Soon the perpetrator of foul deeds perceived   750
That he had never met, in the middle-earth,
A more powerful handgrip from another man—
Not in this world. He in spirit became afraid,
Felt cowered down in heart; yet he could not get away.
He was intent on freeing himself, wished to flee to his refuge,   755
And seek the devils' company. What he met there was not
Like what he had found formerly in his days of life.
Then the brave one, Hygelac's kinsman, remembered
His evening speech; he stood upright,
And laid hold on him firmly. Fingers burst;   760
The giant was striving to escape; the earl stepped further.
The ill-famed one thought, if he could do so,
He would fly to a far-off place and flee away from there
To his fen-retreat: he knew from the grip of the wrathful one
What strength he had. That was a disastrous journey   765
That the pernicious monster ventured to take to Heorot!

    The retainers' hall resounded; to all the Danes,
To the borough-dwellers, to each of the brave ones,
To the earls, terror came. Both of the fierce claimants
Of the hall were in wrath. The building resounded.   770
Then it was a great wonder that the wine-hall
Withstood the death-defying ones, that the beautiful building
Did not fall to the ground: it was so firmly fastened
Both within and without in iron bands,
With skills allowed to smiths. There from the floor flung,   775
As I have heard say, many a mead-bench

golde geregnad, þær þa graman wunnon.

Þæs ne wendon ær witan Scyldinga,

þæt hit a mid gemete manna ænig,

betlic ond banfag, tobrecan meahte, 780

listum tolucan, nymþe liges fæþm

swulge on swaþule. Sweg up astag

niwe geneahhe; Norð-Denum stod

atelic egesa, anra gehwylcum

þara þe of wealle wop gehyrdon, 785

gryreleoð galan Godes ondsacan,

sigeleasne sang, sar wanigean

helle hæfton. Heold hine fæste

se þe manna wæs mægene strengest

on þæm dæge þysses lifes. 790

(XII) Nolde eorla hleo ænige þinga

þone cwealmcuman cwicne forlætan,

ne his lifdagas leoda ænigum

nytte tealde. Þær genehost brægd

eorl Beowulfes ealde lafe, 795

wolde freadrihtnes feorh ealgian,

mæres þeodnes, ðær hie meahton swa.

Hie þæt ne wiston, þa hie gewin drugon,

heardhicgende hildemecgas,

ond on healfa gehwone heawan þohton, 800

sawle secan: þone synscaðan

ænig ofer eorþan irenna cyst,

guðbilla nan, gretan nolde;

ac he sigewæpnum forsworen hæfde,

ecga gehwylcre. Scolde his aldorgedal 805

on ðæm dæge þysses lifes

54

Adorned with gold, where the enraged grappled.

The wise men of the Danes never before thought of it,

That any of men at any time in any wise could

Break it to bits, splendid and adorned with bone,   780

Pull asunder with skills, unless an embrace of fire

Would swallow it in flame. A sound rose up,

Utterly unheard of: on the North-Danes swept

Dreadful horror, on each one of them,

Who heard from the wall a mournful wail,   785

The sound of terrible bellowing of God's enemy,

The cry of defeat, the slave of hell bewailing

The pain he felt. He held the demon firmly,

He who was the strongest in might

Among men in that day of this life.   790

(XII) The champion of the earls would by no means

Allow the murderous visitor to go away alive,

Nor did he account his own life-days as of use

To any of the people. Then each earl of Beowulf

Quickly drew his time-honored heirloom,   795

Would defend the life of his lord,

His glorious chief, if he could do so.

The bold-spirited battle-braving men did not know,

They didn't,—when they were engaged in fighting

And intended to hew every part of his body   800

To seek his soul—, that none of the choicest swords,

Not even the best battle-sword in the world,

Would inflict any harm on that evil-doer,

For by witchcraft he had made the weapons ineffectual,

All of their swords. His departure from life,   805

No matter what might happen on earth,

earmlic wurðan,   ond se ellorgast
on feonda geweald   feor siðian.

   Ða þæt onfunde   se þe fela æror
modes myrðe   manna cynne,   810
fyrene gefremede   —he [wæs] fag wið God—,
þæt him se lichoma   læstan nolde,
ac hine se modega   mæg Hygelaces
hæfde be honda;   wæs gehwæþer oðrum
lifigende lað.   Licsar gebad   815
atol æglæca;   him on eaxle wearð
syndolh sweotol,   seonowe onsprungon,
burston banlocan.   Beowulfe wearð
guðhreð gyfeþe;   scolde Grendel þonan
feorhseoc flêon   under fenhleoðu,   820
secean wynleas wic;   wiste þe geornor,
þæt his aldres wæs   ende gegongen,
dogera dægrim.   Denum eallum wearð
æfter þam wælræse   willa gelumpen.
Hæfde þa gefælsod   se þe ær feorran com,   825
snotor ond swyðferhð,   sele Hroðgares,
genered wið niðe.   Nihtweorce gefeh,
ellenmærþum.   Hæfde East-Denum
Geatmecga leod   gilp gelæsted,
swylce oncyþðe   ealle gebette,   830
inwidsorge,   þe hie ær drugon
ond for þreanydum   þolian scoldon,
torn unlytel.   Þæt wæs tacen sweotol,
syþðan hildedeor   hond alegde,
earm ond eaxle   —þær wæs eal geador   835
Grendles grape—   under geapne hrof.

Was bound to be miserable; and the accursed spirit
Was to travel far into the realm of the fiends.

    Then he who had so far perpetrated many atrocities,
Deeds of affliction of the heart of human race,   810
Realized that he was in a state of strife against God—
That for him the body would not do much service,
But the high-spirited kinsman of Hygelac
Had him in his grip. Each of them to the other
Was loathsome, being alive. The dire demon had lived   815
To feel bodily pain. He had received in one shoulder
An undeniable, deadly wound: the sinews sprang asunder,
The bone-locks burst. To Beowulf was given
The glory in battle; mortally wounded, Grendel
Had to flee from there to be under the marshland,   820
And seek his joyless abode. Therefore, readily he knew
That the end of his life had been reached—
His days were numbered. To all the Danes,
After the bloody fight, jubilee came to pass.
Thus, he who had come from afar earlier,   825
Wise and strong-spirited, had the hall of Hrothgar
Purged and saved from affliction. For the work at night,
He rejoiced at his heroic deeds. The man of the Geats
Fulfilled the boastful promise he had made to the East-Danes.
Thus, he provided remedy for all the distress   830
And sorrow, which they had formerly suffered,
And had to endure for the affliction—the tremendous
Torment inflicted on them. That was a clear token,
When the battle-brave one laid the hand down,
Arm and shoulder—there was all together   835
Grendel's clutching—under the vaulted roof.

(XIII) Ða wæs on morgen   mine gefræge

ymb þa gifhealle   guðrinc monig;

ferdon folctogan   feorran ond nêan   _far + near_

geond widwegas   wundor sceawian,   840

laþes lastas.   No his lifgedal

sarlic þuhte   secga ænegum

þara þe tirleases   trode sceawode,

hu he werigmod   on weg þanon,

niða ofercumen,   on nicera mere   845

fæge ond geflymed   feorhlastas bær.

Ðær wæs on blode   brim weallende,

atol yða geswing   eal gemenged

haton heolfre,   heorodreore weol;

deaðfæge deog,   siððan dreama leas   850

in fenfreoðo   feorh alegde,

hæþene sawle;   þær him hel onfeng.

    Þanon eft gewiton   ealdgesiðas,

swylce geong manig   of gomenwaþe,

fram mere modge   mearum ridan,   855

beornas on blancum.   Ðær wæs Beowulfes

mærðo mæned;   monig oft gecwæð,

þætte suð ne norð   be sæm tweonum

ofer eormengrund   oþer nænig

under swegles begong   selra nære   860

rondhæbbendra,   rices wyrðra.

Ne hie huru winedrihten   wiht ne logon,

glædne Hroðgar,   ac þæt wæs god cyning.

    Hwilum heaþorofe   hleapan leton,

on geflit faran   fealwe mearas,   865

ðær him foldwegas   fægere þuhton,

(XIII) Then in the morning, as I have heard say,
Many a man gathered there around the gift-hall.
From afar and from near, throughout the wide regions,
The folk-leaders came to watch the wonder,   840
The traces left by the hateful foe. His parting from life
Did not seem sad to any of the men,
Who beheld the footprints of the defeated—
How he, disheartened, away from there,
Overcome in a battle, into the mere of water-monsters,   845
Doomed to die and put to flight, bore away his bloody tracks.
There was a pool of water boiling brimful with blood.
Horrid swirl of surfs, all mingled with
Hot pour from gore, was boiling with battle-blood.
Destined for death, he hid in his fen-refuge,   850
When, deprived of mirth, he gave up his life,
His heathen soul: then hell received him.

    The old retainers, and many a young one also,
From there made a joyful journey back again,
From the mere, high-spirited, on horseback—   855
The soldiers on their steeds. There was Beowulf's
Fame extolled; many folks repeatedly said
That, south or north, between the seas,
Over the wide expanse of land, none other
Under the stretch of the sky was a better man   860
For bearing a shield, or deserved a kingdom more.
Yet they did not find fault with their friendly lord,
Gracious Hrothgar, who was a good king.
    Now and again the battle-brave ones let their bay steeds
Gallop and run to compete with one another,   865
Where the footpaths looked fair, not falling short of

cystum cuðe. Hwilum cyninges þegn,
guma gilphlæden, gidda gemyndig,
se ðe ealfela ealdgesegena
worn gemunde, word oþer fand   870
soðe gebunden; secg eft ongan
sið Beowulfes snyttrum styrian,
ond on sped wrecan spel gerade,
wordum wrixlan.
               Welhwylc gecwæð,
þæt he fram Sigemundes secgan hyrde   875
ellendædum, uncuþes fela,
Wælsinges gewin, wide siðas,
þara þe gumena bearn gearwe ne wiston,
fæhðe ond fyrena, buton Fitela mid hine,
þonne he swulces hwæt secgan wolde,   880
êam his nefan, swa hie a wæron
æt niða gehwam nydgesteallan;
hæfdon ealfela eotena cynnes
sweordum gesæged. Sigemunde gesprong
æfter deaðdæge dom unlytel,   885
syþðan wiges heard wyrm acwealde,
hordes hyrde; he under harne stan,
æþelinges bearn, ana geneðde
frecne dæde, ne wæs him Fitela mid;
hwæþre him gesælde, ðæt þæt swurd þurhwod   890
wrætlicne wyrm, þæt hit on wealle ætstod,
dryhtlic iren; draca morðre swealt.
Hæfde aglæca elne gegongen,
þæt he beahhordes brucan moste
selfes dome; sæbat gehleod,   895

Their fame as fine tracks. At times a thane of the king,

One endowed with eloquence, with a store of stories—

He who remembered a multitude of songs,

A great number of old tales—devised another tale   870

With well-woven words: he in turn started to

Sing of the feat of Beowulf with eloquence,

And compose a tale successfully with his skills,

With words set anew.

              He did not miss anything

In telling what he had heard say of Sigemund's*   875

Deeds of valor, many an unknown tale,

The strife of the son of Wæls, his journeys afar,

The feuds and the evil deeds, of which the offspring of men

Had no knowledge—except Fitela with him,

To whom he would not mind revealing such matters,   880

As uncle to his nephew: they were companions

Ever so close in every battle they fought together.

They had together defeated many a clan of giants

With their swords. For Sigemund sprang up

Not a little glory after the day of his death,   885

When, hardy as he was in battle, he killed a serpent

That watched over treasure. Under a gray stone, he,

Son of a prince, ventured all alone upon

The daring deed, nor was Fitela with him.

However, it befell him that the sword pierced   890

The wondrous worm that it stayed stuck on the wall,

The splendid sword did; the dragon died of the deadly stroke.

The fierce fighter, with his valor, had incurred

That he could rejoice at claiming the ring-hoard,

Upon his own will. He loaded his sea-boat,   895

bær on bearm scipes   beorhte frætwa,

Wælses eafera;   wyrm hat gemealt.

    Se wæs wreccena   wide mærost

ofer werþeode,   wigendra hleo,

ellendædum   —he þæs ær onðah—,   900

siððan Heremodes   hild sweðrode,

eafoð ond ellen.   He mid Eotenum wearð

on feonda geweald   forð forlacen,

snude forsended.   Hine sorhwylmas

lemede to lange;   he his leodum wearð,   905

eallum æþellingum   to aldorceare;

swylce oft bemearn   ærran mælum

swiðferhþes sið   snotor ceorl monig,

se þe him bealwa to   bote gelyfde,

þæt þæt ðeodnes bearn   geþeon scolde,   910

fæderæþelum onfon,   folc gehealdan,

hord ond hleoburh,   hæleþa rice,

eþel Scyldinga.   He þær eallum wearð,

mæg Higelaces   manna cynne,

freondum gefægra;   hine fyren onwod.   915

    Hwilum flitende   fealwe stræte

mearum mæton.   Ða wæs morgenleoht

scofen ond scynded.   Eode scealc monig

swiðhicgende   to sele þam hean

searowundor seon;   swylce self cyning   920

of brydbure,   beahhorda weard,

tryddode tirfæst   getrume micle,

cystum gecyþed,   ond his cwen mid him

medostigge mæt   mægþa hose.

(XIV) Hroðgar maðelode   —he to healle geong,   925

Bore into the ship's bosom the dazzling adornments,
Son of Wæls did. The dragon had melted away hot.

    He was among heroes the most widely known
Over many nations, a guardian of the warriors,
For his valorous deeds—the cause of his earlier prosperity—   900
After Heremod's fortune in war became doomed,
When his strength and valor declined: taken by the Jutes,
Heremod was forsworn while in the power of his enemies,
And he was quickly put to death. Swelling sorrows had
Oppressed him too long; he had been to his people,   905
To all princes, source of lifelong care;
Also many a wise man often lamented, in earlier times,
The venture the strong-spirited man had undertaken—
Those who counted on him as remedy for the tribulations,
And hoped that the prince's son would prosper,   910
Receive the legacy from his father, guard the people,
Treasure, and the stronghold, the kingdom of warriors,
The land of the Scyldings.—He,* the kinsman of
Hygelac, there became dearer to his friends,
To all of human race; sin had gotten hold of Heremod.*   915

    At times, competing on horseback, they raced
On the sandy roads, when the morning light
Had approached and hastened. Many a retainer,
Firmly resolved, went to the high hall
To see the strange wonder; the king himself,   920
The guardian of the treasure-hoards with fame for virtues,
Also carried his steps in triumph from his conjugal quarter,
Attended by a large retinue; and his queen with him,
Followed by a train of waiting ladies, trod the path to the mead-hall.
(XIV) Hrothgar spoke—he had gone to the hall,   925

stod on stapole,   geseah steapne hrof

golde fahne   ond Grendles hond—:

   "Ðisse ansyne   Alwealdan þanc

lungre gelimpe!   Fela ic laþes gebad,

grynna æt Grendle;   a mæg God wyrcan   930

wunder æfter wundre,   wuldres Hyrde.

Ðæt wæs ungeara,   þæt ic ænigra me

weana ne wende   to widan feore

bote gebidan,   þonne blode fah

husa selest   heorodreorig stod,   935

wea widscofen   witena gehwylcum

ðara þe ne wendon,   þæt hie wideferhð

leoda landgeweorc   laþum beweredon

scuccum ond scinnum.   Nu scealc hafað

þurh Drihtnes miht   dæd gefremede,   940

ðe we ealle   ær ne meahton

snyttrum besyrwan.   Hwæt, þæt secgan mæg

efne swa hwylc mægþa   swa ðone magan cende

æfter gumcynnum,   gyf heo gyt lyfað,

þæt hyre Ealdmetod   este wære   945

bearngebyrdo.   Nu ic, Beowulf, þec,

secg* betsta,   me for sunu wylle

freogan on ferhþe;   heald forð tela

niwe sibbe.   Ne bið þe nænigra* gad

worolde wilna,   þe ic geweald hæbbe.   950

Ful oft ic for læssan   lean teohhode,

hordweorþunge   hnahran rince,

sæmran æt sæcce.   Þu þe self hafast

dædum* gefremed,   þæt þin dom lyfað

awa to aldre.   Alwalda þec   955

Stood on the steps, watched the steep roof
Glittering with gold, and also Grendel's hand—:
    "For this sight, let thanks be given at once
To the Ruler! I have suffered much from the loathsome foe,
Great torment from Grendel: God may always work	930
Wonder after wonder, the Guardian of glory may.
It was not long ago that I did not expect
Ever to live to see remedy for any of the miseries
For me, when the best of dwellings stood
Besmeared with blood, dreary with dripping gore—	935
Woe widespread for every one of my wise men,
Those who did not expect that they could ever
Defend the folk's fortress from the fiendish foes,
Demons and vile spirits. Now a warrior has,
Through the Lord's might, performed a deed	940
That we all could not accomplish before
With our abilities. Indeed, whoever the woman
Who gave birth to that son of hers, amongst all men,
May say, if she be still alive, that the God of old
Granted special grace on her, when she was	945
About to bear a child. Now, Beowulf,
Best of men, I will love you in my heart,
As a father does his son. From now on, keep well
This new kinship. You will not lack anything,
Of all the worldly goods I have in my possession.	950
Very often I have bestowed reward for less,
Have honored with gifts a man of less worth,
Less bold in battle. With your own deeds you have
Made it clear that your glory will for evermore
Live on. May the Almighty reward you	955

gode forgylde, swa he nu gyt dyde!"
    Beowulf maþelode, bearn Ecgþeowes:
"We þæt ellenweorc estum miclum,
feohtan fremedon, frecne geneðdon
eafoð uncuþes. Uþe ic swiþor, 960
þæt ðu hine selfne geseon moste,
feond on frætewum fylwerigne.
Ic hine hrædlice heardan clammum
on wælbedde wriþan þohte,
þæt he for mundgripe minum scolde 965
licgean lifbysig, butan his lic swice;
ic hine ne mihte, þa Metod nolde,
ganges getwæman, no ic him þæs georne ætfealh,
feorhgeniðlan; wæs to foremihtig
feond on feþe. Hwæþere he his folme forlet 970
to lifwraþe last weardian,
earm ond eaxle; no þær ænige swa þeah
feasceaft guma frofre gebohte;
no þy leng leofað laðgeteona
synnum geswenced, ac hyne sar hafað 975
in nydgripe* nearwe befongen,
balwon bendum; ðær abidan sceal
maga mane fah miclan domes,
hu him scir Metod scrifan wille."
    Ða wæs swigra secg, sunu Ecglafes, 980
on gylpspræce guðgeweorca,
siþðan æþelingas eorles cræfte
ofer heanne hrof hand sceawedon,
feondes fingras; foran æghwylc wæs,
stiðra* nægla gehwylc, style gelicost, 985

With goodness, as He even now has done!"

    Beowulf spoke, son of Ectheow:

"We have more than willingly done the daring work,

The fight, and have boldly braved whatever force

The unknown foe might have. I would rather wish   960

That you could have seen his very presence,

The fiend in all his flourishes, fallen so low!

I thought that I would bind him quickly

On his death-bed with my deadly grip,

That he, on account of my hand-grip, would soon   965

Be writhing, panting for life, unless his body had escaped.

I could not, since God did not will it so,

Keep him from going, nor did I hold him hard enough,

The deadly foe: the fiend was too full of force

To be kept in my grip. However, he let his hand   970

Stay behind as his trace, to preserve his life,

Arm and shoulder; neither thereby, even so,

The cursed creature secured any comfort;

Nor will the loathsome ravager live the longer,

Afflicted by his crimes; but pain has seized   975

Him tightly in its inexorable grip,

With relentless locks; the creature there bearing

The marks of crime must await the grand doom,

What the Lord of light will decree for him."

    Then the son of Ecglaf* became more reticent a man,   980

In boastful outpour on battle-brave deeds,

After the nobles had beheld the hand

Put high over the roof by the strength of an earl,

The fingers of the fiend; to look at from the front,

Each of the strong nails was most like steel;   985

hæþenes handsporu   hilderinces,

egl[u] unheoru;   æghwylc gecwæð,

þæt him heardra nan   hrinan wolde

iren ærgod,   þæt ðæs ahlæcan

blodge beadufolme   onberan wolde.   990

(XV) Ða wæs haten hreþe   Heort innanweard

folmum gefrætwod;   fela þæra wæs,

wera ond wifa,   þe þæt winreced,

gestsele gyredon.   Goldfag scinon

web æfter wagum,   wundorsiona fela   995

secga gehwylcum   þara þe on swylc starað.

Wæs þæt beorhte bold   tobrocen swiðe,

eal inneweard   irenbendum fæst,

heorras tohlidene.   Hrof ana genæs,

ealles ansund,   þe se aglæca   1000

fyrendædum fag,   on fleam gewand,

aldres orwena.   No þæt yðe byð

to befleonne,   fremme se þe wille,

ac gesecan sceal   sawlberendra,

nyde genydde,   niþða bearna,   1005

grundbuendra   gearwe stowe,

þær his lichoma   legerbedde fæst

swefeþ æfter symle.

                Þa wæs sæl ond mæl,

þæt to healle gang   Healfdenes sunu;

wolde self cyning   symbel þicgan.   1010

Ne gefrægen ic þa mægþe   maran weorode

ymb hyra sincgyfan   sel gebæran.

Bugon þa to bence   blædagande,

fylle gefægon;   fægere geþægon

The horrible hand-spur of the heathen harasser

Was frightening; everyone said that no sword,

No matter how hard and well brandished,

Would harm him, that it would have made

The bloody atrocities subside, of the brutish fiend. 990

(XV) Then it was ordered that Heorot be inwardly

Bedecked quickly by hands; there was quite a number

Of men and women who made ready the wine-hall,

The banquet-building. Gold-adorned tapestries shone

On the walls, many a wondrous scene 995

To each man, who gazes on such a sight!

That bright building had been utterly broken—

The whole interior fastened firm by steel bands—

With its hinges cracked. The roof alone remained

Undamaged entirely, which the demonic fiend, 1000

Guilty of gruesome gore, had left in his flight,

Despairing of life. That is not easy

To flee from—let him try who wishes so—,

But he shall seek by necessity

The prepared place, destined for the soul-bearers, 1005

The children of men, the inhabitants of the earth,

Where his body, after the feast of life, will sleep

Fast in the bed of death.

     Then time was ripe

That Healfdene's son* should walk to the hall;

The king himself would partake of the banquet. 1010

I have not heard of people in a greater band,

Who behaved better in attending to their ring-giver.

Then on the bench sat down the glorious ones.

They rejoiced at the feast; their kinsmen,

medoful manig   magas þara*   1015
swiðhicgende   on sele þam hean,
Hroðgar ond Hroþulf.   Heorot innan wæs
freondum afylled;   nalles facenstafas
Þeod-Scyldingas   þenden fremedon.

    Forgeaf þa Beowulfe   bearn Healfdenes   1020
segen gyldenne   sigores to leane,
hroden hildecumbor,*   helm ond byrnan;
mære maðþumsweord   manige gesawon
beforan beorn beran.   Beowulf geþah
ful on flette;   no he þære feohgyfte   1025
for sceotendum   scamigan ðorfte;
ne gefrægn ic freondlicor   feower madmas
golde gegyrede   gummanna fela
in ealobence   oðrum gesellan.
Ymb þæs helmes hrof   heafodbeorge   1030
wirum bewunden   wala* utan heold,
þæt him fela laf   frecne ne meahton
scurheard sceþðan,   þonne scyldfreca
ongean gramum   gangan scolde.
Heht ða eorla hleo   eahta mearas   1035
fætedhleore   on flet têon,
in under eoderas;   þara anum stod
sadol searwum fah,   since gewurþad;
þæt wæs hildesetl   heahcyninges,
ðonne sweorda gelac   sunu Healfdenes   1040
efnan wolde;   næfre on ore læg
widcuþes wig,   ðonne walu feollon.
Ond ða Beowulfe   bega gehwæþres
eodor Ingwina   onweald geteah,

The high-spirited Hrothgar and Hrothulf,*   1015
Pleasantly partook of many a mead-cup,
In the lofty pavilion. Heorot was within
Filled with friends: in those days the Danes were
Not prone to practice perfidy at all.
  Then the son of Healfdene gave to Beowulf   1020
A golden flag of victory as a gift,
An adorned battle-banner, a helmet and a coat of mail;
Many people saw the glorious treasure-sword
Be borne to the hero. Beowulf received
A cup in the hall; for the dispensing of the costly gifts   1025
He had no cause to be baffled in the presence of the warriors.
I have not heard of any other multitude of men
In any other ale-bench who have made a present
Of the four treasures in a manner more friendly.
Around the top of the helmet the rim held   1030
A head-protection outside, bound with metal bands,
That a storm-sweeping sword could not inflict
A severe injury on its wearer, when the warrior
Should make onward move towards his hostile foes.
Then the guardian of the earls ordered to lead   1035
Into the hall eight horses with gold-plated headgears,
Inside the precincts; on one of them stood
A saddle skillfully decorated and adorned with jewels.
That was the war-seat of the high king,
When the son of Healfdene would perform   1040
The play of swords; never in the front failed
The valor of the valiant, each time the vanquished fell.
And then to Beowulf the prince of Ing's kinsmen*
Granted the power to wield on both, the horses

wicga ond wæpna;   het hine wel brucan.   1045
Swa manlice   mære þeoden,
hordweard hæleþa,   heaþoræsas geald
mearum ond madmum,   swa hy næfre man lyhð,
se þe secgan wile   soð æfter rihte.
(XVI) Ða gyt æghwylcum   eorla drihten   1050
þara þe mid Beowulfe   brimlade teah,
on þære medubence   maþðum gesealde,
yrfelafe,   ond þone ænne heht
golde forgyldan,   þone ðe Grendel ær
mane acwealde,   swa he hyra ma wolde,   1055
nefne him witig God   wyrd forstode
ond ðæs mannes mod.   Metod eallum weold
gumena cynnes,   swa he nu git dêð.
Forþan bið andgit   æghwær selest,
ferhðes foreþanc.   Fela sceal gebidan   1060
leofes ond laþes   se þe longe her
on ðyssum windagum   worolde bruceð!
      Þær wæs sang ond sweg   samod ætgædere
fore Healfdenes   hildewisan,
gomenwudu greted,   gid oft wrecen,   1065
ðonne healgamen   Hroþgares scop
æfter medobence   mænan scolde:

". . . Finnes eaferum.   Ða hie se fær begeat,
hæleð Healf-Dena,   Hnæf Scyldinga,
in Freswæle   feallan scolde.*   1070
Ne huru Hildeburh   herian þorfte
Eotena treowe;   unsynnum wearð
beloren leofum   æt þam lindplegan,

72

And the weapons; he ordered him to use them well.   1045
So manfully did the glorious prince,
The hoard-guard of men, recompense for the battle-storms
With horses and treasures, that nobody will ever disparage them—
None who wishes to tell the truth after what is correct.
(XVI) Furthermore, on each of the warriors   1050
Who had undertaken the journey with Beowulf,
The prince at the mead-bench bestowed treasure,
An heirloom; and he ordered to recompense him
With gold—the one whom Grendel had earlier
Slaughtered savagely—as he* would have done more,   1055
Had God in His wisdom and the hero's high spirit
Not forestalled that fate. The Lord has ruled over
The whole of mankind, as He even now does.
Therefore, prudence, forethought of mind,
At all times is best. Many of the beloved and the loathed   1060
He shall live to see—he who for long here
In these days of hardship still enjoys the world!
      There was song and music all mixed together
In the presence of Healfdene's battle-leader;
Harp strings strummed, song often sung,   1065
When Hrothgar's minstrel had to recite in the hall,
Along the mead-benches, his entertaining lines:

". . . the retainers of Finn. When a sudden assault swept on them,
The hero of the Half-Danes, Hnæf of the Scyldings,
Was fated to fall on the Frisian field of slaughter.*   1070
Not indeed had Hildeburh any reason to praise
The faithfulness of Finn's people;* faultless, she became
Deprived of her dear ones at the dashing of shields,

bearnum ond broðrum;   hie on gebyrd hruron,

gare wunde;   þæt wæs geomuru ides!   1075

Nalles holinga   Hoces dohtor

meotodsceaft bemearn,   syþðan morgen com,

ða heo under swegle   geseon meahte

morþorbealo maga,   þær he[o]* ær mæste heold

worolde wynne.   Wig ealle fornam   1080

Finnes þegnas   nemne feaum anum,

þæt he ne mehte   on þæm meðelstede

wig Hengeste   wiht gefeohtan,

ne þa wealafe   wige forþringan

þeodnes ðegne;*   ac hig him geþingo budon,   1085

þæt hie him oðer flet   eal gerymdon,

healle ond heahsetl,   þæt hie healfre geweald

wið Eotena bearn   agan moston,

ond æt feohgyftum   Folcwaldan sunu

dogra gehwylce   Dene weorþode,   1090

Hengestes heap   hringum wenede

efne swa swiðe   sincgestreonum

fættan goldes,   swa he Fresena cyn

on beorsele   byldan wolde.

    "Ða hie getruwedon   on twa healfa   1095

fæste frioðuwære.   Fin Hengeste

elne unflitme   aðum benemde,

þæt he þa wealafe   weotena dome

arum heolde,   þæt ðær ænig mon

wordum ne worcum   wære ne bræce,   1100

ne þurh inwitsearo   æfre gemænden,

ðeah hie hira beaggyfan   banan folgedon

ðeodenlease,   þa him swa geþearfod wæs;

A son and a brother: they fell into fate,

Slaughtered by spears—that was a sorrowful woman.   1075

Not without cause did the daughter of Hoc*

Deplore the decree of destiny, when morning came.

Then she could see under the sky the butchery

Of her blood-kin, where she* used to bathe in the best bliss

The world had bestowed. The battle had carried off   1080

All the thanes of Finn, leaving only a few,

That he could not in the sword-crossing stead

Carry on combat at all against Hengest,

Nor save the survivors in the war

From the prince's thane; but they tendered the terms:*   1085

That they would yield to them another building entirely,

The hall and its high seat, so that they might own

Control of its half with the sons of the Jutes,

And at treasure-dispensing Folcwalda's son*

Should honor the Danes on every occasion,   1090

And treat the troop of Hengest with rings—

With just so much quantity of treasure

Of ornamented gold that he would cheer up

The Frisian folk while within the banquet hall.

    "Then they confirmed the fast compact of peace   1095

On both sides: Finn declared to Hengest

In oaths with an undisputed zeal,

That he would keep the survivors honorably,

After his councilors' decree, that any man there

Would not break the pact in words or deeds,   1100

Nor would ever complain through evil intent, though

They, bereft of their prince, should follow the slayer

Of their ring-giver, when they were compelled by need;

gyf þonne Frysna hwylc   frecnan spræce

ðæs morþorhetes   myndgiend wære,   1105

þonne hit sweordes ecg   seðan* scolde.

    "Ad* wæs geæfned,   ond icge gold

ahæfen of horde.   Here-Scyldinga

betst beadorinca   wæs on bæl gearu.

Æt þæm ade wæs   eþgesyne   1110

swatfah syrce,   swyn ealgylden,

eofer irenheard,   æþeling manig

wundum awyrded;   sume on wæle crungon.

Het ða Hildburh   æt Hnæfes ade

hire selfre sunu   sweoloðe befæstan,   1115

banfatu bærnan   ond on bæl dôn

eame* on eaxle.   Ides gnornode,

geomrode giddum.   Guðrinc astah.

Wand to wolcnum   wælfyra mæst,

hlynode for hlawe;   hafelan multon,   1120

bengeato burston,   ðonne blod ætspranc,

laðbite lices.   Lig ealle forswealg,

gæsta gifrost,   þara ðe þær guð fornam

bega folces;   wæs hira blæd scacen.

(XVII) "Gewiton him ða wigend   wica neosian   1125

freondum befeallen,   Frysland geseon,

hamas ond heaburh.   Hengest ða gyt

wælfagne winter   wunode mid Finne

eal* unhlitme;   eard gemunde,

þeah þe he ne meahte*   on mere drifan   1130

hringedstefnan;   holm storme weol,

won wið winde,   winter yþe beleac

isgebinde,   oþ ðæt oþer com

In case any of the Frisians were to recollect

The murderous hate in speech smacking of audacity,   1105

Then it should be settled by the edge of a sword.

   "The funeral pyre was made ready, and gold

Brought from the hoard; the best of the warriors

Of the Scyldings* was ready on the funeral pyre.

At the funeral pile clearly discernible was   1110

The bloodstained mail-shirt, all-golden image of boar,

The iron-hard boar-figure on helmet; many a prince

Was destroyed by wounds; many a one died in the slaughter.

Then Hildeburh ordered at Hnæf's funeral fire

To commit her own son to the flame,   1115

To burn the bodies, and place him in the fire

Near his uncle shoulder to shoulder: the woman mourned,

And lamented with plaintive songs; the warrior ascended.*

The greatest of funeral fires wound to the skies,

Roared before the barrow; heads melted,   1120

Gashes burst open, while blood poured out,

Grievous wounds of body. The flame swallowed up all—

Most ravenous of spirits—of those that war had carried off

From both peoples: their life force was gone.

(XVII) "Then the warriors, bereft of friends, departed   1125

To go to their dwelling-place—homestead and stronghold—

And seek Friesland. Hengest still stayed on

With Finn for the slaughter-stained winter,

Though unwilling he was. He thought of his land,

Though he could not set sail on the sea   1130

His ring-prowed ship—the sea surged with storm,

Contended with wind; winter locked up the waves

With icy bond, till another year came

gear in geardas,   swa nu gyt dêð,
þa ðe syngales   sele bewitiað,   1135
wuldortorhtan weder.   Ða wæs winter scacen,
fæger foldan bearm;   fundode wrecca,
gist of geardum;   he to gyrnwræce
swiðor þohte   þonne to sælade,
gif he torngemot   þurhteon mihte,   1140
þæt he Eotena bearn   irne* gemunde.
Swa he ne forwyrnde   woroldrædenne,*
þonne him Hunlafing   hildeleoman,
billa selest,   on bearm dyde;
þæs wæron mid Eotenum   ecge cuðe.   1145
Swylce ferhðfrecan   Fin eft begeat
sweordbealo sliðen   æt his selfes ham,
siþðan grimne gripe   Guðlaf ond Oslaf
æfter sæsiðe   sorge mændon,
ætwiton weana dæl;   ne meahte wæfre mod   1150
forhabban in hreþre.   Ða wæs heal roden
feonda feorum,   swilce Fin slægen,
cyning on corþre,   ond seo cwen numen.
Sceotend Scyldinga   to scypon feredon
eal ingesteald   eorðcyninges,   1155
swylce hie æt Finnes ham   findan meahton
sigla, searogimma.   Hie on sælade
drihtlice wif   to Denum feredon,
læddon to leodum."
                    Leoð wæs asungen,
gleomannes gyd.   Gamen eft astah,   1160
beorhtode bencsweg;   byrelas sealdon
win of wunderfatum.   Þa cwom Wealhþeo forð

Unto their dwellings—so does it even now,
Glorious bright weather marks the season,   1135
Punctually as ever. Then the winter was gone,
Fair the lap of earth, the exile was eager to depart,
The visitor from the dwelling; he thought more
About revenge for injury than about sea-journey,
If he could bring about a hostile encounter,   1140
So that he might deal with the Jutes' sons by his sword.
Thus he did not refuse the way of the world,*
When the son of Hunlaf* put on his lap
A battle-beam, the best of swords;
Its blades were well known among the Jutes.   1145
Thus a cruel death by sword befell again
The bold-spirited Finn at his own home,
When Guthlaf and Oslaf* related the grim attack,
The grief after the sea-journey, and charged
For their great share of woes; restless mind might not   1150
Be constrained in heart. Then the hall became crimson
With the blood of enemies; also Finn was slain,
King of the band, and the queen was taken.
The Danish warriors carried to the ships
All the household stuffs of the king of the land   1155
And all the precious jewels they could find
At Finn's dwelling. They brought the noble lady
To the Danes on a voyage, and
Led her to their people."*
                    The lay was sung,
Tale told by a gleeman. Mirth was renewed again,   1160
The convivial noise sounded loud, the cupbearers poured
Wine from the wonder-bowls. Then forth came Wealhtheow,

gan under gyldnum beage,   þær þa godan twegen

sæton suhtergefæderan;   þa gyt wæs hiera sib ætgædere,

æghwylc oðrum trywe.   Swylce þær Unferþ þyle   1165

æt fotum sæt frean Scyldinga;   gehwylc hiora his ferhþe treowde,

þæt he hæfde mod micel,   þeah þe he his magum nære

arfæst æt ecga gelacum.   Spræc ða ides Scyldinga:

  "Onfoh þissum fulle,   freodrihten min,

sinces brytta!   Þu on sælum wes,   1170

goldwine gumena,   ond to Geatum spræc

mildum wordum,   swa sceal man don!

Beo wið Geatas glæd,   geofena gemyndig,

nean ond feorran   þu nu hafast.

Me man sægde,   þæt þu ðe for sunu wolde   1175

hererinc habban.   Heorot is gefælsod,

beahsele beorhta;   bruc þenden þu mote

manigra medo,   ond þinum magum læf

folc ond rice,   þonne ðu forð scyle

metodsceaft seon.   Ic minne can   1180

glædne Hroþulf,   þæt he þa geogoðe wile

arum healdan,   gyf þu ær þonne he,

wine Scildinga,   worold oflætest;

wene ic þæt he mid gode   gyldan wille

uncran eaferan,   gif he þæt eal gemon,   1185

hwæt wit to willan   ond to worðmyndum

umborwesendum ær   arna gefremedon."

Hwearf þa bi bence,   þær hyre byre wæron,

Hreðric ond Hroðmund,   ond hæleþa bearn,

giogoð ætgædere;   þær se goda sæt,   1190

Beowulf Geata,   be þæm gebroðrum twæm.

(XVIII) Him wæs ful boren,   ond freondlaþu

Wearing a golden diadem, to where the brave twain

Sat, nephew and uncle;* then their friendship was still fair,

Each true to the other. There also Unferth the court-speaker   1165

Sat at the feet of the Danish lord; each of them trusted his spirit,

That he had much courage, though he had been unkind to his kinsmen

At times of sword-blow.* Then the queen of the Scyldings spoke:

    "Receive this cup, my noble lord,

Dispenser of treasure! Be you now in mirth,   1170

Prince of men; and speak to the Geatish people

With kind words, as a man must do!

Be gracious to the Geats, mindful of their gifts

You now have near and far.

A man told me that you would have a warrior   1175

For your son. Heorot has been purged,

The bright ring-hall; enjoy many rewards

While you can, and leave people and kingdom

To your kinsmen, when you must go forth

And see the decree of fate. I know my kind Hrothulf,   1180

Son of Halga, will keep the young men

For the sake of honor, if you before he,

Lord of the Scyldings, leave the world.

I expect that he will repay our offspring

With goodness, if he remembers all that—   1185

What favors we earlier did for him as a child,

For the sake of pleasure and honor."*

Then she went to the bench where her sons were,

Hrethric and Hrothmund, and the warriors' sons,

The youths together; there the brave man sat—   1190

Beowulf of the Geats—close by the two brothers.

(XVIII) To him a cup was borne, and friendship

wordum bewægned,　ond wunden gold

estum geeawed,　earmreade twa,

hrægl ond hringas,　healsbeaga mæst　　　　　　　　　1195

þara þe ic on foldan　gefrægen hæbbe.

Nænigne ic under swegle　selran hyrde

hordmaðum hæleþa,　syþðan Hama ætwæg

to þære byrhtan byrig　Brosinga mene,

sigle ond sincfæt;　searoniðas fleah　　　　　　　　　1200

Eormenrices,　geceas ecne ræd.

Þone hring hæfde　Higelac Geata,

nefa Swertinges,　nyhstan siðe,

siðþan he under segne　sinc ealgode,

wælreaf werede;　hyne wyrd fornam,　　　　　　　　　1205

syþðan he for wlenco　wean ahsode,

fæhðe to Frysum.　He þa frætwe wæg,

eorclanstanas　ofer yða ful,

rice þeoden;　he under rande gecranc.

Gehwearf þa in Francna fæþm　feorh cyninges,　　　　1210

breostgewædu　ond se beah somod;

wyrsan wigfrecan　wæl reafedon

æfter guðsceare,　Geata leode,

hreawic heoldon.

　　　　　　　Heal swege onfeng.

Wealhðeo maþelode,　heo fore þæm werede spræc:　　1215

"Bruc ðisses beages,　Beowulf leofa,

hyse, mid hæle,　ond þisses hrægles neot,

þeodgestreona,　ond geþeoh tela,

cen þec mid cræfte,　ond þyssum cnyhtum wes

lara liðe;　ic þe þæs lean geman.　　　　　　　　　　1220

Hafast þu gefered,　þæt ðe feor ond neah

Offered in words, and twisted gold bestowed

With good wishes, along with two arm-ornaments,

Corselet, and rings, the greatest of neck-rings   1195

That I have ever heard about on earth.

I have not heard of any better jewel of men

Under the sky, since Hama carried

To the bright burg a necklace of the Brosings,

A broach and a cup—fled the treacherous enmity   1200

Of Eormenric, and chose an eternal benefit.*

This ring Hygelac of the Geats, nephew* to Swerting,

Had—he had it till most recently—

When under a banner he defended the treasure,

And protected the battle-spoil. Fate took him away,   1205

When he, out of pride, sought for trouble—

Feud with the Frisians. He carried the treasures,

The mighty prince did carry the precious stones

Over the sea brimful of waves; he fell under a shield.

Then the king's body passed into the Franks' possession,*   1210

And his breast-guard and the ring, along with it;

The lowly warmongers plundered those slain,

When carnage was over; the people of the Geats kept

The place filled with bodies.

                 The hall overflowed with sound.

Wealhtheow spoke, she spoke before the company: 1215

"Enjoy this ring, Beowulf, my dear young man,

With prosperity, and enjoy wearing this corselet,

These treasures of people, and prosper well.

Prove yourself with power, and be kind to these boys

In your counsel! I will think of a reward for you for that.   1220

You have brought it about, that far and near

ealne wideferhþ   weras ehtigað,

efne swa side   swa sæ bebugeð,

windgeard, weallas.   Wes þenden þu lifige,

æþeling, eadig.   Ic þe an tela   1225

sincgestreona.   Beo þu suna minum

dædum gedefe,   dreamhealdende.

Her is æghwylc eorl   oþrum getrywe,

modes milde,   mandrihtne hold;

þegnas syndon geþwære,   þeod ealgearo,   1230

druncne dryhtguman   doð swa ic bidde."

      Eode þa to setle.   Þær wæs symbla cyst,

druncon win weras.   Wyrd ne cuþon,

geosceaft grimme,   swa hit agangen wearð

eorla manegum,   syþðan æfen cwom,   1235

ond him Hroþgar gewat   to hofe sinum,

rice to ræste.   Reced weardode

unrim eorla,   swa hie oft ær dydon.

Bencþelu beredon;   hit geondbræded wearð

beddum ond bolstrum.   Beorscealca sum   1240

fus ond fæge   fletræste gebeag.

Setton him to heafdon   hilderandas,

bordwudu beorhtan;   þær on bence wæs

ofer æþelinge   yþgesene

heaþosteapa helm,   hringed byrne,   1245

þrecwudu þrymlic.   Wæs þeaw hyra,

þæt hie oft wæron   an wig gearwe,

ge æt ham ge on herge,   ge gehwæþer þara

efne swylce mæla,   swylce hira mandryhtne

þearf gesælde;   wæs seo þeod tilu.   1250

(XIX) Sigon þa to slæpe.   Sum sare angeald

People will praise you forever and ever,
Even so widely as does the sea, home of the winds,
Surround the walls. While you live, prince,
Be prosperous! I wish you to keep the treasures,   1225
Being duly yours. Be you to my son
Kind in deeds, being so blessed!
Here is each earl faithful to the other,
Kind in heart, loyal to his liege lord.
The thanes are united, people all-willing;   1230
Flushed with wine, the retainers do as I bid."

    Then she returned to her seat. A banquet best in its kind
Went on, in which men drank heartily. They were not aware
Of the grim fate, as it happened to befall
Many of the earls when the evening came;   1235
And the mighty Hrothgar left for his dwelling
To rest for the night; innumerable earls guarded
The hall, as they often had done before.
They cleared the benches away; it became overspread
With beds and cushions. One of the drunken feasters   1240
Lay down on a hall-couch, ready to receive death as his doom.
They had set battle-shields, bright wooden boards,
As pillows. There on the bench were
Over the prince clearly visible
A helmet towering battle-worthy, a corselet woven of rings,   1245
And a spear most warlike. It was their practice
That they were always prepared for battle,
Both at home and in the field, and at any of such
Times as when a trouble had befallen their liege,
Distress coming unexpected; the troop was a good one.   1250
(XIX) Then they fell asleep. One paid heavily for

æfenræste,   swa him ful oft gelamp,

siþðan goldsele   Grendel warode,

unriht æfnde,   oþ þæt ende becwom,

swylt æfter synnum.   Þæt gesyne wearþ,   1255

widcuþ werum,   þætte wrecend þa gyt

lifde æfter laþum,   lange þrage,

æfter guðceare;   Grendles modor,

ides, aglæcwif,   yrmþe gemunde,

se þe wæteregesan   wunian scolde,   1260

cealde streamas,   siþðan Cain wearð

to ecgbanan   angan breþer,

fæderenmæge;   he þa fag gewat,

morþre gemearcod,   mandream flêon,

westen warode.   Þanon woc fela   1265

geosceaftgasta;   wæs þæra Grendel sum,

heorowearh hetelic,   se æt Heorote fand

wæccendne wer   wiges bidan.

Þær him aglæca   ætgræpe wearð;

hwæþre he gemunde   mægenes strenge,   1270

gimfæste gife   ðe him God sealde,

ond him to Anwaldan   are gelyfde,

frofre ond fultum;   ðy he þone feond ofercwom,

gehnægde helle gast.   Þa he hean gewat,

dreame bedæled,   deaþwic sêon,   1275

mancynnes feond.   Ond his modor þa gyt,

gifre ond galgmod   gegan wolde

sorhfulne sið,   sunu deað wrecan.

    Com þa to Heorote,   ðær Hring-Dene

geond þæt sæld swæfun.   Þa ðær sona wearð   1280

edhwyrft eorlum,   siþðan inne fealh

86

His evening rest, as it had happened to them so often
When Grendel ransacked the golden hall,
Perpetrated misdeed till the end came—
Death after his devilish deeds. It became obvious and   1255
Widely known to men that an avenger still
Lived after the loathsome one for a long time,
After the bloody duel: Grendel's mother—
A fiendish female monster—bore in mind the misery,
She who had to inhabit the dreadful water,   1260
The cold streams, when Cain came to be
The sword-slayer of his sole brother—a branch of
The same fatherly root; he then roamed away outlawed,
Fleeing from life's joy among men, marked for murder,
And inhabited a wasteland. From him sprang many   1265
Of the fate-engendered spirits: Grendel was one of them,
The hateful accursed foe that found at Heorot
The watchful warrior awaiting warlike confrontation;
There the fiend laid hold of the one waiting for him.
However, the latter remembered the strength of power,   1270
The bountiful gift, which God had granted him,
And entrusted himself to the Lord for His help,
Solace and support; thus, he overcame the fiend,
And had the hell's demon subdued. Then he left humiliated,
Deprived of mirth, to see the place of his death—   1275
The enemy of mankind did. And yet his mother,
Greedy and gloomy, wanted to embark upon
A venture perilous and avenge her son's death.
    Then she came to Heorot, where the Ring-Danes
Were sleeping all over the hall; then there soon occurred   1280
Turmoil for the earls, when Grendel's mother

Grendles modor.   Wæs se gryre læssa

efne swa micle,   swa bið mægþa cræft,

wiggryre wifes,   be wæpnedmen,

þonne heoru bunden,   hamere geþruen,*   1285

sweord swate fah   swin ofer helme

ecgum dyhtig   andweard scireð.

Ða wæs on healle   heardecg togen

sweord ofer setlum,   sidrand manig

hafen handa fæst;   helm ne gemunde,   1290

byrnan side,   þa hine se broga angeat.

Heo wæs on ofste,   wolde ut þanon,

feore beorgan,   þa heo onfunden wæs;

hraðe heo æþelinga   anne hæfde

fæste befangen,   þa heo to fenne gang.   1295

Se wæs Hroþgare   hæleþa leofost

on gesiðes had   be sæm tweonum,

rice randwiga,   þone ðe heo on ræste abreat,

blædfæstne beorn.   Næs Beowulf ðær,

ac wæs oþer in   ær geteohhod   1300

æfter maþðumgife   mærum Geate.

Hream wearð in Heorote;   heo under heolfre genam

cuþe folme;   cearu wæs geniwod,

geworden in wicun.   Ne wæs þæt gewrixle til,

þæt hie on ba healfa   bicgan scoldon   1305

freonda feorum.

                    Þa wæs frod cyning,

har hilderinc,   on hreon mode,

syðþan he aldorþegn   unlyfigendne,

þone deorestan   deadne wisse.

Hraþe wæs to bure   Beowulf fetod,   1310

Dashed into the hall. The horror was the less,

Even to such a degree as should female strength be,

The warlike threat of a woman, than a warrior's,

When a ring-adorned hammer-forged sword,   1285

A blood-besmeared bill with strong blades,

Cuts the boar over the helmet an opponent wears.*

Then in the hall hard-edged sword was drawn

Over the seats; many a broad shield firm

Was heaved by hand; none could remember his helmet   1290

Or his broad corselet, once terror had gotten hold of him.

She was in haste, and wanted to go out from there,

To save her life, when she was discovered.

Quickly she had one of the men seized

Firmly; then she went to her marshland.   1295

He was the man dearest to Hrothgar

In the position of a retainer on earth,

A valiant shield-bearer, a glorious warrior,

That she killed while in rest. Beowulf was not there,

For a separate lodge had earlier been prepared   1300

For the glorious Geat, when the ring-giving was done.

Outcry arose in Heorot; she had taken, besmeared in blood,

The well-known hand;* care was renewed,

Coming upon the dwelling. That was not a fair deal,

That they, on both sides, had to pay   1305

With the lives of friends!

               Then the old king,

The hoary warrior, was in a troubled mind,

Since he knew that his chief thane

Was no longer alive, his dearest one dead.

Speedily to the hall Beowulf was sent for,   1310

sigoreadig secg.   Samod ærdæge

eode eorla sum,   æþele cempa

self mid gesiðum   þær se snotera bad,

hwæþer him Alwalda   æfre wille

æfter weaspelle   wyrpe gefremman.   1315

Gang ða æfter flore   fyrdwyrðe man

mid his handscale   —healwudu dynede—

þæt he þone wisan   wordum nægde

frean Ingwina,   frægn gif him wære

æfter neodlaðu[m]*   niht getæse.   1320

(XX) Hroðgar maþelode,   helm Scyldinga:

"Ne frin þu æfter sælum!   Sorh is geniwod

Denigea leodum.   Dead is Æschere,

Yrmenlafes   yldra broþor,

min runwita   ond min rædbora,   1325

eaxlgestealla,   ðonne we on orlege

hafelan weredon,   þonne hniton feþan,

eoferas cnysedan.   Swylc scolde eorl wesan,

æþeling ærgod,   swylc Æschere wæs!

Wearð him on Heorote   to handbanan   1330

wælgæst wæfre;   ic ne wat hwæder

atol æse wlanc   eftsiðas teah,

fylle gefægnod.   Heo þa fæhðe wræc,

þe þu gystran niht   Grendel cwealdest

þurh hæstne had   heardum clammum,   1335

forþan he to lange   leode mine

wanode ond wyrde.   He æt wige gecrang

ealdres scyldig,   ond nu oþer cwom

mihtig manscaða,   wolde hyre mæg wrecan,

ge feor hafað   fæhðe gestæled,   1340

The victorious man was. As soon as the day broke,
The noble champion, one of the heroes, went
With his retainers to where the wise man was waiting
To see whether the Lord would ever for him
Bring forth a remedy after the woeful tidings.   1315
Then the battle-brave man walked in on the hall floor,
With his troop—the hall-wood resounded—
So that he might address the wise lord
Of the friends of Ing* in words, ask if to him
The night had been agreeable after his desires.   1320
(XX) Hrothgar spoke, protector of the Scyldings:
"Do not ask about joys! Sorrow is renewed
To the Danish people: Æschere is dead,
Yrmenlaf's elder brother,
My trusted confidant and my counselor,   1325
My comrade—when we in battle protected our
Respective heads, and when the foot-troops clashed,
Dashed against the helmet boars; so should a warrior be,
A man good from old times, as Æschere was!
A wandering murderous sprite has slain him   1330
With her hands in Heorot: I do not know to where
The horrid one took her trip back, glorying in her carrion,
Rejoicing at the feast. She has done revenge on the fight,
In which yesterday night you killed Grendel
In a violent manner with your strong grips,   1335
Because he had dwindled and destroyed my people
Much too long; in the fight he fell down,
Having his life forfeited. And now another
Powerful evil-doer came, would avenge her son,
And has so far made vengeance for the fight—   1340

þæs þe þincean mæg   þegne monegum,

se þe æfter sincgyfan   on sefan greoteþ,—

hreþerbealo hearde;   nu seo hand ligeð,

se þe eow welhwylcra   wilna dohte.

   "Ic þæt londbuend,   leode mine,   1345

selerædende   secgan hyrde,

þæt hie gesawon   swylce twegen

micle mearcstapan   moras healdan,

ellorgæstas.   Ðæra oðer wæs,

þæs þe hie gewislicost   gewitan meahton,   1350

idese onlicnes;*   oðer earmsceapen

on weres wæstmum   wræclastas træd,

næfne he wæs mara   þonne ænig man oðer;

þone on geardagum   Grendel nemdon

foldbuende;   no hie fæder cunnon,   1355

hwæþer him ænig wæs   ær acenned

dyrnra gasta.   Hie dygel lond

warigeað wulfhleoþu,   windige næssas,

frecne fengelad,   ðær fyrgenstream

under næssa genipu   niþer gewiteð,   1360

flod under foldan.   Nis þæt feor heonon

milgemearces,   þæt se mere standeð;

ofer þæm hongiað   hrinde bearwas,

wudu wyrtum fæst   wæter oferhelmað.

Þær mæg nihta gehwæm   niðwundor seon,   1365

fyr on flode.   No þæs frod leofað

gumena bearna,   þæt þone grund wite.

Ðeah þe hæðstapa   hundum geswenced,

heorot hornum trum   holtwudu sece,

feorran geflymed,   ær he feorh seleð,   1370

As it may appear to many a thane,
Who weeps in his heart for his treasure-giver,
A hard heart-bale; now the hand lies low,
That treated you well with all the good things.*

   "I have heard the land-dwellers, my people,   1345
The hall-counselors say so—
That they have seen such two huge
Wanderers in the wasteland, the accursed spirits,
Hold the marshes. One of them was,
According to what they most certainly could know,   1350
In the likeness of a woman; the other wretch
Trod his tracks of exile in the shape of a man,
Except that he was bigger than any other man.
The earth-dwellers called him Grendel
In olden days. They don't know who fathered him,   1355
Whether any before him had been begotten
Of dark spirits. They inhabit a hidden land—
Wolf-infested slopes, windy headlands, and
A perilous fen-path, where the mountain-stream
Falls down in the mist from the headlands   1360
And flows beneath the earth. Not far from here,
A few miles away, stands the mere,
Over which droop trees covered with frost.
The wood darkens the water with entangled roots.
There every night a fearful wonder is seen—   1365
Fire flaring on the water. None alive among men,
No matter how wise, knows how deep it is.
Fleeing from far off, chased by hounds, a stag
May seek a holt-wood to hide his strong horns;
Yet he will rather give up his life, lingering   1370

aldor on ofre,   ær he in wille,

hafelan [hydan].*   Nis þæt heoru stow!

Þonon yðgeblond   up astigeð

won to wolcnum,   þonne wind styreþ

lað gewidru,   oð þæt lyft drysmaþ,   1375

roderas reotað.   Nu is se ræd gelang

eft æt þe anum.   Eard git ne const,

frecne stowe,   ðær þu findan miht

[fela]sinnigne* secg;   sec gif þu dyrre!

Ic þe þa fæhðe   feo leanige,   1380

ealdgestreonum,   swa ic ær dyde,

wundnum* golde,   gyf þu on weg cymest."

(XXI) Beowulf maþelode,   bearn Ecgþeowes:

"Ne sorga, snotor guma!   Selre bið æghwæm,

þæt he his freond wrece,   þonne he fela murne.   1385

Ure æghwylc sceal   ende gebidan

worolde lifes;   wyrce se þe mote

domes ær deaþe;   þæt bið drihtguman

unlifgendum   æfter selest.

Aris, rices weard,   uton hraþe feran   1390

Grendles magan   gang sceawigan.

Ic hit þe gehate;   no he on helm losaþ,

ne on foldan fæþm,   ne on fyrgenholt,

ne on gyfenes grund,   ga þær he wille.

Ðys dogor þu   geþyld hafa   1395

weana gehwylces,   swa ic þe wene to."

        Ahleop ða se gomela,   Gode þancode,

mihtigan Drihtne,   þæs se man gespræc.

Þa wæs Hroðgare   hors gebæted,

wicg wundenfeax.   Wisa fengel   1400

94

On the bank, than plunge his head into the pool
To save his life;* that is not a pleasant place!
From there surging waves rise up,
Darkening the clouds, while the wind swirls,
Threatening storms, till the air turns choking 1375
And the sky howls. Now the remedy is at hand
Again only from you. You don't know the dwelling yet,
The dangerous place, where you might find
The sinful creature; seek if you dare!
I will reward you with riches for the fight, 1380
With ancient treasures, as I have done before,
With twisted gold, if you come away."
(XXI) Beowulf spoke, son of Ecgtheow:
"Do not be in grief, wise man! It is better for any man
That he avenge his friend than he mourn much. 1385
Each of us must live to see the end
Of worldly life; let him, who may, attain glory
Before his death: that is best for a fighting man,
After he has done with his living days to leave behind.
Arise, guardian of the kingdom. Let us go quickly 1390
And see the track of Grendel's kinswoman.
I promise you this: she will not escape into a refuge,
Nor into the bosom of the earth, nor into a mountain-wood,
Nor to the bottom of the sea, go where she may!
This day do have patience 1395
For each of the woes, as I hope you will."
    Then the old man leapt up, thanked God,
The mighty Lord, for what the man had spoken.
For Hrothgar then a horse was saddled—
The steed with braided mane. The wise king 1400

geatolic gende;   gumfeþa stop
lindhæbbendra.   Lastas wæron
æfter waldswaþum   wide gesyne,
gang ofer grundas,   þær heo* gegnum for
ofer myrcan mor,   magoþegna bær   1405
þone selestan   sawolleasne
þara þe mid Hroðgare   ham eahtode.
Ofereode þa   æþelinga bearn
steap stanhliðo,   stige nearwe,
enge anpaðas,   uncuð gelad,   1410
neowle næssas,   nicorhusa fela;
he feara sum   beforan gengde
wisra monna   wong sceawian,
oþ þæt he færinga   fyrgenbeamas
ofer harne stan   hleonian funde,   1415
wynleasne wudu;   wæter under stod
dreorig ond gedrefed.   Denum eallum wæs,
winum Scyldinga,   weorce on mode
to geþolianne,   ðegne monegum,
oncyð eorla gehwæm,   syðþan Æscheres   1420
on þam holmclife   hafelan metton.
Flod blode weol   —folc to sægon—,
hatan heolfre.   Horn stundum song
fuslic fyrdleoð.   Feþa eal gesæt.
     Gesawon ða æfter wætere   wyrmcynnes fela,   1425
sellice sædracan,   sund cunnian,
swylce on næshleoðum   nicras licgean,
ða on undernmæl   oft bewitigað
sorhfulne sið   on seglrade,
wyrmas ond wildeor.   Hie on weg hruron,   1430

Rode in a stately manner; a troop on foot marched,
The band of shield-bearers. The footprints were
Clearly traceable along the woodland paths,
The track over the ground, where she had gone straight
Over the dark moor, bearing the best   1405
Of thanes no longer blessed with soul—
Of those who had with Hrothgar kept watch over home.
Then the offspring of noble princes* traversed
Steep stony slopes, narrow lanes,
Deserted paths, an unknown trail,   1410
Precipitous headlands, many an abode of water-monsters;
He rode ahead with a handful of his
Wise counselors to investigate the terrain,
Till he suddenly found the mountain trees
Leaning over a gray stone—   1415
A wood deprived of joy. Water stagnated underneath—
Dreary and turbid; to all the Danes,
The retainers of the Scyldings, to many thanes,
It was painful in heart to endure, to each of the men
It was a moment of grief, when they saw   1420
Æschere's head put on the cliff by the waterside.
The water was bubbling with blood—people saw—
Hot still. The horn sounded time and again
The war song prepared. The entire troop sat down.
    Then they saw in the water many of the serpents' kin   1425
And sinister sea-snakes swimming in the pool,
Also the water-monsters lying on the headlands,
Which in the morning-tide often venture on a
Perilous journey in the sea: those serpents and wild beasts.
They rushed on the way, fierce and enraged: 1430

bitere ond gebolgne;   bearhtm ongeaton,
guðhorn galan.   Sumne Geata leod
of flanbogan   feores getwæfde,
yðgewinnes,   þæt him on aldre stod
herestræl hearda;   he on holme wæs   1435
sundes þe sænra,   ðe hyne swylt fornam.
Hræþe wearð on yðum   mid eoferspreotum
heorohocyhtum   hearde genearwod,
niða genæged,   ond on næs togen,
wundorlic wægbora;   weras sceawedon   1440
gryrelicne gist.   Gyrede hine Beowulf
eorlgewædum,   nalles for ealdre mearn;
scolde herebyrne   hondum gebroden,
sid ond searofah,   sund cunnian,
seo ðe bancofan   beorgan cuþe,   1445
þæt him hildegrap   hreþre ne mihte,
eorres inwitfeng   aldre gesceþðan;
ac se hwita helm   hafelan werede,
se þe meregrundas   mengan scolde,
secan sundgebland   since geweorðad,   1450
befongen freawrasnum,   swa hine fyrndagum   *in days gone by.*
worhte wæpna smið,   wundrum teode,
besette swinlicum,   þæt hine syðþan no
brond ne beadomecas   bitan ne meahton.
Næs þæt þonne mætost   mægenfultuma,   1455
þæt him on ðearfe lah   ðyle Hroðgares;
wæs þæm hæftmece   Hrunting nama;
þæt wæs an foran   ealdgestreona;
ecg wæs iren,   atertanum fah,
ahyrded heaþoswate;   næfre hit æt hilde ne swac   1460

They had heard the sound, the war-horn singing.

A man of the Geats deprived one of them

Of life with an arrow shot from his bow,

Of its sinew for swimming, for the strong war-arrow

Stuck in it for life; it was in the water   1435

Slower in swimming, for it was now in the grip of death.

Speedily it was ransacked hard on the waves

With sword-hooked barbed boar-spears,

Assailed violently, and drawn to the bluff—

The wonder-causing wave-roamer; people beheld   1440

The horrid monster. Beowulf put on

His armor; he had no anxiety about his life;

The battle-corselet woven link by link by hand,

Broad and bearing crafty design, should now delve into water—

The armor that could protect his body   1445

So that no hostile grasp might harm his breast,

Nor any malicious grip of an angry one might injure his life;

But the glittering helmet protected the head—

The helmet that should scour the floors of the mere

And visit the vortex—being adorned with treasure   1450

And encircled with splendid bands, as the weapon-smith

Wrought it in olden days, shaping it wondrously,

Adorning it with boar-figures, so that since then

No sword or battle-maces could batter it.

Then it was not the smallest of mighty helps   1455

That Hrothgar's court speaker* lent him in need:

The hilted sword was called Hrunting.

That was an old legacy of ancient treasury.

Its blade was iron, decorated with poison-stripes,

And hardened with bloodshed; never at battle it had   1460

manna ængum   þara þe hit mid mundum bewand,

se ðe gryresiðas   gegan dorste,

folcstede fara;   næs þæt forma sið,

þæt hit ellenweorc   æfnan scolde.

Huru ne gemunde   mago Ecglafes   1465

eafoþes cræftig,   þæt he ær gespræc

wine druncen,   þa he þæs wæpnes onlah

selran sweordfrecan;   selfa ne dorste

under yða gewin   aldre geneþan,

drihtscype dreogan;   þær he dome forleas,   1470

ellenmærðum.   Ne wæs þæm oðrum swa,

syðþan he hine to guðe   gegyred hæfde.

(XXII) Beowulf maðelode,   bearn Ecgþeowes:

"Geþenc nu, se mæra   maga Healfdenes,

snottra fengel,   nu ic eom siðes fus,   1475

goldwine gumena,   hwæt wit geo spræcon,

gif ic æt þearfe   þinre scolde

aldre linnan,   þæt ðu me a wære

forðgewitenum   on fæder stæle.

Wes þu mundbora   minum magoþegnum,   1480

hondgesellum,   gif mec hild nime;

swylce þu ða madmas,   þe þu me sealdest,

Hroðgar leofa,   Higelace onsend.

Mæg þonne on þæm golde ongitan   Geata dryhten,

geseon sunu Hrædles,   þonne he on þæt sinc starað,   1485

þæt ic gumcystum   godne funde

beaga bryttan,   breac þonne moste.

Ond þu Unferð læt   ealde lafe,

wrætlic wægsweord,   widcuðne man

heardecg habban;   ic me mid Hruntinge   1490

Failed any of those who wielded it in their hands—
One that dared to enter upon perilous expeditions,
And run into a crowd of swarming foes. It was not
The first time that it should enact a work of valor.
Indeed, the son of Ecglaf,* of mighty strength,   1465
Did not remember what he had earlier spoken,
Drunk with wine, when he lent the weapon
To a better warrior. He himself dared not
Risk his life under the turbulence of waves
To perform bravery; there he lost his glory,   1470
Fame for courage. It was not so with the other,
When he had made himself all ready for the fight.
(XXII) Beowulf spoke, son of Ecgtheow:
"Think now, glorious son of Healfdene,
Wise king, now that I am ready for the venture,   1475
Prince of men, of what we two talked about earlier:
That, if at your need I should lose my life,
You would always be in the place of a father
For me, when I am gone.
Be you the guardian of my young retainers,   1480
My companions, if the battle should carry me off.
Also, the treasures that you have given me,
Dear Hrothgar, send them to Hygelac.
Then the lord of the Geats will perceive on the gold,
The son of Hrethel will, when he looks on that treasure,   1485
That I had found a good ring-giver
With manly virtues, and enjoyed while I could.
And let Unferth the wide-known man have
The old heirloom, the splendid sword with ornaments,
Hard of edge; I will attain glory   1490

dom gewyrce, oþðe mec deað nimeð!"

    Æfter þæm wordum   Weder-Geata leod

efste mid elne,—   nalas ondsware

bidan wolde;   brimwylm onfeng

hilderince.   Ða wæs hwil dæges,   1495

ær he þone grundwong   ongytan mehte.

    Sona þæt onfunde   se ðe floda begong

heorogifre beheold   hund missera,

grim ond grædig,   þæt þær gumena sum

ælwihta eard   ufan cunnode.   1500

Grap þa togeanes,   guðrinc gefeng

atolan clommum;   no þy ær in gescod

halan lice;   hring utan ymbbearh,

þæt heo þone fyrdhom   ðurhfon ne mihte,

locene leoðosyrcan   laþan fingrum.   1505

Bær þa seo brimwylf,   þa heo to botme com,

hringa þengel   to hofe sinum,

swa he ne mihte,   no he þeah modig wæs,*

wæpna gewealdan,   ac hine wundra þæs fela

swencte on sunde,   sædeor monig   1510

hildetuxum   heresyrcan bræc,

ehton aglæcan.   Ða se eorl ongeat,

þæt he in niðsele   nathwylcum wæs,

þær him nænig wæter   wihte ne sceþede,

ne him for hrofsele   hrinan ne mehte   1515

færgripe flodes;   fyrleoht geseah,

blacne leoman   beorhte scinan.

Ongeat þa se goda   grundwyrgenne,

merewif mihtig;   mægenræs forgeaf

hildebille,   hond sweng ne ofteah,   1520

With Hrunting, or death will carry me off!"

    After these words the man of the Weather-Geats
Hastened with courage—he would not wait
For an answer: the surge of the water received
The warrior. Then was it a long while of the day   1495
That he could see the floor of the mere.

    Soon that which had occupied the watery region
For half of a hundred years, fiercely ravenous,
Grim and greedy, found that there a certain man
From above was exploring the dwelling of the demons.   1500
She then gripped and seized the warrior towards her
With her horrid clutches; yet she could not injure
The wholesome body inside; the ring-mail protected outside,
That she could not pierce the battle-wear,
The shirt of interlocked rings, with her loathsome fingers.   1505
Then the she-wolf of the sea, when she came to the bottom,
Brought the prince of the rings to her dwelling.
So he could not—no matter how brave he was—
Wield his weapons; but many of the monsters molested him
In the water, and many of the underwater brutes   1510
Battered his battle-wear with their bulging tusks,
The fiends followed him. Then the warrior perceived
That he was in a certain hall of hostility,
Where no downpour of water would fall on him,
Nor a sudden sweep of flood could drown him,   1515
For the hall was roofed. He saw fire-light,
A blazing gleam burn brightly.
Then the brave man saw the accursed of the deep,
The mighty mere-woman; he gave such powerful swing
To his battle-sword—his hand did not deny the blow—   1520

þæt hire on hafelan   hringmæl agol
grædig guðleoð.   Ða se gist onfand,
þæt se beadoleoma   bitan nolde,
aldre sceþðan,   ac seo ecg geswac
ðeodne æt þearfe;   ðolode ær fela   1525
hondgemota,   helm oft gescær,
fæges fyrdhrægl;   ða wæs forma sið
deorum madme,   þæt his dom alæg.
Eft wæs anræd,   nalas elnes læt,
mærða gemyndig   mæg Hy[ge]laces.   1530
Wearp ða wundenmæl   wrættum gebunden
yrre oretta,   þæt hit on eorðan læg,
stið ond stylecg;   strenge getruwode,
mundgripe mægenes.   Swa sceal man don,
þonne he æt guðe   gegan þenceð   1535
longsumne lof;   na ymb his lif cearað.
    Gefeng þa be eaxle   —nalas for fæhðe mearn—
Guð-Geata leod   Grendles modor;
brægd þa beadwe heard,   þa he gebolgen wæs,
feorhgeniðlan,   þæt heo on flet gebeah.   1540
Heo him eft hraþe   andlean forgeald
grimman grapum   ond him togeanes feng;
oferwearp þa werigmod   wigena strengest,
feþecempa,   þæt he on fylle wearð.
Ofsæt þa þone selegyst   ond hyre seax geteah   1545
brad ond brunecg;   wolde hire bearn wrecan,
angan eaferan.   Him on eaxle læg
breostnet broden;   þæt gebearh feore,
wið ord ond wið ecge   ingang forstod.
Hæfde ða forsiðod   sunu Ecgþeowes   1550

That the ring-sword, falling on her head, made
A grim sound. Then the visitor found out
That the sword would not serve its purpose,
Injure life, but the sword had failed to serve
The prince in his need; many a hand-grapple it had   1525
Gone through earlier, and often cut through the helmet
And fight-wear of the fated; it was the first time
For the fine treasure when its glory had failed.
Still he was determined; Hygelac's kinsman was
Not loose in courage, but intent on attaining glory.   1530
He threw away the sword bound with carved ornaments—
The angry warrior did—that it lay on the ground,
Strong and steel-edged; he counted on his own strength,
The handgrip of his might. So must a man act,
When in a battle he thinks of obtaining the glory   1535
That will last long; he did not care about his life.
　　　Then the man of the War-Geats gripped Grendel's
Mother by her shoulder; he never shrank from the fight.
Then the battle-brave one, when he was enraged,
Did fling the deadly fiend, and she fell on the floor.   1540
She speedily paid back for his painful punishment
With her grim grips, and grappled with him.
Then the strongest of fighters, the foot-warrior,
Stumbled in exhaustion, and he happened to fall.
Then she sat upon the hall-visitor, and drew her short sword, 1545
Broad and bright-edged; she wanted to avenge her son,
Her sole offspring. On his shoulder lay
The woven mail-shirt, which protected his life;
It prevented sharp point and edge from piercing.
Thus the son of Ecgtheow, the champion of the Geats,   1550

under gynne grund,   Geata cempa,

nemne him heaðobyrne   helpe gefremede,

herenet hearde,   ond halig God

geweold wigsigor;   witig Drihten,

rodera Rædend   hit on ryht gesced   1555

yðelice,   syþðan he eft astod.

(XXIII) Geseah ða on searwum   sigeeadig bil,

eald sweord eotenisc,   ecgum þyhtig,

wigena weorðmynd;   þæt wæs wæpna cyst,

buton hit wæs mare   ðonne ænig mon oðer   1560

to beadulace   ætberan meahte,

god ond geatolic,   giganta geweorc.

He gefeng þa fetelhilt,   freca Scyldinga

hreoh ond heorogrim   hringmæl gebrægd,

aldres orwena,   yrringa sloh,   1565

þæt hire wið halse   heard grapode,

banhringas bræc; (bil eal ðurhwod   *sword*

fægne flæschoman;   heo on flet gecrong.

Sweord wæs swatig,   secg weorce gefeh.

Lixte se leoma,   leoht inne stod,   1570

efne swa of hefene   hadre scineð

rodores candel.   He æfter recede wlat;

hwearf þa be wealle,   wæpen hafenade

heard be hiltum   Higelaces ðegn

yrre ond anræd,—   næs seo ecg fracod   1575

hilderince,   ac he hraþe wolde

Grendle forgyldan   guðræsa fela

ðara þe he geworhte   to West-Denum

oftor micle   ðonne on ænne sið,

þonne he Hroðgares   heorðgeneatas   1580

Might have perished under the wide plain of earth,

Had his battle-wear not lent him help—

The hard metal-woven net—and the Holy God

Brought about victory; the Lord in His wisdom,

The Ruler of the heavens, rightly decided it   1555

With ease, for he stood up again.

(XXIII) Then he saw among the battle-gear a ferocious falchion,

An ancient sword with strong edges, made by giants—

The glory of warriors. That was the best of weapons,

Except that it was greater than any other man   1560

Could bear to battle for warlike wielding,

Strong and splendid, wrought by giants.

He gripped the linked hilt—the hero of the Scyldings did—

Rough and fierce; he drew the ring-sword,

Despairing of life, angrily struck,   1565

That it dug into her deep on the neck,

And broke the bone-ring; the falchion went smartly through

The body of the fated; she fell on the floor.

The bill was bloody, the man rejoiced at his work.

 The gleam brightened, while the light stayed within,   1570

Even as the candle of the sky shines clearly

From the heaven. He looked around the hall;

Then he walked along the wall, and lifted the weapon

Hard by the hilt—the thane of Hygelac,

In anger and determination. The sword was not useless   1575

To the warrior; but he wished to pay back

Speedily to Grendel for many of the assaults

Which he had perpetrated on the West-Danes,

Much too often—more than on one occasion,

When he slew Hrothgar's hearth-companions   1580

sloh on sweofote,   slæpende fræt

folces Denigea   fyftyne men,

ond oðer swylc   ut offerede,

laðlicu lac.   He him þæs lean forgeald,   *saw*

reþe cempa,   to ðæs þe he on ræste geseah   1585

guðwerigne   Grendel licgan,

aldorleasne,   swa him ær gescod

hild æt Heorote.   Hra wide sprong,

syþðan he æfter deaðe   drepe þrowade,

heorosweng heardne,   ond hine þa heafde becearf.   1590

    Sona þæt gesawon   snottre ceorlas,

þa ðe mid Hroðgare   on holm wliton,

þæt wæs yðgeblond   eal gemenged,

brim blode fah.   Blondenfeaxe,

gomele ymb godne   ongeador spræcon,   1595

þæt hig þæs æðelinges   eft ne wendon,

þæt he sigehreðig   secean come

mærne þeoden;   þa ðæs monige gewearð,

þæt hine seo brimwylf   abroten hæfde.

Ða com non dæges.   Næs ofgeafon   1600

hwate Scyldingas;   gewat him ham þonon

goldwine gumena.   Gistas setan

modes seoce   ond on mere staredon;

wiston ond ne wendon,   þæt hie heora winedrihten

selfne gesawon.   *Then, meanwhile,*

    Þa þæt sweord ongan   1605

æfter heaþoswate   hildegicelum,

wigbil wanian;   þæt wæs wundra sum,

þæt hit eal gemealt   ise gelicost,

ðonne forstes bend   Fæder onlæteð,

While asleep, and devoured the sleeping
Fifteen men of the Danish folk,
And carried off another such number,
As hideous booties. For that he paid him requital—
The wrathful warrior did—when he saw Grendel   1585
Lying lifeless, as if in rest, wornout with war—
So much had he been injured beforehand
From the fight at Heorot. The body spread wide,
When he suffered a blow after death,
The strong sweep of the sword, and his head fell, chopped off.   1590
    Soon the wise men saw—
Those who with Hrothgar were gazing on the water—
That the tossing wave was entirely stirred up,
Bubbling with blood. The gray-haired ones,
The aged men around the good king, spoke in unison   1595
That they could not hope to see the prince again—
Expect that he would come back victorious to seek
The glorious king: then many men decided that
Surely the she-wolf of the mere had killed him.
Then the ninth hour of the day came. The valiant Danes   1600
Left the headland; the prince of the men departed
For home from there. The visitors sat,
Downcast in spirit, and stared on the mere;
They wished, yet not expected, that they would see
Their dear lord again.
              Then the sword began to   1605
Droop, the biting falchion did, from the battle blood,
As icicles melt away. It was one of the wonders
That it all melted down most like ice,
When the Father unlocks the fetter of frost,

onwindeð wælrapas, se geweald hafað   1610

sæla ond mæla; þæt is soð Metod.

Ne nom he in þæm wicum, Weder-Geata leod,

maðmæhta ma, þeh he þær monige geseah,

buton þone hafelan ond þa hilt somod

since fage; sweord ær gemealt,   1615

forbarn brodenmæl; wæs þæt blod to þæs hat,

ættren ellorgæst, se þær inne swealt.

Sona wæs on sunde se þe ær æt sæcce gebad

wighryre wraðra, wæter up þurhdeaf;

wæron yðgebland eal gefælsod,   1620

eacne eardas, þa se ellorgast

oflet lifdagas ond þas lænan gesceaft.

Com þa to lande lidmanna helm   *seafearer's leader*

swiðmod swymman; sælace gefeah,

mægenbyrþenne þara þe he him mid hæfde.   1625

Eodon him þa togeanes, Gode þancodon,

ðryðlic þegna heap, þeodnes gefegon,

þæs þe hi hyne gesundne geseon moston.

Ða wæs of þæm hroran helm ond byrne

lungre alysed. Lagu drusade,   *Lake settled,*   1630

wæter under wolcnum, wældreore fag.   *clouds*

Ferdon forð þonon feþelastum

ferhþum fægne, foldweg mæton,

cuþe stræte; cyningbalde men

from þæm holmclife hafelan bæron   1635

earfoðlice heora æghwæþrum

felamodigra; feower scoldon   *four*

on þæm wælstenge weorcum geferian

to þæm goldsele Grendles heafod,

Loosens the water-locks—He has the control 1610
Of the shifting seasons: the true Maker He is.
He did not take in that dwelling, the man of the Weather-Geats,
More of the treasures, though he saw many there,
But the head and also the hilt that shone with ornaments.
The sword blade had already melted; the ornamented sword 1615
Had been burnt up, for the blood was hot to such a degree.
The accursed spirit was venomous, who died therein.
Soon the one who had lived through the fight to see the fall
Of the fiends was swimming; he swam through the water upward.
The surging waves had been entirely purged— 1620
The large domain—when the accursed spirit left
The days of living and this world that fleets away.
    Then to the land came the seafarers' guardian,
The stouthearted man swam. He was pleased with his booty,
With the heavy load he was carrying with him. 1625
Then they went together, thanked God,
The mighty band of thanes; they rejoiced that
They could see their lord safe and sound again.
Then from the strong one the helmet and the coat of mail
Were removed soon; the lake remained still, 1630
The water under the clouds, stained with blood of the slain.
They marched forth from there with light steps.
Rejoicing in spirit, they measured the path,
The well-acquainted road; the men of kingly bravery
Bore the head from the waterside cliff 1635
With difficulty for each of them,
Valiant though they were. Four of them had to
Carry Grendel's head to the gold-hall
On a shaft of spear, with difficulty,

oþ ðæt semninga   to sele comon   1640
frome fyrdhwate   feowertyne (19)
Geata gongan;   gumdryhten mid
modig on gemonge   meodowongas træd.
Ða com in gan   ealdor ðegna,
dædcene mon   dome gewurþad,   1645
hæle hildedeor,   Hroðgar gretan.
Þa wæs be feaxe   on flet boren
Grendles heafod,   þær guman druncon,
egeslic for eorlum   ond þære idese mid,
wliteseon wrætlic;   weras on sawon.   1650
(XXIV) Beowulf maþelode,   bearn Ecgþeowes:
"Hwæt, we þe þas sælac,   sunu Healfdenes,
leod Scyldinga,   lustum brohton
tires to tacne,   þe þu her to locast.
Ic þæt unsofte   ealdre gedigde,   1655
wigge under wætere,   weorc geneþde
earfoðlice;   ætrihte wæs
guð getwæfed,   nymðe mec God scylde.
Ne meahte ic æt hilde   mid Hruntinge
wiht gewyrcan,   þeah þæt wæpen duge;   1660
ac me geuðe   ylda Waldend,
þæt ic on wage geseah   wlitig hangian
eald sweord eacen   —oftost wisode
winigea leasum—,   þæt ic ðy wæpne gebræd.
Ofsloh ða æt þære sæcce,   þa me sæl ageald,   1665
huses hyrdas.   Þa þæt hildebil
forbarn brogdenmæl,   swa þæt blod gesprang,
hatost heaþoswata.   Ic þæt hilt þanan
feondum ætferede,   fyrendæda wræc,

Until presently to the hall came 1640
The fourteen of the warlike brave Geats.
Among them, the lord of men, in their company,
Walked in high spirit, toward the mead-hall.
Then came in the prince of thanes,
The man daring in deeds, exalted with glory, 1645
The battle-brave hero, to greet Hrothgar.
Then, held by hair, into the hall was brought
Grendel's head, where people were drinking,
Horrifying to the earls, and to the lady, too,
This ghastly sight; people looked on it. 1650
(XXIV) Beowulf spoke, son of Ecgtheow:
"What! Son of Healfdene, lord of the Scyldings,
We are pleased to have brought this booty for you,
As a token of glory that you here now look at.
I, who have scarcely come through it alive, 1655
The fight under the water, ventured on the work
With difficulty: the fight would have been put
To an end right away, had it not been for God's protection.
In the fight I could not accomplish anything
With Hrunting,* though that weapon may be a mighty one; 1660
But the Ruler of men granted me
That I saw on the wall an ancient sword hanging,
Beautiful and mighty—most often He has led
The friendless—that I on that cause drew the weapon.
Then I slew the keepers of the house in the fight, 1665
When proper time permitted me. Then the battle-bill,
The ornamented sword, burnt up, as that blood spurted forth—
The hottest of battle blood. I carried that hilt from there,
Away from the fiends: I avenged their atrocious deeds,

deaðcwealm Denigea,   swa hit gedefe wæs.   1670

Ic hit þe þonne gehate,   þæt þu on Heorote most
sorhleas swefan   mid þinra secga gedryht,
ond þegna gehwylc   þinra leoda,
duguðe ond iogoþe,   þæt þu him ondrædan ne þearft,
þeoden Scyldinga,   on þa healfe,   1675
aldorbealu eorlum,   swa þu ær dydest."

    Ða wæs gylden hilt   gamelum rince,
harum hildfruman,   on hand gyfen,
enta ærgeweorc;   hit on æht gehwearf
æfter deofla hryre   Denigea frean,   1680
wundorsmiþa geweorc;   ond þa þas worold ofgeaf
gromheort guma,   Godes ondsaca,*
morðres scyldig,   ond his modor eac,
on geweald gehwearf   woroldcyninga
ðæm selestan   be sæm tweonum   1685
ðara þe on Scedenigge   sceattas dælde.
    Hroðgar maðelode,   hylt sceawode,
elde lafe,   on ðæm wæs or writen
fyrngewinnes,   syðþan flod ofsloh,
gifen geotende,   giganta cyn,   1690
frecne geferdon;   þæt wæs fremde þeod
ecean Dryhtne;   him þæs endelean
þurh wæteres wylm   Waldend sealed.
Swa wæs on ðæm scennum   sciran goldes
þurh runstafas   rihte gemearcod,   1695
geseted ond gesæd,   hwam þæt sweord geworht,
irena cyst,   ærest wære,
wreoþenhilt ond wyrmfah.
                    Ða se wisa spræc

114

Slaughter of the Danes, as it was a proper thing to do.   1670

Then I pledge to you that you may sleep in Heorot,

Free from care with the company of your men,

And each of the thanes of your people may, too,

Your tried warriors and fledglings; that you need not

Fear for them, prince of the Scyldings, on their behalf,   1675

Death of the earls, as you earlier did."

   Then the golden hilt was given to the old warrior,

To the hoary war-chief, into his hand,

That ancient work of giants; after the fall of demons,

It passed into the possession of the lord of the Danes,   1680

That wonder-smiths' handiwork; and when the hostile-hearted churl,

That adversary of God, gave up this world,

Guilty of murder, and his mother, too,

It passed into the control of the king of the world,

The best of those between the seas, of those   1685

Who had dispensed treasures in the Danish realm.

   Hrothgar spoke—he beheld the hilt,

The time-honored heirloom, on which was engraved

The origin of an ancient strife, when the flood,

The sweeping surges, destroyed the race of giants.   1690

They incurred a terrible result. That was a nation

Estranged from the eternal Lord: for that reason

The Ruler gave them retribution—flood to drown them.

So was on the sword-guard of bright gold

Rightly marked in runic letters, set down and told,   1695

For whom that sword, the best of irons,

Had first been made, its hilt twisted and ornamented

With serpentine figures—

                    Then the wise man spoke,

sunu Healfdenes —swigedon ealle—:

"Þæt, la, mæg secgan se þe soð ond riht 1700

fremeð on folce, feor eal gemon,

eald eþelweard, þæt ðes eorl wære

geboren betera! Blæd is aræred

geond widwegas, wine min Beowulf,

ðin ofer þeoda gehwylce. Eal þu hit geþyldum healdest, 1705

mægen mid modes snyttrum, Ic þe sceal mine gelæstan _wile_

freode, swa wit furðum spræcon. Ðu scealt to frofre weorþan

eal langtwidig leodum þinum,

hæleðum to helpe. Ne wearð Heremod swa

eaforum Ecgwelan, Ar-Scyldingum; 1710

ne geweox he him to willan, ac to wælfealle

ond to deaðcwalum Deniga leodum;

breat bolgenmod beodgeneatas,

eaxlgesteallan, oþ þæt he ana hwearf,

mære þeoden, mondreamum from, 1715

ðeah þe hine mihtig God mægenes wynnum,

eafeþum stepte, ofer ealle men

forð gefremede. Hwæþere him on ferhþe greow

breosthord blodreow; nallas beagas geaf

Denum æfter dome; dreamleas gebad, 1720

þæt he þæs gewinnes weorc þrowade,

leodbealo longsum. Ðu þe lær be þon,

gumcyste ongit. Ic þis gid be þe

awræc wintrum frod. Wundor is to secganne,

hu mihtig God manna cynne 1725

þurh sidne sefan snyttru bryttað,

eard ond eorlscipe; he ah ealra geweald.

Hwilum he on lufan læteð hworfan

Son of Healfdene did—all were silent—:

"Indeed, so may a man say, he who performs truth and justice   1700

To his people and bears in mind all far back—

An old guardian of the land: this earl was

Born to prove better than any! Your glory is exalted

Throughout the distant regions, my friend Beowulf,

Your glory all over the nations. You steadily hold it all,   1705

Your strength with wisdom of mind. I shall fulfill my friendship

To you, as we have recently spoken together. You shall

Truly become a long-lasting solace for your own nation,

And prop for the people. Heremod did not turn out so

For Ecgwela's offspring, for the Honor-Scyldings;*   1710

He grew not to be a joy for them, but turned out

Slaughter and destruction for the Danish people;

Enraged, he killed his table companions,

His shoulder-to-shoulder pals, till he became an outcast,

A king in glory, yet far away from the joy of mingling   1715

With people, though the mighty God may have exalted him

With the pleasure of power, and advanced him to be over all men.

Yet his heart grew bloodthirsty in spirit toward them.

No rings did he give to the Danes for their glory;

Deprived of joy, he lived on to suffer   1720

Distress of the strife, the long-term affliction

To his people. Let this teach you a lesson,

And understand what manly virtues are. Wise with winters,

I have told this tale for your sake. It is a wonder to say

How the mighty God in his bounteous will   1725

Dispenses wisdom, land, and nobility

To mankind: He owns the power over all.

Sometimes He lets the mind of a man

monnes modgeþonc   mæran cynnes,

seleð him on eþle   eorþan wynne   1730

to healdanne   hleoburh wera,

gedeð him swa gewealdene   worolde dælas,

side rice,   þæt he his selfa ne mæg

his unsnyttrum   ende geþencean.

Wunað he on wiste;   no hine wiht dweleð   1735

adl ne yldo,   ne him inwitsorh

on sefan sweorceð,   ne gesacu ohwær

ecghete eoweð,   ac him eal worold

wendeð on willan;   he þæt wyrse ne con,

(XXV) oð þæt him on innan   oferhygda dæl   1740

weaxeð ond wridað;   þonne se weard swefeð,

sawele hyrde;   bið se slæp to fæst,

bisgum gebunden,   bona swiðe neah,

se þe of flanbogan   fyrenum sceoteð.

Þonne bið on hreþre   under helm drepen   1745

biteran stræle   —him bebeorgan ne con—,

wom wundorbebodum   wergan gastes;

þinceð him to lytel,   þæt he lange heold,

gytsað gromhydig,   nallas on gylp seleð

fætte beagas,   ond he þa forðgesceaft   1750

forgyteð ond forgymeð,   þæs þe him ær God sealde,

wuldres Waldend,   weorðmynda dæl.

Hit on endestæf   eft gelimpeð,

þæt se lichoma   læne gedreoseð,

fæge gefealleð;   fehð oþer to,   1755

se þe unmurnlice   madmas dæleþ,

eorles ærgestreon,   egesan ne gymeð.

Bebeorh þe ðone bealonið,   Beowulf leofa,

Of noble birth move in love,

Gives him worldly joy in his homeland, 1730

A stronghold of men as his domain,

Renders regions in the world so subject to his rule,

A large kingdom that he himself cannot conceive

An end to it all, due to his unwiseness.

He lives in prosperity: neither disease nor old age 1735

Hinders him at all, nor a sad thought throws

Dark shadow in his mind, nor hostility anywhere

Breeds a deadly feud, but to him the whole world

Moves along as he wishes; he knows nothing worse—

(XXV) Till in his mind a great deal of arrogance 1740

Grows and flourishes; then the overseer sleeps,

The soul's guardian does. That sleep is too deep,

Bound in its troubles, a slayer very near—

One who from an arrow-bow shoots him unnoticed.

Then is he hit in his heart under the helmet 1745

With the sharp arrow—no way to protect himself—

With the crooked cryptic commands of the accursed spirit;

What he has long held seems trivial to him.

He covets furiously, does not honorably dispense

Ornamented treasures, and he forgets and neglects 1750

His future state, as God, the Lord of glory,

Previously gave him a great deal of honor.

It comes to pass in turn in the end

That the fleeting body declines,

Falls fated; another seizes the earl's 1755

Ancient treasure—one who unsparingly dispenses

The treasures, and does not heed to fear.

Protect yourself against that wickedness, dear Beowulf,

secg betsta,   ond þe þæt selre geceos,

ece rædas;   oferhyda ne gym,   1760

mære cempa.   Nu is þines mægnes blæd

ane hwile;   eft sona bið,

þæt þec adl oððe ecg   eafoþes getwæfeð,

oððe fyres feng,   oððe flodes wylm,

oððe gripe meces,   oððe gares fliht,   1765

oððe atol yldo;   oððe eagena bearhtm

forsiteð ond forsworceð;   semninga bið,

þæt ðec, dryhtguma,   deað oferswyðeð.

Swa ic Hring-Dena   hund missera

weold under wolcnum   ond hig wigge beleac   1770

manigum mægþa   geond þysne middangeard,

æscum ond ecgum,   þæt ic me ænigne

under swegles begong   gesacan ne tealde.

Hwæt, me þæs on eþle   edwenden cwom,

gyrn æfter gomene,   seoþðan Grendel wearð,   1775

ealdgewinna,   ingenga min;

ic þære socne   singales wæg

modceare micle.   Þæs sig Metode þanc,

ecean Dryhtne,   þæs ðe ic on aldre gebad,

þæt ic on þone hafelan   heorodreorigne   1780

ofer eald gewin   eagum starige!

Ga nu to setle,   symbelwynne dreoh

wigge weorþad;   unc sceal worn fela

maþma gemænra,   siþðan morgen bið."

    Geat wæs glædmod,   geong sona to,   1785

setles neosan,   swa se snottra heht.

Þa wæs eft swa ær   ellenrofum,

fletsittendum   fægere gereorded

Best of men, and choose the better—
The eternal good counsels; do not indulge in arrogance,   1760
Glorious champion! The glory of your might is here now
Only for a while; soon will it be
That disease or sword will deprive you of strength,
Or fire's swallowing, or flood's surging,
Or sword's attack, or spear's flight,   1765
Or dire old age; or brightness of eyes
Will diminish and grow dim; shortly will it be
That death, warrior, will overpower you.
So I have ruled the Ring-Danes for half of a century
Beneath the clouds, and have protected them in war,   1770
With spears and swords, against many tribes
All over this middle-earth, so that I have thought that
None could be my adversary beneath the sky's expanse.
Alas, reversal of it came to me in my homeland,
Grief after joy, when Grendel appeared—   1775
That old adversary of mine came to invade.
I continually suffered great sorrow of soul for
The devastation he caused. May God, the eternal Lord,
Be thanked, for that I have ever come to experience
That I look on that blood-stained head   1780
With my own eyes, after the old strife!
Go now to your seat, and enjoy the delightful feast,
Distinguished in battle; a great deal of treasures
We shall share, when morning comes."
    The Geat was glad at heart, went soon to   1785
Seek his seat, as the wise man commanded.
Then a feast was fairly prepared again as before,
For the brave men sitting about in the hall,

niowan stefne.

       Nihthelm geswearc

deorc ofer dryhtgumum.   Duguð eal aras;   1790

wolde blondenfeax   beddes neosan,

gamela Scylding.   Geat unigmetes wel,

rofne randwigan,   restan lyste;

sona him seleþegn   siðes wergum,

feorrancundum,   forð wisade,   1795

se for andrysnum   ealle beweotede

þegnes þearfe,   swylce þy dogore

heaþoliðende   habban scoldon.

    Reste hine þa rumheort;   reced hliuade

geap ond goldfah;   gæst inne swæf,   1800

oþ þæt hrefn blaca   heofones wynne

bliðheort bodode.   Ða com beorht scacan

[scima ofer sceadwa];   scaþan onetton,

wæron æþelingas   eft to leodum

fuse to farenne;   wolde feor þanon   1805

cuma collenferhð   ceoles neosan.

    Heht þa se hearda   Hrunting beran

sunu Ecglafes,   heht his sweord niman,

leoflic iren;   sægde him þæs leanes þanc,

cwæð, he þone guðwine   godne tealde,   1810

wigcræftigne,   nales wordum log

meces ecge;   þæt wæs modig secg.

Ond þa siðfrome,   searwum gearwe

wigend wæron;   eode weorð Denum

æþeling to yppan,   þær se oþer wæs,   1815

hæle hildedeor   Hroðgar grette.

(XXVI) Beowulf maþelode,   bearn Ecgþeowes:

All over again—

        A veil of night lowered—

Dark over the warriors; the whole band of retainers arose.   1790

The gray-haired one, the aged Scylding, wished to

Retire in bed. The Geat, the brave shield-warrior,

Was pleased to rest well without measure.

Soon a hall-thane showed forth the way to him,

Weary of venture, coming from a far-off land;   1795

He for courtesy's sake attended to all the needs

Of the thane—such as at that time

The seafaring warriors should have.

    Then the big-hearted man rested. The building soared high,

Vaulted and gold-adorned; the guest slept within,   1800

Till the black raven blithe of heart announced

The joy of heaven. Then came the bright beam,

[Light over the shadows];* the warriors hastened,

The nobles were eager to set out to sail

To their people again; the visitor, bold of spirit,   1805

Wished to seek his ship far from there.

    Then the brave one bade to bear Hrunting

To the son of Ecglaf,* asked him to take back his sword,

His dear iron, thanked him for the favor rendered,

Said that he reckoned it a good battle-companion,   1810

Powerful in war, never in words found fault

With the sword—that was a gracious man.*

And then the warriors were eager to depart,

Ready with arms. The prince honored by the Danes

Went to the high seat, where the other was;   1815

The battle-brave warrior greeted Hrothgar.

(XXVI) Beowulf spoke, son of Ecgtheow:

"Nu we sæliðend   secgan wyllað
feorran cumene,   þæt we fundiaþ
Higelace secan.   Wæron her tela,   1820
willum bewenede;   þu us wel dohtest.
Gif ic þonne on eorþan   owihte mæg
þinre modlufan   maran tilian,
gumena dryhten,   ðonne ic gyt dyde,
guðgeweorca,   ic beo gearo sona.   1825
Gif ic þæt gefricge   ofer floda begang,
þæt þec ymsittend   egesan þywað,
swa þec hetende   hwilum dydon,
ic ðe þusenda   þegna bringe,
hæleþa to helpe.   Ic on Higelace wat,   1830
Geata dryhten,   þeah ðe he geong sy,
folces hyrde,   þæt he mec fremman wile
wordum ond weorcum,   þæt ic þe wel herige
ond þe to geoce   garholt bere,
mægenes fultum,   þær ðe bið manna þearf.   1835
Gif him þonne Hreþric   to hofum Geata
geþingeð, þeodnes bearn,   he mæg þær fela
freonda findan;   feorcyþðe beoð
selran gesohte   þæm þe him selfa deah."
    Hroðgar maþelode   him on ondsware: 1840
"Þe þa wordcwydas   wigtig Drihten
on sefan sende;   ne hyrde ic snotorlicor   wise/ly
on swa geongum feore   guman þingian.
Þu eart mægenes strang,   ond on mode frod,
wis wordcwida.   Wen ic talige,   1845
gif þæt gegangeð,   þæt ðe gar nymeð,
hild heorugrimme,   Hreþles eaferan,

124

"Now we seafarers coming from far off
Wish to say that we are anxious to
Return to Hygelac. We have been well treated   1820
Here to our desire. You have dealt with us well.
If then on earth I may in any way
Earn more of your heart's love,
Lord of men, than I have done heretofore
With warlike deeds, I should be ready soon.   1825
If I hear of that beyond the stretch of the sea,
That your neighbors threaten you with terrors,
As your enemies have done in the past,
I will bring a thousand thanes to you,
Men to your aid. I know of Hygelac,   1830
Lord of the Geats, though he is young
To be the guardian of a people, that he will support me
With words and deeds, so that I may honor you well
And bring a forest of spears to your aid,
Augmenting your strength, where you have need of men.   1835
If then Hrethric, your princely son, decides to visit
The court of the Geats, he can find there
Many friends; far countries are even better to seek
For one, who himself is a man of worth."
     Hrothgar spoke to him in answer: 1840
"The Lord in His wisdom sent those words
Into your mind; I have not heard a man
In so young an age speak more wisely.
You are a man of great strength, prudent mind,
And wise words! I consider it likely,   1845
If it happens that spear, sword-fierce battle,
Takes the son of Hrethel,*

125

adl oþðe iren   ealdor ðinne,

folces hyrde,   ond þu þin feorh hafast,

þæt þe Sæ-Geatas   selran næbben   1850

to geceosenne   cyning ænigne,

hordweard hæleþa,   gyf þu healdan wylt

maga rice.   Me þin modsefa

licað leng swa wel,   leofa Beowulf.

Hafast þu gefered,   þæt þam folcum sceal,   1855

Geata leodum   ond Gar-Denum,

sib gemæne,   ond sacu restan,

inwitniþas,   þe hie ær drugon,

wesan, þenden ic wealde   widan rices,

maþmas gemæne,   manig oþerne   1860

godum gegrettan   ofer ganotes bæð;

sceal hringnaca   ofer heafu bringan

lac ond luftacen.   Ic þa leode wat

ge wið feond ge wið freond   fæste geworhte,

æghwæs untæle   ealde wisan."   1865

    Ða git him eorla hleo   inne gesealde,

mago Healfdenes,   maþmas twelfe;

het hine mid þæm lacum   leode swæse

secean on gesyntum,   snude eft cuman.

Gecyste þa   cyning æþelum god,   1870

þeoden Scyldinga,   ðegn betstan

ond be healse genam;   hruron him tearas

blondenfeaxum.   Him wæs bega wen,

ealdum infrodum,   oþres swiðor,

þæt hie seoððan [no]   geseon moston,   1875

modige on meþle.   Wæs him se man to þon leof,

þæt he þone breostwylm   forberan ne mehte,

Sickness or sword seizes your lord,

The guardian of people, and you retain your life,

That the Sea-Geats will not have any man   1850

Better to choose as their king, as guardian of

Their treasure, if you wish to hold the kingdom

That belongs to your kinsmen. Your inner soul has long

Pleased me so well, dear Beowulf.

You have brought it about that peace shall   1855

Be shared by two nations, people of the Geats

And the Spear-Danes, and strife shall cease,

Hostile acts that they have done so far.

While I rule the wide kingdom, treasures

Shall be shared; many a man shall greet   1860

Another with gifts over the gannet's bath-pool;

The ring-prowed ship will bring over the seas

Gifts and friendly tokens; I know your people

Both with foe and with friend are firmly disposed,

Follow old ways, faultless in every respect."   1865

    And then the protector of earls gave him within,

The son of Healfdene did, twelve treasures.

He bade him to go to his dear people

With the gifts safely, and come again quickly.

Then the good king of noble descent,   1870

The prince of the Scyldings, kissed the best of thanes,

And hugged him by the neck; tears fell from

The gray-haired man: for the wise old man, there was

Expectation of two things, of one of them more,

That they henceforth would not be allowed to see each other   1875

In such bold spirit at meeting. The man was so dear to him

That he could not restrain his heart's welling,

ac him on hreþre   hygebendum fæst
æfter deorum men   dyrne langað
beorn wið blode.

                   Him Beowulf þanan,   1880
guðrinc goldwlanc,   græsmoldan træd
since hremig;   sægenga bad
agendfrean,   se þe on ancre rad.
Þa wæs on gange   gifu Hroðgares
oft geæhted;   þæt wæs an cyning,   1885
æghwæs orleahtre,   oþ þæt hine yldo benam
mægenes wynnum,   se þe oft manegum scod.
(XXVII) Cwom þa to flode   felamodigra,
hægstealdra heap;   hringnet bæron,
locene leoðosyrcan.   Landweard onfand   1890
eftsið eorla,   swa he ær dyde;
no he mid hearme   of hliðes nosan
gæstas grette,   ac him togeanes rad,
cwæð þæt wilcuman   Wedera leodum
scaþan scirhame   to scipe foron.   1895
Þa wæs on sande   sægeap naca
hladen herewædum,   hringedstefna,
mearum ond mðmum;   mæst hlifade
ofer Hroðgares   hordgestreonum.
He þæm batwearde   bunden golde   1900
swurd gesealde,   þæt he syðþan wæs
on meodubence   maþme þy weorþra,
yrfelafe.   Gewat him on naca
drefan deop wæter,   Dena land ofgeaf.
Þa wæs be mæste   merehrægla sum,   1905
segl sale fæst;   sundwudu þunede;

But firmly tied by heart-strings in his bosom,

Hidden longing after the dear man

Burned in his blood.

                        Away from him there Beowulf,   1880

Warrior wearing gold adornment, walked on the grassy earth,

Exulting with his treasure. The ship awaited

Its lordly owner, that rode at anchor.

Then on the way the gift of Hrothgar was

Praised often; that was a peerless king,   1885

Flawless in every way, till age deprived him

Of the joys of strength—age that often injured many.

(XXVII) Then came to the sea the band of

Brave young men; they bore ring-nets,

Interlocked mail-jackets. The coastguard perceived   1890

The return of the warriors, as he had done before;

He did not greet the guests with harsh words

From the cliff's bluff, but rode down toward them,

And said that the warriors in bright armor on their way

To the ship would be welcome to the people of the Geats.   1895

Then on the sand was the sea-spacious ship

Loaded with war-gears, the ring-prowed ship,

With horses and treasures; the mast stood high—

High over Hrothgar's treasures hoarded up.

He gave to the boat-guard a sword bound   1900

In gold, that he thenceforth was the more

Honored at mead-bench for the treasure

He had received. The ship embarked to stir up

The deep water; it left the land of the Danes.

Then on the mast was a sail, the sea-garment   1905

Was fastened by a rope; the ship creaked.

no þær wegflotan   wind ofer yðum

siðes getwæfde;   sægenga for,

fleat famigheals   forð ofer yðe,

bundenstefna   ofer brimstreamas,   1910

þæt hie Geata clifu   ongitan meahton,

cuþe næssas;   ceol up geþrang

lyftgeswenced,   on lande stod.

Hraþe wæs æt holme   hyðweard geara,

se þe ær lange tid   leofra manna   1915

fus æt faroðe   feor wlatode;

sælde to sande   sidfæþme scip

oncerbendum fæst,   þy læs hym yþa ðrym

wudu wynsuman   forwrecan meahte.

Het þa up beran   æþelinga gestreon,   1920

frætwe ond fætgold;   næs him feor þanon

to gesecanne   sinces bryttan,

Higelac Hreþling,   þær æt ham wunað

selfa mid gesiðum   sæwealle neah.

  Bold wæs betlic,   bregorof cyning,   1925

heah in healle,*   Hygd swiðe geong,

wis, welþungen,   þeah ðe wintra lyt

under burhlocan   gebiden hæbbe,

Hæreþes dohtor;   næs hio hnah swa þeah,

ne to gneað gifa   Geata leodum,   1930

maþmgestreona.   Mod Þryðo* wæg,

fremu folces cwen,   firen ondrysne;

nænig þæt dorste   deor geneþan

swæsra gesiða,   nefne sinfrea,

þæt hire an dæges   eagum starede;   1935

ac him wælbende   weotode tealde

There wind was no hindrance for the ship
To journey over the waves; the ship fared,
Floated, foamy-necked, forth over the wave,
Boat with bound prow over the sea-streams,   1910
Till they could see the cliffs of the Geats,
Familiar headlands. The ship pressed onward,
And, driven by the wind, stood on land to moor.
A sea-guard was swiftly ready at the harbor,
He who had watched out far on the sea   1915
For a long time, eager to receive dear men;
He* moored the spacious ship to the sand
Firmly by anchor-ropes, for fear that the force of the waves
Pull the fair wooden vessel away from them.
Then he ordered that the treasure of the nobles be borne,   1920
Ornaments and plated gold; it was not far from there
For them to visit the treasure-dispenser,
Hrethel's son, Hygelac, where at home he dwelt
Close by the sea wall, himself with his retainers.

    The building was imposing, the king majestic,   1925
Seated high in the hall. Hygd* was very young,
Wise, and well-accomplished, though she, Hæreth's
Daughter, had spent few winters in the enclosure of
The fortress; she was not niggardly, though,
Nor too sparing of gifts, of treasures, for the people   1930
Of the Geats. A good queen of the people,
She kept in mind the temper of Thryth, her cruel deed:*
None so brave as to dare to venture,
Among her nearby guards—except her lord—*
To cast his eyes on her in daylight,   1935
But would reckon a deadly bond ordained,

handgewriþene;   hraþe seoþðan wæs

æfter mundgripe   mece geþinged,

þæt hit sceadenmæl   scyran moste,

cwealmbealu cyðan.   Ne bið swylc cwenlic þeaw   1940

idese to efnanne,   þeah ðe hio ænlicu sy,

þætte freoðuwebbe   feores onsæce

æfter ligetorne   leofne mannan.

Huru þæt onhohsnode   Hemminges mæg;   *Offa*

ealodrincende   oðer sædan,   1945

þæt hio leodbealewa   læs gefremede,

inwitniða,   syððan ærest wearð

gyfen goldhroden   geongum cempan,

æðelum diore,   syððan hio Offan flet

ofer fealone flod   be fæder lare   1950

siðe gesohte;   ðær hio syððan well

in gumstole,   gode mære,

lifgesceafta   lifigende breac,

hiold heahlufan   wið hæleþa brego,

ealles moncynnes   mine gefræge   1955

þone selestan   bi sæm tweonum,

eormencynnes.   Forðam Offa wæs

geofum ond guðum,   garcene man,

wide geweorðod,   wisdome heold

eðel sinne;   þonon Eomer woc   1960

hæleðum to helpe,   Hemminges mæg,

nefa Garmundes,   niða cræftig.

(XXVIII) Gewat him ða se hearda   mid his hondscole

sylf æfter sande   sæwong tredan,

wide waroðas.   Woruldcandel scan,   *The world's candle*   1965

sigel suðan fus.   Hi sið drugon,

Having his wrists twisted: swiftly afterwards
He was fated by the sword, after the arrest—
That a patterned sword had to settle it—
Deadly evil made known. Such is not a queen-like practice   1940
For a woman to follow, though she may be peerless,
That a peace-weaver should deprive a dear man
Of his life on the ground of an unsubstantiated blame.*
However, Hemming's kinsman*put an end to it;
Ale-drinkers have given another account—   1945
That she practiced less harm to the people,
Fewer evil deeds, when for the first time she happened
To be given, gold-adorned, to the young warrior,
Of noble descent when by her father's counsel
She sought the hall of Offa on a voyage over   1950
The palely brown billows. There on the throne she,
Afterwards well renowned for her goodness,
Made use of her destined life while living;
She harbored deep love for the prince of warriors—*
According to what I have heard, the choicest   1955
Of the whole human race between the seas,
Of mankind, for the reason that Offa was a man
With spear-like bravery with gifts and wars,
Widely honored, and ruled his native land wisely.
From him was born Eomer, who was to be   1960
A prop for warriors—Hemming's kinsman,
Grandson of Garmund, granted with gift in waging wars.*
(XXVIII) Then the brave one walked with his band,
Treading on the sand over the plain by the sea,
The wide shore stretched. The world's light-giver shone,   1965
The sun hastened from the south. They made their way,

elne geeodon,   to ðæs ðe eorla hleo,

bonan Ongenþeoes   burgum in innan,

geongne guðcyning   godne gefrunon

hringas dælan.   Higelace wæs   1970

sið Beowulfes   snude gecyðed,

þæt ðær on worðig   wigendra hleo,

lindgestealla,   lifigende cwom,

heaðolaces hal   to hofe gongan.

Hraðe wæs gerymed,   swa se rica bebead,   1975

feðegestum   flet innanweard.

    Gesæt þa wið sylfne   se ða sæcce genæs,

mæg wið mæge,   syððan mandryhten

þurh hleoðorcwyde   holdne gegrette,

meaglum wordum.   Meoduscencum hwearf   1980

geond þæt healreced   Hæreðes dohtor,

lufode ða leode,   liðwæge bær

hæleðum to handa.   Higelac ongan

sinne geseldan   in sele þam hean

fægre fricgcean,   hyne fyrwet bræc,   1985

hwylce Sæ-Geata   siðas wæron:

    "Hu lomp eow on lade,   leofa Biowulf,

þa ðu færinga   feorr gehogodest

sæcce secean   ofer sealt wæter,

hilde to Hiorote?   Ac ðu Hroðgare   1990

widcuðne wean   wihte gebettest,

mærum ðeodne?   Ic ðæs modceare

sorhwylmum seað,   siðe ne truwode

leofes mannes;   ic ðe lange bæd,

þæt ðu þone wælgæst   wihte ne grette,   1995

lete Suð-Dene   sylfe geweorðan

Anxiously walked to where the protector of earls,

The slayer of Ongentheow,* the brave young war-king,

As they had heard say, dealt out the rings

In his stronghold. The coming of Beowulf   1970

Was quickly announced to Hygelac,

That there in his domain the defender of warriors,

His shield-companion, who had come alive

Safe and sound from battle, was approaching the court.

The hall was quickly cleared within, as the mighty   1975

One bade, for the guests to arrive on foot.

     Then he who had survived the fight sat with the king,

Kinsman with kinsman, after he greeted his liege lord,

His trusty friend, in ceremonious speech with solemn

Words. Hæreth's daughter* moved about   1980

Through that hall-building with mead-bowls,

Genially tended on the people, and bore a jar of drink

To pour for the men. Hygelac began to

Inquire of his companion with courtesy

In the high hall—curiosity pressed hard on him—   1985

What the adventures of the Sea-Geats had been:

    "How was your journey, dear Beowulf,

When you suddenly resolved to seek

Battle far off over the salt water,

The fight at Heorot? Did you somehow provide   1990

Remedy for the wide-known woe for Hrothgar,

The renowned prince? I for that was restless in care,

Unable to suppress surging worries, didn't trust

The venture of a dear man; I entreated you long

That you make no attempt to assault the damned spirit,   1995

Let the South-Danes settle for themselves

note spelling

guðe wið Grendel. | Gode ic þanc secge,   *God again!*
þæs ðe ic ðe gesundne   geseon moste."
— Biowulf maðelode,   bearn Ecgðioes: ✳
"Þæt is undyrne,   dryhten Higelac,   2000
micel* gemeting,   monegum fira,
hwylc [orleg]hwil   uncer Grendles
wearð on ðam wange,   þær he worna fela
Sige-Scyldingum   sorge gefremede,
yrmðe to aldre;   ic ðæt eall gewræc,   2005
swa begylpan ne þearf   Grendeles maga
ænig ofer eorðan   uhthlem þone,
se ðe lengest leofað   laðan cynnes,
facne bifongen. | Ic ðær furðum cwom
to ðam hringsele   Hroðgar gretan;   *ring-hall*   2010
sona me se mæra   mago Healfdenes,
syððan he modsefan   minne cuðe,
wið his sylfes sunu   setl getæhte.
Weorod wæs on wynne;   ne seah ic widan feorh
under heofones hwealf   healsittendra   2015
medudream maran.   Hwilum mæru cwen,
friðusibb folca,   flet eall geondhwearf,
bædde byre geonge;   oft hio beahwriðan
secge sealde,   ær hie to setle geong.
Hwilum for duguðe   dohtor Hroðgares   2020
eorlum on ende   ealuwæge bær,
þa ic Freaware   fletsittende
nemnan hyrde,   þær hio nægled sinc
hæleðum sealde.   Sio gehaten is,
geong, goldhroden,   gladum suna Frodan;   2025
hafað þæs geworden   wine Scyldinga,

By waging a fight with Grendel. I thank God
For allowing me to see you sound and safe."
    Beowulf spoke, son of Ecgtheow:
"It is not a hidden matter, lord Hygelac,   2000
The big match, for many of the men,
What a time of fight between us two, I and Grendel,
Happened in that place, where he had caused
A great many sorrows for the Victory-Scyldings,
Miseries for ever; I avenged that all,   2005
So that any of Grendel's kinsfolk over
The earth need not boast of that din at dawn,
Whoever lives longest of the loathsome race,
Soaked in sin. I first arrived there
At the ring-hall to greet Hrothgar;   2010
Soon the renowned son of Healfdene,
When he knew my intention,
Assigned me a seat his sons might deserve.
The company was in joy; I had never seen till then
Under the heaven-vault a greater mirth over mead   2015
Of those gathered in a hall. Now and again the renowned queen,
Peace-pledge of the people, moved about the entire hall,
Cheering the young men; often she handed
A ring-band to a man, before she went to her seat.
Now and again the daughter of Hrothgar bore   2020
The ale-cup to the retainers, to all the earls, taking turns,
Whom I heard those sitting in the hall
Call Freawaru, when she handed the studded
Bowl to the warriors. She is promised to wed,
Young and gold-adorned, the gracious son of Froda;*   2025
The friend of the Scyldings, the guardian of the kingdom,

rices hyrde,   ond þæt ræd talað,

þæt he mid ðy wife   wælfæhða dæl,

sæcca gesette. \Oft seldan hwær

æfter leodhryre   lytle hwile   2030

bongar bugeð,   þeah seo bryd duge!

Mæg þæs þonne ofþyncan   ðeodne Heaðo-Beardna

ond þegna gehwam   þara leoda,

þonne he mid fæmnan   on flett gæð,

dryhtbearn Dena,   duguða biwenede;   2035

on him gladiað   gomelra lafe,

heard ond hringmæl   Heaða-Beardna gestreon,

þenden hie ðam wæpnum   wealdan moston,

[XXIX–XXX] oð ðæt hie forlæddan   to ðam lindplegan

swæse gesiðas   ond hyra sylfra feorh.   2040

Þonne cwið æt beore   se ðe beah gesyhð,

eald æscwiga,   se ðe eall geman,

garcwealm gumena   —him bið grim sefa—,

onginneð geomormod   geongum cempan

þurh hreðra gehygd   higes cunnian,   2045

wigbealu weccean,   ond þæt word acwyð:

'Meaht ðu, min wine,   mece gecnawan,

þone þin fæder   to gefeohte bær

under heregriman   hindeman siðe,

dyre iren,   þær hyne Dene slogon,   2050

weoldon wælstowe,   syððan Wiðergyld læg,

æfter hæleþa hryre,   hwate Scyldungas?

Nu her þara banena   byre nathwylces

frætwum hremig   on flet gæð,

morðres gylpeð,   ond þone maðþum byreð,   2055

þone þe ðu mid rihte   rædan sceoldest.'

Has decided on that, and considers it a wise policy

That he settle a great deal of deadly feuds and conflicts

By means of this woman. Hardly in any nation,

After the fall of a prince, the deadly spear rests 2030

Even for a little while, though the bride may be good.

Then it may displease the prince of the Heatho-Bards

And each of the thanes of that people,

When he, the wedding attendant of the Danes

Nobly feasted, goes into the hall with the woman; 2035

On them will shine the old heirlooms, the hard and

Ring-adorned treasure that belonged to the Heatho-Bards

While they could wield the weapons,*

[XXIX–XXX] Till they led to destruction, to war,

Their dear companions' lives and their own selves'. 2040

Then upon seeing the treasure at beer drinking, an old warrior,

The one who remembers all—many a man's death by the spear—

Will speak, grim in his heart full of sorrow—

Will begin to make a trial of a young warrior

In his spirit by imparting the thought in his heart, 2045

To arouse warlike spirit, and will utter this word:

"My friend, can you recognize that sword,

The precious iron, which your father bore to battle

Wearing a warlike mask for the last time,

Where the Danes, the fierce Scyldings, slew him, 2050

And took control of the battle-field,

When Withergyld* lay dead, after the fall of the warriors?

Now here the son of a certain one of his slayers

Walks in the hall, exulting with his adornments,

Boasts of the butchery, and bears the treasure 2055

That should have been yours by right."

Manað swa ond myndgað   mæla gehwylce

sarum wordum,   oð ðæt sæl cymeð,

þæt se fæmnan þegn   fore fæder dædum

æfter billes bite   blodfag swefeð,   2060

ealdres scyldig;   him se oðer þonan

losað lifigende,   con him land geare.

Þonne bioð abrocene   on ba healfe

aðsweord eorla;   syððan Ingelde

weallað wælniðas,   ond him wiflufan   2065

æfter cearwælmum   colran weorðað.

Þy ic Heaðo-Beardna   hyldo ne telge,

dryhtsibbe dæl   Denum unfæcne,

freondscipe fæstne.   Ic sceal forð sprecan

gen ymbe Grendel,   þæt ðu geare cunne,   2070

sinces brytta,   to hwan syððan wearð

hondræs hæleða.   Syððan heofones gim

glad ofer grundas,   gæst yrre cwom,   *maddened spirit came*

eatol æfengrom,   user neosan,

ðær we gesunde   sæl weardodon.   2075

Þær wæs Hondsciô   hild onsæge,

feorhbealu fægum;   he fyrmest læg,

gyrded cempa;   him Grendel wearð,

mærum maguþegne   to muðbonan,

leofes mannes   lic eall forswealg.   2080

No ðy ær ut ða gen   idelhende

bona blodigtoð,   bealewa gemyndig,

of ðam goldsele   gongan wolde;

ac he mægnes rof   min costode,

grapode gearofolm.   Glof hangode   2085

sid ond syllic,   searobendum fæst;

So will he incite and remind on each occasion
With sore words, till the time comes
That the woman's thane, for his father's deeds,
Receives a sword-blow to fall down blood-stained, 2060
With his life forfeited. The other escapes
From there alive, knows the land well.
Then on both sides, the pledges made by the earls
Will be broken; thereupon deadly hate will well up
In Ingeld, and after the surging of sorrow 2065
The love he feels for his wife will turn cold.
Therefore, I do not consider the loyalty of the Heatho-Bards,
Their share in the alliance with the Danes, free from deceit—
Nor their friendship firmly fixed. I shall speak forth
Further about Grendel, that you may readily know, 2070
Dispenser of treasure, what since came about with
The hand-to-hand grapple of the fighters. When heaven's jewel*
Had glided over the grounds, the enraged ghost came,
Ghastly and hostile in the dark, to seek us out,
Where, unharmed, we were guarding the hall. 2075
There the fight was fatal to Hondscio,* deadly to him,
For he was one doomed to die. He, an armed warrior,
Was the first one to lie dead; Grendel proved himself
A slayer by gorging, for the glorious young retainer,
For he devoured the entire body of the beloved man. 2080
The slayer with blood-stained teeth, intent on
Devastation, was not ready to leave the gold-hall—
Not quite yet, without a booty grabbed in his hand;
But he, monstrously powerful, attacked me,
And instantly took me in his grip. His glove hung 2085
Wide and eerie, fastened by cunning clasps;

sio wæs orðoncum   eall gegyrwed

deofles cræftum   ond dracan fellum.

He mec þær on innan   unsynnigne,

dior dædfruma,   gedon wolde   2090

manigra sumne;   hyt ne mihte swa,

syððan ic on yrre   uppriht astod.

To lang ys to reccenne,   hu ic ðam leodsceaðan

yfla gehwylces   ondlean forgeald;

þær ic, þeoden min,   þine leode   2095

weorðode weorcum.   He on weg losade,

lytle hwile   lifwynna breac;

hwæþre him sio swiðre   swaðe weardade

hand on Hiorte,   ond he hean ðonan,

modes geomor   meregrund gefeoll.   2100

Me þone wælræs   wine Scildunga

fættan golde   fela leanode,

manegum maðmum,   syððan mergen com,

ond we to symble   geseten hæfdon.

Þær wæs gidd ond gleo.   Gomela Scilding,   2105

felafricgende,   feorran rehte;

hwilum hildedeor   hearpan wynne,

gomenwudu grette,   hwilum gyd awræc

soð ond sarlic,   hwilum syllic spell

rehte æfter rihte   rumheort cyning;   2110

hwilum eft ongan   eldo gebunden,

gomel guðwiga   gioguðe cwiðan,

hildestrengo;   hreðer inne weoll,

þonne he wintrum frod   worn gemunde.

Swa we þær inne   ondlangne dæg   2115

niode naman,   oð ðæt niht becwom

It had been all contrived with ingenuity—
With the devil's devices and the dragon's peels.
He would put me, one of many, therein—
The fierce perpetrator of evil deeds would—   2090
Though guiltless I was. He could not do so,
For I in anger had stood up tall and stalwart.
It is too long to recount how I paid back
To the folk-ravager what's due for his evil deeds.
I have done honor to your nation, my prince,   2095
By doing what I did there. He escaped away—
Only to brook the joy of life a little while.
However, his right hand remained behind
In Heorot, and he, crest-fallen, from there,
Sad of heart, sank to the floor of the mere.   2100
The lord of the Scyldings rewarded me
For the deadly fight greatly with plated gold,
With many treasures, when morning came
And we sat down for a feast.
There was song and jubilee; the old Scylding,*   2105
Informed well, told tales from far-off times.
Now and again the battle-brave one strummed the harp,
Partook of the joy in the mirthful wood, to tell
Sometimes a tale true and sad, sometimes a strange story—
The great-hearted king recounted in a rightful manner;   2110
At times, again, fettered with age,
The old warrior began to lament the lapse of his youth,
His martial prowess; his heart surged within, as he
Recalled many a thing from the winters he had lived.
Thus we took pleasure therein the entire day,   2115
Till another night came back to men.

oðer to yldum. Þa wæs eft hraðe

gearo gyrnwræce Grendeles modor,

siðode sorhfull; sunu deað fornam,

wighete Wedra. Wif unhyre 2120

hyre bearn gewræc, beorn acwealde

ellenlice; þær wæs Æschere,

frodan fyrnwitan, feorh uðgenge.

Noðer hy hine ne moston, syððan mergen cwom,

deaðwerigne Denia leode, 2125

bronde forbærnan, ne on bęl hladan,

leofne mannan; hio þæt lic ætbær

feondes fæðmum under firgenstream.

Þæt wæs Hroðgare hreowa tornost

þara þe leodfruman lange begeate. 2130

Þa se ðeoden mec ðine life

healsode hreohmod, þæt ic on holma geþring

eorlscipe efnde, ealdre geneðde,

mærðo fremede; he me mede gehet.

Ic ða ðæs wælmes, þe is wide cuð, 2135

grimne gryrelicne grundhyrde fond.

Þær unc hwile wæs hand gemæne;

holm heolfre weoll, ond ic heafde becearf

in ðam guðsele Grendeles modor

eacnum ecgum; unsofte þonan 2140

feorh oðferede; næs ic fæge þa gyt;

ac me eorla hleo eft gesealde

maðma menigeo, maga Healfdenes.

(XXXI) Swa se ðeodkyning þeawum lyfde;

nealles ic ðam leanum forloren hæfde, 2145

mægnes mede, ac he me maðmas geaf,

Then Grendel's mother in her turn was
Swiftly ready to revenge the injuries done,
Made a journey, mortified; death had taken her son,
Martial hate of the Weather-Geats had.   2120
The female monster avenged her brat:
Brutally she butchered a warrior; that was
Æschere, wise old counselor deprived of life.
When morning came, they could not, the people
Of the Danes could not, burn him, death-weary,   2125
In the fire, nor could they put on a pyre
Their beloved man: she had borne off his body
In her fiendish embrace down into a mountain-stream.
That was for Hrothgar the most painful of sorrows,
Which had long befallen the people's guardian.   2130
Then the prince, troubled in heart, entreated me,
For the sake of your name, to perform a heroic deed,
Risk my life, and fulfill a glorious achievement,
In the watery tumult; he promised me reward.
Then I found the keeper of the abysmal deep   2135
That is widely known, the grim and horrid one.
There between us two was hand-grapple awhile.
Water bubbled with blood, and in that battle-hall
I severed the head of Grendel's mother
With a mighty sword. Barely from there   2140
I bore away my life; I was not then doomed to die yet,
But the protector of earls bestowed on me again
A great many treasures, Healfdene's son did.
(XXXI) So the people's king lived in good customs.
I had not lost the gifts at all, the reward of my strength,   2145
But he gave me treasures—Healfdene's son did—

sunu Healfdenes,   on minne sylfes dom;

ða ic ðe, beorncyning,   bringan wylle,

estum geywan.   Gen is eall æt ðe

lissa gelong;   ic lyt hafo   2150

heafodmaga   nefne, Hygelac, ðec."

    Het ða in beran   eafor heafodsegn,

heaðosteapne helm,   hare byrnan,

guðsweord geatolic,   gyd æfter wræc:

"Me ðis hildesceorp   Hroðgar sealde,   2155

snotra fengel;   sume worde het,

þæt ic his ærest ðe   est gesægde;

cwæð þæt hyt hæfde   Hiorogar cyning,

leod Scyldunga   lange hwile;

no ðy ær suna sinum   syllan wolde,   2160

hwatum Heorowearde,   þeah he him hold wære,

breostgewædu.   Bruc ealles well!"

    Hyrde ic þæt þam frætwum   feower mearas

lungre, gelice   last weardode,

æppelfealuwe;   he him est geteah   2165

meara ond maðma.   Swa sceal mæg don,

nealles inwitnet   oðrum bregdon

dyrnum cræfte,   deað renian

hondgesteallan.   Hygelace wæs

niða heardum   nefa swyðe hold,   2170

ond gehwæðer oðrum   hroþra gemyndig.

Hyrde ic þæt he ðone healsbeah   Hygde gesealde,

wrætlicne wundurmaððum,   ðone þe him Wealhðeo geaf,

ðeodnes dohtor,   þrio wicg somod

swancor ond sadolbeorht;   hyre syððan wæs   2175

æfter beahðege   breost geweorðod.

In accordance with what I myself deemed suitable.
I will bring these to you, my brave king,
And present them gladly. All is still
Dependent on your favor; I have few   2150
Close kinsmen, except you, Hygelac."
    Then he ordered to bring in the boar-head banner,
The helmet towering in battle, the gray mail-shirt,
The splendid sword, and then spoke thus:
"Hrothgar gave this battle-wear to me,   2155
The wise king did; he commanded emphatically
That I should first tell you about this gift;
He said that King Heorogar* had kept it,
Lord of the Scyldings had, for a long time;
Not so readily would he* have given the breast-wear   2160
To his son, bold Heoroweard,* although he had been
Loyal to his father. Enjoy it all well!"
    I have heard that four swift-paced horses followed
The treasures, alike all in apple-fallow;
He made a gift to him of both—   2165
The horses and the treasures; so must kinsmen act,
Must never weave the net of malice for each other
With hidden craft, or plot for the deaths of
Close companions. To Hygelac was his nephew
Very trust-worthy for his hardiness at battles,   2170
And each to the other was mindful of being helpful.
I have heard that he gave the neck-ring—the splendid
Jewel of wonder Wealhtheow had given him—
To Hygd, a prince's daughter, along with three horses,
Graceful and saddle-bright; since then her breast   2175
Was adorned with the ring she received then.

Swa bealdode   bearn Ecgðeowes,

guma guðum cuð,   godum dædum,

dreah æfter dome,   nealles druncne slog

heorðgeneatas;   næs him hreoh sefa,   2180

ac he mancynnes   mæste cræfte

ginfæstan gife,   þe him God sealde,

heold hildedeor.   Hean wæs lange,

swa hyne Geata bearn   godne ne tealdon,

ne hyne on medobence   micles wyrðne   2185

drihten Wedera   gedon wolde;

swyðe wendon,   þæt he sleac wære,

æðeling unfrom.   Edwenden cwom

tireadigum menn   torna gehwylces.

Het ða eorla hleo   in gefetian,   2190

heaðorof cyning,   Hreðles lafe

golde gegyrede;   næs mid Geatum ða

sincmaðþum selra   on sweordes had;

þæt he on Biowulfes   bearm alegde,

ond him gesealde   seofan þusendo,   2195

bold ond bregostol.   Him wæs bam samod

on ðam leodscipe   lond gecynde,

eard, eðelriht,   oðrum swiðor

side rice   þam ðær selra wæs.

Eft þæt geiode   ufaran dogrum   2200

hildehlæmmum,   syððan Hygelac læg,

ond Heardrede   hildemeceas

under bordhreoðan   to bonan wurdon,

ða hyne gesohtan   on sigeþeode

hearde hildefrecan,   Heaðo-Scilfingas,   2205

niða genægdan   nefan Hererices—

Thus the son of Ecgtheow proved himself valiant.
A man with warlike fame and praised for brave deeds,
He acted in pursuit of glory. He never slew drunken
Hearth-companions;* his temper was not fierce,   2180
But he, brave in battle, with the greatest strength
Among mankind, kept the bounteous gift that
God had granted him. He had long been of low esteem;
So the Geatish people did not consider him much of a man,
Nor would the lord of the Weathers make him   2185
Entitled to much merit-mark on the mead bench.
They very much thought that he was a sluggard—feeble
Though born a prince. Change came to the man of glory
For each of the afflictions he had to go through.

    Then the guardian of the earls, the battle-brave king,   2190
Ordered to bring in the heirloom of Hrethel*
Bedecked with gold; for the Geats then
There was no finer treasure in the shape of a sword.
He laid that down on Beowulf's lap,
And gave him seven thousand [hides of land],   2195
A hall, and a princely seat. To both of them alike
Land had been bequeathed as inborn right in the country,
The ancestral domain, though for the other more
Expansive was the realm, for he was higher in status.

    It happened afterwards in later days that,   2200
When Hygelac lay slain in the clashes of battle,
And the battle-swords became the bane
Of Heardred* under the shield-covering—
When the War-Scylfings, the hardy warriors,
Sought him out in the victorious people   2205
And fiercely attacked Hereric's nephew—*

149

syððan Beowulfe   brade rice

on hand gehwearf;   he geheold tela

fiftig wintra   —wæs ða frod cyning,

eald eþelweard—,   oð ðæt an ongan   2210

deorcum nihtum   draca ricsian,

se ðe on heaum hæþe*   hord beweotode,

stanbeorh steapne;   stig under læg

eldum uncuð.   Þær on innan giong

niðða nathwylc,   se þe neh gefealg   2215

hæðnum horde,   hond wæge nam,

sid, since fah;   ne he þæt syððan bemað,

þeah ðe he slæpende   besyred wurde

þeofes cræfte;   þæt sie ðiod onfand,

bigfolc beorna,   þæt he gebolgen wæs.*   2220

(XXXII) Nealles mid gewealdum   wyrmhord abræc,

sylfes willum,   se ðe him sare gesceod,

ac for þreanedlan   þeow nathwylces

hæleða bearna   heteswengeas fleah,

ærnes þearfa,   ond ðær inne fealh,   2225

secg synbysig.   Sona onfunde

þæt [þær] ðam gyste   [gry]rebroga stod;

hwæðre [earm]sceapen . . . .

. . . . sceapen

. . . .   þa hyne se fær begeat.   2230

Sincfæt . . . . .   Þær wæs swylcra fela

in ðam eorðhuse   ærgestreona,

swa hy on geardagum   gumena nathwylc,

eormenlafe   æþelan cynnes,

þanchycgende   þær gehydde,   2235

deore maðmas.   Ealle hie deað fornam

Then to Beowulf was the wide realm
Passed on for reign. He ruled well
For fifty winters—he was a wise king,
An old guardian of the land—till a certain creature,   2210
A dragon, began to hold sway in the dark nights,
Which had kept watch over a hoard on the high heath,*
A steep stone-barrow. A path lay underneath,
Unknown to men. Thereon went in
One of the human species, one who made his way   2215
To the heathen hoard; his hand took a large cup,
A shining treasure. He could not hide it thereafter,
Though sleeping, the dragon happened to be tricked
By the thief's treachery, for the people found out—
Those dwelling near did—, that he was enraged.*   2220
(XXXII) He who sorely injured the dragon did not break
Into the serpent's hoard of his own accord, on his own will,
But for dire distress: the slave of someone of
The children of men fled hateful blows,
In need of a refuge, and made his way therein,   2225
The man burdened with guilt. [. . . . .
. . . .
. . . .
. . . .
. . . .   2230
. . . .]* There was a great deal of
Such ancient treasures in that earth-cave,
As in the olden days a certain one of mankind
Had thoughtfully hidden them there,
An enormous legacy of a noble race,   2235
The precious treasures. Death had taken them all

ærran mælum,   ond se an ða gen
leoda duguðe,   se ðær lengest hwearf,
weard winegeomor,   wende þæs ylcan,
þæt he lytel fæc   longgestreona   2240
brucan moste.   Beorh eallgearo
wunode on wonge   wæteryðum neah,
niwe be næsse,   nearocræftum fæst.
Þær on innan bær   eorlgestreona
hringa hyrde   hordwyrðne dæl,   2245
fættan goldes,   fea worda cwæð:
    "Heald þu nu, hruse,   nu hæleð ne mostan,
eorla æhte!   Hwæt, hyt ær on ðe
gode begeaton;   guðdeað fornam,
feorhbealo frecne,   fyra gehwylcne   2250
leoda minra,   þara ðe þis lif ofgeaf,
gesawon seledream.   [Ic] nah hwa* sweord wege
oððe feormie   fæted wæge,
dryncfæt deore;   duguð ellor sceoc.
Sceal se hearda helm   hyrsted golde,   2255
fætum befeallen;   feormynd swefað,
þa ðe beadogriman   bywan sceoldon;
ge swylce seo herepad,   sio æt hilde gebad
ofer borda gebræc   bite irena,
brosnað æfter beorne.   Ne mæg byrnan hring   2260
æfter wigfruman   wide feran,
hæleðum be healfe.   Næs hearpan wyn,
gomen gleobeames,   ne god hafoc
geond sæl swingeð,   ne se swifta mearh
burhstede beateð.   Bealocwealm hafað   2265
fela feorhcynna   forð onsended!"

In bygone days, and the only one still alive,

Of the clansmen, he had stirred there longest,

Guardian mourning after friends; he expected the same—

That he would be able to enjoy the ancient treasure   2240

Not for a long while. A mound fully prepared

Stood on the plain near the sea-waves, newly built

By the headland, and fixed by an art of forbidding access.

Thereto the keeper of the rings bore in a portion of

The earls' treasures worth to be hoarded—plated gold.   2245

Then he spoke a few words:

　　"Hold now, you earth, the heroes' property,

Now men may not! What, good men obtained it,

First from you. War-death, the dreadful deadly evil,

Has carried off every one of my men, of my people;   2250

Each has left this life, of those who have seen the hall-joy.

I do not have anyone who would carry my sword

Or would polish my ornamented flagon,

My dear drinking bowl. All the retainers are gone elsewhere.

The strong helmet must remain bereft of fair-wrought ornament,   2255

Of its gold plates: the burnishing men sleep in death,

Who should polish the battle mask that it may shine.

And also the mail-coat, which at war lived through

The clashing of shields and the cutting of swords,

Decays after the warrior; the ring-mail cannot   2260

Journey with the battle-leader going far away,

Shoulder to shoulder with his warriors. There is no joy

Of a harp, no delight in the glee-wood; nor does a good hawk

Fly through the hall, nor do a swift horse's pounding hooves

Beat the courtyard to resound. Baleful death has   2265

Sent forth many of the living men!"

Swa giomormod   giohðo mænde

an æfter eallum,   unbliðe hwearf

dæges ond nihtes,   oð ðæt deaðes wylm

hran æt heortan.   Hordwynne fond   2270

eald uhtsceaða   opene standan,

se ðe byrnende   biorgas seceð,

nacod niðdraca,   nihtes fleogeð

fyre befangen;   hyne foldbuend

swiðe ondrædað.   He gesecean sceall   2275

hord on hrusan,   þær he hæðen gold

warað wintrum frod;   ne byð him wihte ðy sel.

    Swa se ðeodsceaða   þreo hund wintra

heold on hrusan   hordærna sum

eacencræftig,   oð ðæt hyne an abealch   2280

mon on mode;   mandryhtne bær

fæted wæge,   frioðowære bæd

hlaford sinne.   Ða wæs hord rasod,

onboren beaga hord,   bene getiðad

feasceaftum men;   frea sceawode   2285

fira fyrngeweorc   forman siðe.   *former ancient work*

    Þa se wyrm onwoc,   wroht wæs geniwad;

stonc ða æfter stane,   stearcheort onfand

feondes fotlast;   he to forð gestop

dyrnan cræfte   dracan heafde neah.   2290

Swa mæg unfæge   eaðe gedigan

wean ond wræcsið,   se ðe waldendes

hyldo gehealdeþ!   Hordweard sohte   *The hoard's guardia*

georne æfter grunde,   wolde guman findan,

þone þe him on sweofote   sare geteode;   2295

hat ond hreohmod   hlæw oft ymbehwearf

Thus, sad of thought, he uttered words of sorrow,
The one left alone after all were gone, moved about
Joyless day and night, till the surging of death
Touched his heart. The old depredator-at-dawn   2270
Found the delightful treasures stand open,
The one who, while burning, seeks barrows,
The naked malevolent dragon that flies by night,
Enwrapped in fire; the land-dwellers
Dread him dearly. He is wont to visit   2275
The hoard in the earth, where he, grown wary over the winters,
Guards the heathen gold—a task bringing no benefit.
 Thus for three hundred years the people's ravager
Had occupied in the earth one of the treasure-houses,
Magnificently large, till one man made his heart   2280
Inflamed with rage: he bore to his master
A gold-plated flagon, and pleaded to his lord
For peaceful pardon. Then was the hoard explored,
The hoard of rings diminished, the petition granted
To the poor man: his lord cast his eyes on   2285
The ancient work of men, for the first time.
 When the serpent awoke, the strife was renewed.
Then he* swiftly moved along a rock, and, hard-hearted,
Found his foe's foot-track; he had footed forward
In stealthy steps too close to the dragon's head.   2290
So may a man not doomed yet easily come through
His woe and exile—he who is guarded
By God's grace! The hoard's guardian searched
Eagerly along the ground: he wished to find the man,
Who had dealt with him unfairly while he was asleep.   2295
Hot and fierce in mood, he often moved about

ealne utanweardne;   ne ðær ænig mon

on þære westenne.   Hwæðre wiges gefeh,

beaduwe weorces;   hwilum on beorh æthwearf,

sincfæt sohte;   he þæt sona onfand,   2300

ðæt hæfde gumena sum   goldes gefandod,

heahgestreona.   Hordweard onbad

earfoðlice,   oð ðæt æfen cwom;

wæs ða gebolgen   beorges hyrde,

wolde se laða   lige forgyldan   2305

drincfæt dyre.   Þa wæs dæg sceacen

wyrme on willan;   no on wealle læng

bidan wolde,   ac mid bæle for,

fyre gefysed.   Wæs se fruma egeslic

leodum on lande,   swa hyt lungre wearð   2310

on hyra sincgifan   sare geendod.

(XXXIII) Ða se gæst ongan   gledum spiwan,   *mouster*

beorht hofu bærnan;   bryneleoma stod

eldum on andan;   no ðær aht cwices

lað lyftfloga   læfan wolde.   2315

Wæs þæs wyrmes wig   wide gesyne,

nearofages nið   nean ond feorran,

hu se guðsceaða   Geata leode

hatode ond hynde;   hord eft gesceat,

dryhtsele dyrnne,   ær dæges hwile.   2320

Hæfde landwara   lige befangen,

bæle ond bronde;   beorges getruwode,

wiges ond wealles;   him seo wen geleah.

Þa wæs Biowulfe   broga gecyðed

snude to soðe,   þæt his sylfes ham,   *(own home)*   2325

bolda selest,   brynewylmum mealt,

All outside the mound—there was no man to be found
In the wilderness; however, he rejoiced at rampage,
The act of waging war. At times he turned to the barrow,
And searched for the precious cup; he soon found out   2300
That a certain man had tampered with his gold,
The splendid treasure. The hoard-watcher waited
Impatiently till the evening came.
Then the warden of the barrow became enraged,
The hostile foe wished to pay back with flame for   2305
The dear drinking-bowl lost. Then the day was gone,
To the joy of the serpent: he would not wait long
On the wall, but went forth with fire,
Prepared with flame. The beginning was terrifying
To the people of the land, as it was forthwith to lead   2310
To a grievous end brought upon their treasure-giver.
(XXXIII) Then the stranger began to spew flame
And burn the bright houses—the glow of fire shone forth
To the horror of men; the loathsome flier
Would never leave anything to remain alive there.   2315
The assault of the serpent was seen far and wide,
The malicious marauding from near and from afar,
How much the fight-monger hated and humiliated
The people of the Geats. He hastened again to his hoard,
His hidden hall of splendor, before daylight broke.   2320
He had entrapped the people of the land in flame,
With fire and burning: he had trust in his barrow,
His valor, and the wall; his faith failed him.
    Then the horror was made known to Beowulf
Straightaway in truth—that his own dwelling,   2325
The best of buildings, the gift-seat of the Geats,

157

gifstol Geata. Þæt ðam godan wæs

hreow on hreðre, hygesorga mæst;

wende se wisa, þæt he Wealdende

ofer ealde riht ecean Dryhtne 2330

bitre gebulge; breost innan weoll

þeostrum geþoncum, swa him geþywe ne wæs.

Hæfde ligdraca leoda fæsten,

ealond utan, eorðweard ðone

gledum forgrunden; him ðæs guðkyning, 2335

Wedera þioden, wræce leornode.

    Heht him þa gewyrcean wigendra hleo

eallirenne, eorla dryhten,

wigbord wrætlic; wisse he gearwe,

þæt him holtwudu helpan ne meahte, 2340

lind wið lige. Sceolde lændaga

æþeling ærgod ende gebidan,

worulde lifes, ond se wyrm somod,

þeah ðe hordwelan heolde lange.

Oferhogode ða hringa fengel, 2345

þæt he þone widflogan weorode gesohte,

sidan herge; no he him þa sæcce ondred,

ne him þæs wyrmes wig for wiht dyde,

eafoð ond ellen, forðon he ær fela

nearo neðende niða gedigde, 2350

hildehlemma, syððan he Hroðgares,

sigoreadig secg, sele fælsode,

ond æt guðe forgrap Grendeles mægum

laðan cynnes.

        No þæt læsest wæs

hondgemota, þær mon Hygelac sloh, 2355

Had melted in the surge of fire. That was distress in heart
To the good man, the greatest sadness within;
The wise man thought that he might have
Bitterly offended the Ruler, the eternal Lord,   2330
By a breach of the old law: his breast surged within
With gloomy thoughts, as was unusual to him.
The fire-dragon had destroyed the stronghold of people,
The shoreline land without, the fortress itself
With flames; for that the warrior-king,   2335
The prince of the Weather-Geats, planned to punish him.
   Then the protector of the warriors, the lord of earls,
Ordered them to make a wondrous shield,
Entirely of iron: he readily knew
That wood from forest, a linden shield, could not   2340
Help him against fire. The non-paralleled prince
Was bound to live to see the end of the transitory days,
Of worldly life—and the serpent also, though
He had long guarded the hoard of wealth.
Then the king of rings scorned to make an assault   2345
At the far-reaching flier with a flock of men,
A bulky band; he did not fear a battle for himself,
And did not make much out of the war-faring of the serpent,
His strength and valor, because he had previously
Gone through many battles, venturing on difficulty,   2350
The clashes of war, since the time when he, a man
Blessed with victory, had purged the hall of Hrothgar,
And at a fight had crushed the clan of Grendel
Of the hateful line.
                    Nor was that the smallest
Of his close combats, in which Hygelac was slain,   2355

syððan Geata cyning   guðe ræsum,

freawine folca   Freslondum on,

Hreðles eafora   hiorodryncum swealt,

bille gebeaten.   Þonan Biowulf com

sylfes cræfte,   sundnytte dreah;   2360

hæfde him on earme   ana þritig

hildegeatwa,   þa he to holme [st]ag.*

Nealles Hetware   hremge þorfton

feðewiges,   þe him foran ongean

linde bæron;   lyt eft becwom   2365

fram þam hildfrecan   hames niosan.

Oferswam ða sioleða bigong   sunu Ecgðeowes,

earm anhaga,   eft to leodum;

þær him Hygd gebead   hord ond rice,

beagas ond bregostol;   bearne ne truwode,   2370

þæt he wið ælfylcum   eþelstolas

healdan cuðe,   ða wæs Hygelac dead.

No ðy ær feasceafte   findan meahton

æt ðam æðelinge   ænige ðinga,

þæt he Heardrede   hlaford wære,   2375

oððe þone cynedom   ciosan wolde;

hwæðre he hine on folce   freondlarum heold,

estum mid are,   oð ðæt he yldra wearð,

Weder-Geatum weold.

　　　　　　　　　　Hyne wræcmæcgas

ofer sæ sohtan,   suna Ohteres;   2380

hæfdon hy forhealden   helm Scylfinga,

þone selestan   sæcyninga

þara ðe in Swiorice   sinc brytnade,

mærne þeoden.   Him þæt to mearce wearð;

When the king of the Geats, people's lord and friend,
Son of Hrethel, died in the storm of a battle,
In Friesland, in a falchion-biting fight,
Struck by a sword. From there Beowulf came
By his sheer strength, crossing the strokes of the waves;   2360
He had on his arm the battle-gear of thirty
Of his opponents, when he set out to the sea.*
The Hetware* had no cause to be exultant in
The battle on foot, those who bore their shields
In front, against him; few came back alive again   2365
From that warrior, and returned to their homes.
Then Ecgtheow's son swam across the watery expanse,*
A forlorn solitary man, back to his people;
Then Hygd offered him treasure and the kingdom,
Rings and the royal seat; she had no faith in her son—   2370
That he would be able to maintain the ancestral thrones
Against foreign troops, now that Hygelac was dead.
Yet the poor lordless people could not prevail
Upon the princely nobleman by any means
That he would consent to be lord to Heardred,   2375
Or that he would accept the kingly power.*
But he upheld Heardred among people by friendly counsel,
With good will built on honor, till the latter grew older
And ruled the Weather-Geats.
                         The exiled men sought
Heardred across the sea, the sons of Ohthere* did.   2380
They had rebelled against the protector of the Scylfings,*
The mightiest of the sea kings that dispensed
Treasure in the land of the Swedes—a renowned prince.
To Heardred that happened to mark the end of his life;

he þær for feorme   feorhwunde hleat,   2385
sweordes swengum,   sunu Hygelaces;
ond him eft gewat   Ongenðioes bearn
hames niosan,   syððan Heardred læg,
let ðone bregostol   Biowulf healdan,
Geatum wealdan.   Þæt wæs god cyning!   2390
(XXXIV) Se ðæs leodhryres   lean gemunde
uferan dogrum,   Eadgilse wearð
feasceaftum freond;   folce gestepte
ofer sæ side   sunu Ohteres,
wigum ond wæpnum;   he gewræc syððan   2395
cealdum cearsiðum,   cyning ealdre bineat.
Swa he niða gehwane   genesen hæfde,
sliðra geslyhta,   sunu Ecgðiowes,
ellenweorca,   oð ðone anne dæg,
þe he wið þam wyrme   gewegan sceolde.   *dragon*   2400
    Gewat þa twelfa sum   torne gebolgen
dryhten Geata   dracan sceawian;
hæfde þa gefrunen,   hwanan sio fæhð aras,
bealonið biorna;   him to bearme cwom
maðþumfæt mære   þurh ðæs meldan hond.   2405
Se wæs on ðam ðreate   þreotteoða secg,
se ðæs orleges   or onstealde,
hæft hygegiomor,   sceolde hean ðonon
wong wisian.   He ofer willan giong
to ðæs ðe he eorðsele   anne wisse,   2410
hlæw under hrusan   holmwylme neh,
yðgewinne;   se wæs innan full
wrætta ond wira.   Weard unhiore,
gearo guðfreca,   goldmaðmas heold,

For his hospitality there he received a mortal wound,   2385
Hygelac's son did, by the strokes of a sword.
And the son of Ongentheow* departed again
To seek his home after Heardred lay dead,
Leaving Beowulf behind to sit on the royal seat
And rule the Geats. That was a good king!   2390
(XXXIV) He kept in mind requital for the calamity
In later days, and became a friend to
The all-bereft Eadgils; with his people he supported
The son of Ohthere* over the wide sea,
With warriors and weapons; he avenged afterwards   2395
By a bitter careworn expedition, and took the king's life.*
Thus he had survived each of the battles,
The fierce combats, the son of Ecgtheow had,
Of the works of valor, till that one day,
On which he had to fight with the serpent.   2400
     Then, aroused to anger, the lord of the Geats—
One of twelve—went to look upon the dragon.
He had then learnt from where the disaster arose,
The dire affliction of men: the renowned treasure cup,
Through the informer's hand, had come to his possession.   2405
He was the thirteenth man in the troop—
The one who had brought about the beginning of the broil;
The sad slave, the wretched one, had to from there
Show the way to the place. Against his wish he went
To where he knew a certain earth-hall—   2410
The cave under the ground near the sea-surge,
The tossing waves; within, it was overflowing
With ornaments and fineries. The dreadful guard,
The alert fighter, old under the earth,

eald under eorðan;   næs þæt yðe ceap   2415
to gegangenne   gumena ænigum.

   Gesæt ða on næsse   niðheard cyning;
þenden hælo abead   heorðgeneatum,
goldwine Geata.   Him wæs geomor sefa,
wæfre ond wælfus,   wyrd ungemete neah,   2420
se ðone gomelan   gretan sceolde,
secean sawle hord,   sundur gedælan
lif wið lice;   no þon lange wæs
feorh æþelinges   flæsce bewunden.

   Biowulf maþelade,   bearn Ecgðeowes: 2425
"Fela ic on giogoðe   guðræsa genæs,
orleghwila;   ic þæt eall gemon.
Ic wæs syfanwintre,   þa mec sinca baldor,
freawine folca,   æt minum fæder genam;
heold mec ond hæfde   Hreðel cyning,   2430
geaf me sinc ond symbel,   sibbe gemunde;
næs ic him to life   laðra owihte,
beorn in burgum,   þonne his bearna hwylc,
Herebeald ond Hæðcyn   oððe Hygelac min.
Wæs þam yldestan   ungedefelice   2435
mæges dædum   morþorbed stred,
syððan hyne Hæðcyn   of hornbogan,
his freawine,   flane geswencte,
miste mercelses   ond his mæg ofscet,
broðor oðerne   blodigan gare.   2440
Þæt wæs feohleas gefeoht,   fyrenum gesyngad,
hreðre hygemeðe;   sceolde hwæðre swa þeah
æðeling unwrecen   ealdres linnan.
Swa bið geomorlic   gomelum ceorle

164

Kept the golden treasures. That was not an object   2415
That any man could attain in an easy bargain.

    Then on the headland sat the battle-brave king,
While the prince of the Geats wished good luck for
His hearth-companions. He was sad in heart,
Uneasy, yet ready for death, the fate being so near   2420
That should come upon the old man,
Try to reach the hoard of soul, and part asunder
Life from the body; not for long afterwards
The prince's life was enclosed in flesh.

    Beowulf spoke, son of Ecgtheow: 2425
"In youth I survived many of the battle-storms,
Of the times of war—I remember that all.
I was seven years old, when the prince of the rings—
The friendly lord of the people—took me from my father:
King Hrethel took charge of me and kept me,   2430
Gave me treasure and feast, remembered our kinship;
In his lifetime I was never any less dear to him
As a man at arms in his stronghold than any of his sons—
Herebeald, Hæthcyn, or Hygelac, my dear lord.
For the eldest a violent death-bed was spread   2435
Inappropriately by the deeds of a kinsman—
When Hæthcyn struck him down, his friendly lord,
With an arrow shot from his horn-bow,
Missed the mark, and shot his kinsman dead—
One brother killed another, with the bloody arrow-shaft.   2440
That was a fight inexpiable, unfortunately perpetrated,
Wearying to the heart; yet so did it happen, no matter
How a prince had to lose his life without being avenged.
So heart chilling it is for a hoary man

to gebidanne, / þæt his byre ride   2445
giong on galgan; þonne he gyd wrece,
sarigne sang, þonne his sunu hangað
hrefne to hroðre, ond he him helpe ne mæg,
eald ond infrod, ænige gefremman.
Symble bið gemyndgad morna gehwylce   2450
eaforan ellorsið; oðres ne gymeð
to gebidanne burgum in innan
yrfeweardas, þonne se an hafað
þurh deaðes nyd dæda gefondad.
Gesyhð sorhcearig on his suna bure   2455
winsele westne, windge reste
reote berofene; ridend swefað,
hæleð in hoðman; nis þær hearpan sweg,
gomen in geardum, swylce ðær iu wæron.
(XXXV) Gewiteð þonne on sealman, sorhleoð gæleð   2460
an æfter anum; þuhte him eall to rum,
wongas ond wicstede. Swa Wedra helm
æfter Herebealde heortan sorge
weallinde wæg; wihte ne meahte
on ðam feorhbonan fæghðe gebetan;   2465
no ðy ær he þone heaðorinc hatian ne meahte
laðum dædum, þeah him leof ne wæs.
He ða mid þære sorhge, þe him to sar belamp,*
gumdream ofgeaf, Godes leoht geceas;
eaferum læfde, swa deð eadig mon,   2470
lond ond leodbyrig, þa he of life gewat.
Þa wæs synn ond sacu Sweona ond Geata
ofer wid wæter wroht gemæne,
herenið hearda, syððan Hreðel swealt,

To endure that his son should swing so young   2445
Upon the hanging gallows; then he may utter a dirge,
A mournful song, when his son is hanging
For the joy of the raven, and he cannot perform
Any help to him, though himself old and wise.
The death of his son is incessantly remembered   2450
Upon each sunrise; he does not care to
Wait for another heir to succeed in his
Stronghold, when the one, through the mandate
Of death, has undergone all experiences.
The sorrowful man sees in his son's dwelling   2455
A wine-hall wasted, a windy bedroom
Deprived of joy—the riders sleep,
The warriors in the grave; no sound of the harp,
No joy in the dwelling is there, as there were before.
(XXXV) He then goes to bed, and sings a song of sorrow—   2460
A man longing for a man;* the fields and the homestead—
All seemed hollow to him. Thus the protector
Of the Weather-Geats bore in his heart grief
Welling after Herebeald; he could by no means
Settle the feud by retribution on the slayer;   2465
None the sooner could he chastise the warrior*
For his hateful deeds, though he was not dear to him.
Then with the grief that had befallen him too bitterly*
He gave up joy among men, and chose God's light:
He left for his sons land and towns, as does   2470
A prosperous man, when he departed from life.
Then there was hostility and strife between Swedes and Geats
Across the wide water, a feud affecting both sides,
A severe belligerent enmity, when Hrethel died.

oððe him Ongenðeowes   eaferan wæran   2475
frome fyrdhwate,   freode ne woldon
ofer heafo healdan,   ac ymb Hreosnabeorh
eatolne inwitscear   oft gefremedon.
Þæt mægwine   mine gewræcan,
fæhðe ond fyrene,   swa hyt gefræge wæs,   2480
þeah ðe oðer his   ealdre gebohte,
heardan ceape;   Hæðcynne wearð,
Geata dryhtne,   guð onsæge.
Þa ic on morgne gefrægn   mæg oðerne
billes ecgum   on bonan stælan,   2485
þær Ongenþeow   Eofores niosað;
guðhelm toglad,   gomela Scylfing
hreas heoroblac;*   hond gemunde
fæhðo genoge,   feorhsweng ne ofteah.
Ic him þa maðmas,   þe he me sealde,   2490
geald æt guðe,   swa me gifeðe wæs,
leohtan sweorde;   he me lond forgeaf,
eard eðelwyn.   Næs him ænig þearf,
þæt he to Gifðum   oððe to Gar-Denum
oððe in Swiorice   secean þurfe   2495
wyrsan wigfrecan,   weorðe gecypan;
symle ic him on feðan   beforan wolde,
ana on orde,   ond swa to aldre sceall
sæcce fremman,   þenden þis sweord þolað,
þæt mec ær ond sið   oft gelæste,   2500
syððan ic for dugeðum   Dæghrefne wearð
to handbonan,   Huga cempan;
nalles he ða frætwe   Frescyninge,
breostweorðunge   bringan moste,

And the sons of Ongentheow* were   2475
Bold and battle-brave, and did not wish to maintain
Friendship over the seas; but around Hreosnabeorh*
They often perpetrated dire malicious slaughter.
That my kinsmen redressed with vengeance,
The hostile deed and crime, as it was well-known,   2480
Though one of them paid with his life,
A dear cost; the war turned out fatal
For Hæthcyn, the lord of the Geats.*
Then I have heard one kinsman* in the morning
Avenged the other* on the slayer with the edge of a sword,   2485
When Ongentheow attacked Eofor;*
The battle-helm split, the old Scylfing
Fell mortally wounded;* his* hand remembered
Numerous feuds, and did not withhold deadly blow.
With my shining sword I have repaid   2490
At battle those treasures that he* gave me,
As was granted me by fate; he gave me land,
The joy of estate bequeathed. There was no need
For him to seek a warrior with less worth
From among the Gifthas* or the Spear-Danes   2495
Or the Swedes, and buy him with treasure;
I would always march ahead of him in his troop,
Alone in the front, and thus throughout my life shall
Fulfill my task at battle, while this sword holds out,
That at all times has never failed to serve me,   2500
Since I in the presence of the troops became
The hand-slayer of Dæghrefn,* the Frankish champion—
He could not bring the adornments,
The breast-ornament, to the king of the Frisians,

ac in campe gecrong   cumbles hyrde,   2505

æþeling on elne;   ne wæs ecg bona,   *sword - blade*

ac him hildegrap   heortan wylmas,

banhus gebræc.   Nu sceall billes ecg,   *wrecked the bone - house*

hond ond heard sweord   ymb hord wigan."

Beowulf maðelode,   beotwordum spræc   *boast*   2510

niehstan siðe: "Ic geneðde fela

guða on geogoðe;   gyt ic wylle,

frod folces weard   fæhðe secan,

mærðu fremman,   gif mec se mansceaða

of eorðsele   ut geseceð."   2515

Gegrette ða   gumena gehwylcne,

hwate helmberend,   hindeman siðe,

swæse gesiðas: "Nolde ic sweord beran,

wæpen to wyrme,   gif ic wiste hu   *dragon*

wið ðam aglæcean   elles meahte   2520

gylpe wiðgripan,   swa ic gio wið Grendle dyde;   *as I did with Grendel*

ac ic ðær heaðufyres   hates wene,

oreðes ond attres;   forðon ic me on hafu

bord ond byrnan.   Nelle ic beorges weard

oferfleon* fotes trem,   ac unc furður sceal   2525

weorðan æt wealle,   swa unc wyrd geteoð,

Metod manna gehwæs.   Ic eom on mode from,

þæt ic wið þone guðflogan   gylp ofersitte.

Gebide ge on beorge   byrnum werede,

secgas on searwum,   hwæðer sel mæge   2530

æfter wælræse   wunde gedygan

uncer twega.   Nis þæt eower sið,

ne gemet mannes,   nefne min anes,

þæt he wið aglæcean   eofoðo dæle,

But in the battle fell down, keeper of the banner,   2505

A valorous prince; nor was he slain by my sword,

But my fierce handgrip crushed his pulsating heart—

The flesh covering his bones; now shall the sharp blade,

Hand, and a strong sword do the battle to get the hoard."

    Beowulf spoke, spoke in words full of boast   2510

For the last time: "I ventured upon many a

Battle in my youthful days; still shall I,

An old guardian of the folk, be glad to fight

To attain a glorious feat, if a heinous ravager

Come out of the earth-hall to confront me."   2515

    Then he greeted each of the men,

The bold helmet-wearers for the last time,

His dear companions: "I would not bear a sword,

A weapon, to the worm, if I knew how I could

Otherwise against the fierce foe fulfilling devastation   2520

Grapple with pledge, as I did with Grendel long ago.

But I expect here the hot-burning battle-flame,

Harsh breath and venomous air; that is why I carry

This shield, this coat of mail. I will not flee a step

From the barrow's ward, but it shall for us both henceforth   2525

Happen on the wall as fate dictates for us—

That governs each man's life. My resolution is such that

I scorn to utter an oath against the winged foe.

Wait on the barrow, well protected by your mail-coats,

You, men at arms—to find which of us can better   2530

Endure the wounds inflicted in the deadly encounter

Between the two of us: this is not your undertaking,

Nor is it fitting for any man except me alone,

That he should exert his strength against the monster,

eorlscype efne. | Ic mid elne sceall 2535
gold gegangan, oððe guð nimeð,
feorhbealu frecne frean eowerne!"
    Aras ða bi ronde rof oretta,
heard under helme, hiorosercean bær
under stancleofu, strengo getruwode 2540
anes mannes; ne bið swylc earges sið!
Geseah ða be wealle se ðe worna fela,
gumcystum god, guða gedigde,
hildehlemma, þonne hnitan feðan,
stondan stanbogan, stream ut þonan 2545
brecan of beorge; wæs þære burnan wælm
heaðofyrum hat, ne meahte horde neah
unbyrnende ænige hwile
deop gedygan for dracan lege.
Let ða of breostum, ða he gebolgen wæs, 2550
Weder-Geata leod word ut faran,
stearcheort styrmde; stefn in becom
heaðotorht hlynnan under harne stan.
Hete wæs onhrered, hordweard oncniow
mannes reorde; næs ðær mara fyrst 2555
freode to friclan. From ærest cwom
oruð aglæcean ut of stane,
hat hildeswat; hruse dynede.
Biorn under beorge bordrand onswaf
wið ðam gryregieste, Geata dryhten; 2560
ða wæs hringbogan heorte gefysed
sæcce to seceanne. Sweord ær gebræd
god guðcyning, gomele lafe,
ecgum unslaw; | æghwæðrum wæs

Fulfill a man's job. With valor I shall   2535
Obtain wealth, or war—dire destroyer of life—will
Take your lord away from you!"
　　　Then the brave warrior up rose by his shield.
Hardy under helmet, he bore his battle-wear
Under the stone-cliffs, trusting the strength   2540
Of one man: such is not what a coward can do!
Then by the wall he saw—he who had come through
Many a battle, brave with manly virtues,
Battle-clashes when the bands on foot beat together—
A stone-arch standing, from where a stream   2545
Bursting out of the barrow; there was surging of a flow,
Hot with deadly flame. He could not
Stay unburned by the dragon's flame
Even for a while at the cave near the hoard.
Swollen with rage, the man of the Weather-Geats   2550
Then let a word burst out of his breast—
Strong-hearted, he shouted. His voice rang clear in battle,
And it resounded in under the gray stone.
Hate was aroused; the hoard's ward knew that
It was man's speech. There was no more time to   2555
Ask for appeasement. First came forth
The breath of the fierce ravager out of the stone,
The burning battle-fume; the earth rumbled.
The man under the barrow, the lord of the Geats,
Swung his shield's rim against the detestable stranger;   2560
Then the heart of the coiled creature was aroused
To burn after battle. The good warrior-king
Had drawn his sword, an ancient heirloom,
Not dull of edge. For each of them was terror

173

bealohycgendra   broga fram oðrum.   2565

Stiðmod gestod   wið steapne rond

winia bealdor,   ða se wyrm gebeah

snude tosomne;   he on searwum bad.

Gewat ða byrnende   gebogen scriðan,

to gescipe scyndan.   Scyld wel gebearg   2570

life ond lice   læssan hwile

mærum þeodne,   þonne his myne sohte,

ðær he þy fyrste   forman dogore

wealdan moste,   swa him wyrd ne gescraf

hreð æt hilde.   Hond up abræd   2575

Geata dryhten,   gryrefahne sloh

incge-lafe,   þæt sio ecg gewac

brun on bane,   bat unswiðor,

þonne his ðiodcyning   þearfe hæfde,

bysigum gebæded.

                          Þa wæs beorges weard   2580

æfter heaðuswenge   on hreoum mode,

wearp wælfyre;   wide sprungon   *battle-fire billowed + spewed*

hildeleoman.   Hreðsigora ne gealp

goldwine Geata;   guðbill geswac

nacod æt niðe,   swa hyt no sceolde,   2585

iren ærgod.   Ne wæs þæt eðe sið,

þæt se mæra   maga Ecgðeowes

grundwong þone   ofgyfan wolde;

sceolde ofer willan   wic eardian

elles hwergen,   swa sceal æghwylc mon   2590

alætan lændagas.   Næs ða long to ðon,

þæt ða aglæcean   hy eft gemetton.

Hyrte hyne hordweard,   hreðer æðme weoll,

From the other, each being intent on destroying the other.   2565

Stout-hearted stood he with his shield aloft,

The lord of friends, when the serpent swiftly coiled

Its whole body; he waited in full preparation.

Then, burning in flame, it went gliding coiled,

Hastening to its fate. The shield well protected   2570

The life and body of the renowned prince

For a while, but not long as he had purported.

There, for the first time in the days of his life,

He could not assert his claim for triumph at battle,

As fate's decree was not so. The lord of the Geats   2575

Uplifted his hand, struck the multi-colored beast

With his mighty heirloom, that the blade failed,

Gleaming on the bone, bit not so thoroughly

As the king of the folk had need for it,

Oppressed by an ordeal.

                    Then the barrow's ward   2580

Was in a fierce spirit after the battle-stroke, and

Spewed deadly fire; the battle-flames

Spread wide. The gold-giving friend of the Geats

Boasted of no glorious feat; the battle-sword, drawn

For fight, had failed—as it should never have,   2585

Iron good all the way till then. Nor was that an easy journey,

One that the renowned son of Ecgtheow would

Be willing to take to give up his tie to the land.

He, against his wish, had to take up a dwelling-place

Elsewhere, as each man must depart, leaving his   2590

Fleeting days behind. It was not long till

The two mighty opponents met together again.

The hoard's ward took heart, his heart heaved in breathing,

niwan stefne;   nearo ðrowode

fyre befongen,   se ðe ær folce weold.   2595

Nealles him on heape   handgesteallan,

æðelinga bearn,   ymbe gestodon

hildecystum,   ac hy on holt bugon,   *ran to the woods*

ealdre burgan.   Hiora in anum weoll

sefa wið sorgum;   sibb æfre ne mæg   *sorrow*   2600

wiht onwendan   þam ðe wel þenceð.

(XXXVI) Wiglaf wæs haten,   Weoxstanes sunu,

leoflic lindwiga,   leod Scylfinga,   *valued warrior*

mæg Ælfheres;   geseah his mondryhten

under heregriman   hat þrowian.   2605

Gemunde ða ða are,   þe he him ær forgeaf,

wicstede weligne   Wægmundinga,

folcrihta gehwylc,   swa his fæder ahte;

ne mihte ða forhabban,   hond rond gefeng,

geolwe linde,   gomel swyrd geteah;   2610

þæt wæs mid eldum   Eanmundes laf,

suna Ohteres;   þam æt sæcce wearð,

wræccan wineleasum   Weohstan bana

meces ecgum,   ond his magum ætbær

brunfagne helm,   hringde byrnan,   2615

ealdsweord etonisc;   þæt him Onela forgeaf,

his gædelinges   guðgewædu,   *? war - gear*

fyrdsearo fuslic,—   no ymbe ða fæhðe spræc,

þeah ðe he his broðor bearn   abredwade.

He [ðā]* frætwe geheold   fela missera,   2620

bill ond byrnan,   oð ðæt his byre mihte

eorlscipe efnan   swa his ærfæder;

geaf him ða mid Geatum   guðgewæda,

Once again. Surrounded by flames, he who had once
Ruled a nation came to suffer hard-to-endure pain.   2595
Not at all did the co-fighters of his—
Those sons of the nobles—stand around him in band
With warlike valor; but they fled to the wood,
And saved their lives. Among them all, there was one
Who felt a surge of grief in his heart: a man can never   2600
Annul the ties of kinship, if he is one who thinks rightly.
(XXXVI) His name was Wiglaf, son of Weohstan,
An admirable shield-warrior, a man of the Scylfings,
A kinsman of Ælfhere.* He saw his liege lord
Suffer from heat, under his battle-mask.   2605
He then remembered what property he had given him before,
The rich dwelling-place of the Wægmundings,*
Each of the folk-rights, such as his father had possessed.
He could not then hold himself; his hand gripped his shield,
The brown linden, and he drew his time-honored sword.   2610
That was, as known to men, an heirloom of Eanmund,
Ohthere's son, whom—a friendless exile—
Weohstan happened to slay at battle
With his sword's edge, thereafter carrying to his kinsmen
The shining helmet, the ringed mail-coat,   2615
And the old sword giants made. Onela gave it to him,
And the battle-garments of his kinsman,
Ready battle-gear; he did not speak about the feud,
Despite that he had killed the son of his own brother.*
He kept the battle-gear for many half-years,   2620
Sword and mail-shirt, till his son could
Attain warriorhood, as his old father had done.
Then he gave him among the Geats every single piece

æghwæs unrim, þa he of ealdre gewat

frod on forðweg. Þa wæs forma sið 2625

geongan cempan, þæt he guðe ræs

mid his freodryhtne fremman sceolde.

Ne gemealt him se modsefa, ne his mæges laf

gewac æt wige; þæt se wyrm onfand,

syððan hie togædre gegan hæfdon. 2630

Wiglaf maðelode, wordrihta fela

sægde gesiðum —him wæs sefa geomor—:

"Ic ðæt mæl geman, þær we medu þegun,

þonne we geheton ussum hlaforde

in biorsele, ðe us ðas beagas geaf, 2635

þæt we him ða guðgetawa gyldan woldon,

gif him þyslicu þearf gelumpe,

helmas ond heard sweord. Ðe he usic on herge geceas

to ðyssum siðfate sylfes willum,

onmunde usic mærða, ond me þas maðmas geaf, 2640

þe he usic garwigend gode tealde,

hwate helmberend, þeah ðe hlaford us

þis ellenweorc ana aðohte

to gefremmanne, folces hyrde,

for ðam he manna mæst mærða gefremede, 2645

dæda dollicra. Nu is se dæg cumen,

þæt ure mandryhten mægenes behofað,

godra guðrinca; wutun gongan to,

helpan hildfruman, þenden hyt sŷ,

gledegesa grim. God wat on mec, 2650

þæt me is micle leofre, þæt minne lichaman

mid minne goldgyfan gled fæðmie.

Ne þynceð me gerysne, þæt we rondas beren

Of the battle-gear, when he was about to leave life behind,

An old man on his way forth. That was the first time for   2625

The young warrior to partake in the storm of battle,

Shoulder to shoulder with his noble lord.

His spirit did not melt, nor did his father's heirloom

Fail at war; the serpent perceived that, when

They had come to confront each other in strife.   2630

    Wiglaf spoke, addressed his companions

With many words of truth—he was sad at heart—:

"I remember that time, when we drank mead.

On such an occasion we pledged to our lord

In the beer-hall, who gave us the rings,   2635

That we would repay him with our battle-gears,

With helmet and hard sword, if such a need should

Befall him. For this reason he chose us from his army

For this expedition by the will of his own,

Took us worthy of glory, and gave me these treasures,   2640

For he considered us to be good spear-wielders,

Brave helmet-wearers—although our lord,

People's guardian, intended to perform

The work of glory all by himself, for he had attained

The foremost feats of glory among men—the greatest   2645

Of all daring deeds. Now is the day come that

Our liege lord is in need of the strength of

Good warriors. Let us go where we should,

To help our battle-leader, though heat there may be—

The grim horror of fire. God knows, as for me,   2650

That I would rather choose to let my body

Be engulfed in flame with my ring-giver.

It does not seem right that we bear our shields

eft to earde,   nemne we æror mægen
fane gefyllan,   feorh ealgian   2655
Wedra ðeodnes.   Ic wat geare,
þæt næron ealdgewyrht,   þæt he ana scyle
Geata duguðe   gnorn þrowian,
gesigan æt sæcce;   urum sceal sweord ond helm,
byrne ond beaduscrud,   bam gemæne."   2660
    Wod þa þurh þone wælrec,   wigheafolan bær
frean on fultum,   fea worda cwæð:
"Leofa Biowulf,   læst eall tela,
swa ðu on geoguðfeore   geara gecwæde,
þæt ðu ne alæte   be ðe lifigendum   2665
dom gedreosan;   scealt nu dædum rof,
æðeling anhydig,   ealle mægene
feorh ealgian;   ic ðe fullæstu."
    Æfter ðam wordum   wyrm yrre cwom,
atol inwitgæst,   oðre siðe   2670
fyrwylmum fah   fionda niosian,
laðra manna.   Ligyðum forborn
bord wið rond,   byrne ne meahte
geongum garwigan   geoce gefremman,
ac se maga geonga   under his mæges scyld   2675
elne geeode,   þa his agen wæs
gledum forgrunden.   Þa gen guðcyning
mærða gemunde,   mægenstrengo sloh
hildebille,   þæt hyt on heafolan stod
niþe genyded;   Nægling forbærst,   2680
geswac æt sæcce   sweord Biowulfes
gomol ond grægmæl.   Him þæt gifeðe ne wæs,
þæt him irenna   ecge mihton

Back to home, unless we first could

Finish off this foe, and protect the life   2655

Of the prince of the Geats. I know well

That his past deeds do not warrant that he must

Suffer affliction all alone among the Geatish host,

And fall in battle. We shall share sword and helmet,

Mail-coat and battle-gear, for common use among us."   2660

      Then he waded through the stifling smoke, wearing

A helmet, to help his lord, and spoke, sparing words:

"Dear Beowulf, carry out all well—

So said you long ago in your youth,

That you would not, while you are alive,   2665

Let glory decline. Now, strong-willed prince,

Brave in deeds, you must defend your life

In all your strength; I shall help you."

      When these words were over, the wrathful ward came,

The horrid foe in malevolence, a second time,   2670

To attack his enemies, the hated men, all flashing

In a surge of flame. The streak of fire fared forth,

Burnt the shield down to the boss; the battle-shirt

Could not lend any help to the young spear-fighter,

But the young man slid secure and bold   2675

Under his kinsman's shield, when his own was

Burnt down by the flame. Then the warrior-king

Rekindled his zeal for glory, let his battle-sword

Cleave in strong sweep, that it got stuck on the head,

Bearing the heat of his hate. Nægling* broke—   2680

The sword of Beowulf failed at battle,

Time-honored and gray with age; it was not granted

That the blades of iron-made swords could be of

helpan æt hilde;   wæs sio hond to strong,

se ðe meca gehwane   mine gefræge   2685

swenge ofersohte,   þonne he to sæcce bær

wæpen wundrum heard;   næs him wihte ðe sel.

  Þa wæs þeodsceaða þriddan siðe,   *ravager of the people*

frecne fyrdraca   fæhða gemyndig,

ræsde on ðone rofan,   þa him rum ageald,   2690

hat ond heaðogrim,   heals ealne ymbefeng

biteran banum;   he geblodegod wearð

sawuldriore,   swat yðum weoll.

(XXXVII) Ða ic æt þearfe gefrægn   þeodcyninges

andlongne eorl   ellen cyðan,   2695

cræft ond cenðu,   swa him gecynde wæs.

Ne hedde he þæs heafolan,   ac sio hand gebarn   *pay attention/care*

modiges mannes,   þær he his mæges healp,

þæt he þone niðgæst   nioðor hwene sloh,

secg on searwum,   þæt ðæt sweord gedeaf   *skilled warrior* 2700

fah ond fæted,   þæt ðæt fyr ongon

sweðrian syððan.   Þa gen sylf cyning

geweold his gewitte,   wæll-seaxe gebræd

biter ond beaduscearp,   þæt he on byrnan wæg;

forwrat Wedra helm   wyrm on middan.   *dragon* 2705

Feond gefyldan   —ferh ellen wræc—,

ond hi hyne þa begen   abroten hæfdon,

sibæðelingas;   swylc sceolde secg wesan,   *partners in nobility*

þegn æt ðearfe!   Þæt ðam þeodne wæs

siðast sigehwile   sylfes dædum,   2710

worlde geweorces.   Ða sio wund ongon,

þe him se eorðdraca   ær geworhte,   *caused/inflicted earth-burner*

swelan ond swellan;   he þæt sona onfand,   *scald + swell*

Any help to him at battle; his hand was too strong,

The hand that, as I have heard, surpassed any sword   2685

In its stroke, even when he bore to battle

A weapon hardened with wounds:* he was no better off for it.

    Then, for the third time, the ravager of people,

The fearsome fire-dragon, intent on devilish devastation,

Rushed upon the valiant one, when it was given a chance,   2690

Hot and full of hatred. It took his entire neck in the grip

Of its piercing teeth; he turned bloody all over

With the stream of life's water flowing down in flood.

(XXXVII) Then, I have heard, in the presence of his king's need,

The warrior proved his valorous zeal, standing beside his lord,   2695

With his strength and bravery he was born with.

He didn't care about his head, but the hand of the brave

Man got burnt while he was helping his kinsman,

That he struck the malevolent foe somewhat lower,

The man at arms did, so that the sword sank in,   2700

Shining and adorned, that the fire began to

Subside henceforth. Then the king himself still

Had control of his senses, drew his deadly dagger,

Biting and battle-sharp, which he carried on his war-coat;

The guardian of the Geats cut through the worm in the middle.   2705

They had felled their foe—their valor had driven out its life—

And they both together had quelled it down,

The noble kinsmen had. Such should a man be—

A thane at need should. That was for the prince

The last of the victories he had attained by his deeds—   2710

Work in the world. Then the wound, which

The earth-dragon had inflicted on him earlier,

Began to burn and swell; he soon found it out

þæt him on breostum   bealoniðe weoll   *welling*

attor on innan.   Ða se æðeling giong,   *poison inside*   2715

þæt he bi wealle   wishycgende   *wise*

gesæt on sesse;   seah on enta geweorc,   *sat on a bench*

hu ða stanbogan   stapulum fæste   *giant fort*   *natural stone arch*

ece eorðreced   innan healde.   *earthwork*

Hyne þa mid handa   heorodreorigne,   2720

þeoden mærne   þegn ungemete till,

winedryhten his   wætere gelafede   *his friendly lord*

hilde sædne   ond his helm onspeon.   *unbuckled his helmet*

✱ [Biowulf maþelode—   he ofer benne spræc,   *despite mortal injury*

wunde wælbleate;   wisse he gearwe,   *(ready?)*   2725

þæt he dæghwila   gedrogen hæfde,

eorðan wynne;   ða wæs eall sceacen

dogorgerimes,   deað ungemete neah—:   *allotted time of life*

"Nu ic suna minum   syllan wolde

guðgewædu,   þær me gifeðe swa   *? armour ?*   2730

ænig yrfeweard   æfter wurde

lice gelenge.   Ic ðas leode heold

fiftig wintra;   næs se folccyning,

ymbesittendra   ænig ðara,

þe mec guðwinum   gretan dorste,   2735

egesan ðêon.   Ic on earde bad

mælgesceafta,   heold min tela,   *?*

ne sohte searoniðas,   ne me swor fela   *never fomented quarrels*

aða on unriht.   Ic ðæs ealles mæg

feorhbennum seoc   gefean habban;   2740

forðam me witan ne ðearf   Waldend fira

morðorbealo maga,   þonne min sceaceð

lif of lice.   Nu ðu lungre geong

That in his breast, deep inside, venom was welling up
With fierce rage. Then the wise prince walked   2715
To sit down on a seat near the wall;
He looked on the giants' work—
How the ancient earth dwelling had held within
The stone-arches firmly secured by the columns.
Then the thane, boundlessly good, with his hand   2720
Washed the renowned prince, besmeared with blood—
His friend and dear lord, wearied out in battle—,
With water, and untied his helmet.

    Beowulf spoke—uttered words despite the wound,
The uncurable cut; he knew all too well   2725
That he had passed through all his days of life,
His earthly joy; when the whole number of days
Had been exhausted, death was to be imminent:
"Now I would have given to my son
My battle-gear, had such been granted me—   2730
An heir who would live on afterwards
With fleshly legacy. I have ruled my people
For fifty winters: there was no folk-king,
None among those of the neighboring peoples,
Who dared to challenge me with his battle forces,   2735
Or threaten with fear. I have waited on this land
For the dictum of destiny, kept my share properly,
Sought no crafty dealings, nor have sworn for my sake
Many oaths wrongfully. In all of this I, though
Weakened with mortal wounds, can have joy;   2740
For there is no cause for the Lord of men to blame me
For slaughter of kinsmen, when life passes away
From my body. Go you now forthwith,

hord sceawian   under harne stan,
Wiglaf leofa,   nu se wyrm ligeð,   2745
swefeð sare wund,   since bereafod.
Bio nu on ofoste,   þæt ic ærwelan,
goldæht ongite,   gearo sceawige
swegle searogimmas,   þæt ic ðy seft mæge
æfter maððumwelan   min alætan   2750
lif ond leodscipe,   þone ic longe heold."
(XXXVIII) Ða ic snude gefrægn   sunu Wihstanes
æfter wordcwydum   wundum dryhtne
hyran heaðosiocum,   hringnet beran,
brogdne beadusercean   under beorges hrof.   2755
Geseah ða sigehreðig,   þa he bi sesse geong,
magoþegn modig   maððumsigla fealo,
gold glitinian   grunde getenge,
wundur on wealle,   ond þæs wyrmes denn,
ealdes uhtflogan,   orcas stondan,   2760
fyrnmanna fatu,   feormendlease,
hyrstum behrorene;   þær wæs helm monig
eald ond omig,   earmbeaga fela
searwum gesæled.   Sinc eaðe mæg,
gold on grunde   gumcynnes gehwone   2765
oferhigian,   hyde se ðe wylle.
Swylce he siomian geseah   segn eallgylden
heah ofer horde,   hondwundra mæst,
gelocen leoðocræftum;   of ðam leoma stod,
þæt he þone grundwong   ongitan meahte,   2770
wræte giondwlitan.   Næs ðæs wyrmes þær
onsyn ænig,   ac hyne ecg fornam.
Ða ic on hlæwe gefrægn   hord reafian,

Have a look at the hoard under the gray stone,

Dear Wiglaf, now the serpent is sprawled dead,   2745

Sleeps sorely wounded, deprived of treasure.

Be now in haste, that I may see the ancient riches,

The golden treasure, and clearly examine

The bright jewels finely wrought, so I may,

With more comfort at the abundance of treasure,   2750

Leave my life and my people, whom I have ruled long."

(XXXVIII) Then, I have heard, the son of Weohstan,

Upon hearing these words, quickly obeyed his lord,

Wounded and wearied in battle, and bore his ring-net,

His woven battle-shirt, beneath the roof of the barrow.   2755

Then the victorious one saw, when he went near a seat,

The brave young thane did, many of the precious jewels,

Gold glittering on the ground strewn all over,

Wondrous things on the wall, and the den of the serpent,

Of the old pre-dawn flier, and the cups standing,   2760

The vessels of the men of old, remaining unpolished,

Stripped of their adornments. There was many a helmet

Old and rusty, a multitude of arm-coverings

Skillfully twisted.—Treasure can easily overpower

Anyone of mankind, gold in the ground can,   2765

No matter who may wish to hide it.—

Also he saw a banner wrought of gold

Hanging high over the hoard, the most wondrous work

Woven by handcraft; from it light shone forth,

So that he could see the surface of the floor,   2770

Detect every ornate thing thereon. No trace of the dragon

Was to be seen there, for a sword had carried him off.

Then, I have heard, the sole man plundered

eald enta geweorc   anne mannan,
him on bearm hladon   bunan ond discas   2775
sylfes dome;   segn eac genom,
beacna beorhtost.   Bill ær gescod
—ecg wæs iren—   ealdhlafordes
þam ðara maðma   mundbora wæs
longe hwile,   ligegesan wæg   2780
hatne for horde,   hioroweallende
middelnihtum,   oð þæt he morðre swealt.
   Ar wæs on ofoste,   eftsiðes georn,
frætwum gefyrðred;   hyne fyrwet bræc,
hwæðer collenferð   cwicne gemette   2785
in ðam wongstede   Wedra þeoden
ellensiocne,   þær he hine ær forlet.
He ða mid þam maðmum   mærne þioden,
dryhten sinne   driorigne fand
ealdres æt ende;   he hine eft ongon   2790
wæteres weorpan,   oð þæt wordes ord
breosthord þurhbræc.   [Biorncyning spræc]*
gomel on giohðe   —gold sceawode—:
"Ic ðara frætwa   Frean ealles ðanc,
Wuldurcyninge   wordum secge,   2795
ecum Dryhtne,   þe ic her on starie,
þæs ðe ic moste   minum leodum
ær swyltdæge   swylc gestrynan.
Nu ic on maðma hord   mine bebohte
frode feorhlege,   fremmað gena   2800
leoda þearfe;   ne mæg ic her leng wesan.
Hatað heaðomære   hlæw gewyrcean
beorhtne æfter bæle   æt brimes nosan;

188

The hoard, the old work of the giants in the barrow;
He heaped up cups and plates on his lap   2775
Upon his choice; he also took the banner—
The brightest of beacons. His old lord's sword—
Its blade was of iron—earlier wounded
The one who had been the warden of the treasures
For a long time, who had brought the terror of flame   2780
Burning hot for the hoard, welling fiercely
In the middle of night, till he died a violent death.

    The messenger was in haste, eager to return,
Impelled by the treasures; anxiety oppressed him—
Whether he, bold in spirit, would find the prince   2785
Of the Weather-Geats drained out of strength still alive
In that place where earlier he had left him.
He then found the renowned prince, his lord
Besmeared in blood, along with the treasures,
At the end of his life. He again began to   2790
Sprinkle water on him, till bits of words
Burst out through his breast. [The hero-king spoke,]*
An old man in grief—casting his eyes on the gold—:
"I thank the Lord of all, the King of glory,
The eternal Lord, in my own words,   2795
For the treasures that I gaze on here,
For my having been allowed to obtain such
For my people, before I breathe my last breath.
Now I have exhausted my life in old age
For the hoard of treasures, you further attend to   2800
The need of my people; I cannot be here long.
Bid the battle-glorious men to build a burial mound,
A splendid one, after the pyre, on a sea promontory;

se scel to gemyndum   minum leodum

heah hlifian   on Hronesnæsse,   2805

þæt hit sæliðend   syððan hatan

Biowulfes biorh,   ða ðe brentingas

ofer floda genipu   feorran drifað."

   Dyde him of healse   hring gyldenne

þioden þristhydig,   þegne gesealde,   2810

geongum garwigan,   goldfahne helm,

beah ond byrnan,   het hyne brucan well:

"Þu eart endelaf   usses cynnes,

Wægmundinga;   ealle wyrd forsweop

mine magas   to metodsceafte,   2815

eorlas on elne;   ic him æfter sceal."

   Þæt wæs þam gomelan   gingæste word

breostgehygdum,   ær he bæl cure,

hate heaðowylmas;   him of hræðre gewat

sawol secean   soðfæstra dom.   2820

(XXXIX) Ða wæs gegongen   guman unfrodum

earfoðlice,   þæt he on eorðan geseah

þone leofestan   lifes æt ende

bleate gebæran.   Bona swylce læg,

egeslic eorðdraca   ealdre bereafod,   2825

bealwe gebæded.   Beahhordum leng

wyrm wohbogen   wealdan ne moste,

ac hine irenna   ecga fornamon,

hearde, heaðoscearpe*   homera lafe,

þæt se widfloga   wundum stille   2830

hreas on hrusan   hordærne neah.

Nalles æfter lyfte   lacende hwearf

middelnihtum,   maðmæhta wlonc

It is to tower high at the Whale's Headland,
As a memorial for my people,   2805
So that the sea-faring men afterwards may call it
Beowulf's tomb—those who will sail ships across
The mist of the flooding waves from afar."
        The brave-hearted prince took his golden ring
From his neck, and gave it to the thane,   2810
To the young spear-warrior, and his gold-adorned helmet,
Bracelet and battle-gear, and bade him to use them well:
"You are the last one in our family line,
The Wægmundings; Fate has swept off all
My kinsmen to the decree of destiny,   2815
All the earls valorous; I shall follow them."
        That was for the old man the last word he uttered,
Coming from his heart, before he took to the pyre,
Hot and hostile flame; his soul departed from his heart
To seek the glory of the truth-bound ones.   2820
(XXXIX) Then it came to pass to the young man
With all the pain, that he on earth had to watch
His dearest lord at the end of his life
Go away pitiably. His slayer was also lying,
The dreadful earth-dragon deprived of life,   2825
Overpowered by death. The twining serpent
Could not have control over the ring-hoard long,
For the swords' blades had taken him away,
The strong battle-sharp* leavings of hammers,
That the far-flier, quelled by his wounds,   2830
Had fallen on the earth near the treasure.
Never again did he move about, flying in the air
At midnight, glorying in his precious properties,

ansyn ywde,   ac he eorðan gefeoll

for ðæs hildfruman)   hondgeweorce.)   2835

Huru þæt on lande   lyt manna ðah

mægenagendra   mine gefræge,

þeah ðe he dæda gehwæs   (dyrstig)wære,

þæt he wið attorsceaðan   oreðe geræsde,

oððe hringsele)   hondum styrede,   2840

gif he wæccende   weard onfunde

buon on beorge.   Biowulfe wearð

dryhtmaðma dæl   deaðe forgolden;

hæfde æghwæðer   ende gefered

lænan lifes.   Næs ða lang to ðon,   2845

þæt ða hildlatan   holt ofgefan,

tydre treowlogan)   tyne ætsomne,

ða ne dorston ær   dareðum lacan

on hyra mandryhtnes   miclan þearfe;

ac hy scamiende   scyldas bæran,   2850

guðgewædu)   þær se gomela læg;

wlitan on Wilaf.   He gewergad sæt,

feðecempa   frean eaxlum neah,

wehte hyne wætre;   him wiht ne speow.

Ne meahte he on eorðan,   ðeah he uðe wel,   2855

on ðam frumgare)   feorh gehealdan,)

ne ðæs Wealdendes)   wiht oncirran;)

wolde dom)Godes   dædum rædan

gumena gehwylcum,   swa he nu gen dêð.

      Þa wæs æt ðam geongan   grim andswaru   2860

eðbegete   þam ðe ær his elne forleas.

Wiglaf maðelode,   Weohstanes sunu,

secg)sarigferð   —seah on unleofe—:

And show his shape, for he had fallen on the earth,
Thanks to the feat the warlord's hands performed.   2835
Indeed, according to what I have heard, no man
Of mighty achievements on earth, no matter how
Daring in all his deeds, did thrive in an attempt
To make a rush against the breath of the fatal foe
Or disrupt the hall of treasures with his hands,   2840
If he discovered the keeper dwelling in the barrow
Wake up. A share of the lordly treasures came
To be Beowulf's, to be paid for only by his death:
Each had reached the end of his journey, as a part
Of the fleeting life. Then it was not long before   2845
The wary watchers unfit for war left the wood,
The cowardly traitors, ten of them, all told,
Who had not dared before to fight with their spears
In the face of their liege lord's great need:
But they, feeling ashamed, bore their shields   2850
And battle-garments to where the old man lay,
And they looked on Wiglaf. Wearied out, he was sitting,
A fighter on foot, near the shoulders of his lord;
He tried to awaken him with water—all to no avail.
He could not on earth, though he wished so much,   2855
Keep hold of the strain of life in his liege lord,
Nor change anything already ordained by the Ruler:
God's decree would rule the deeds
For each of the men, as it now still does.
        Then one who had lost courage earlier was   2860
Bound to receive a grim answer from the young man.
Wiglaf spoke, son of Weohstan,
A grief-stricken man, looking on the unlovely ones:

"Þæt, la, mæg secgan   se ðe wyle soð specan,

þæt se mondryhten,   se eow ða maðmas geaf,   2865

eoredgeatwe,   þe ge þær on standað,

—þonne he on ealubence   oft gesealde

healsittendum   helm ond byrnan,

þeoden his þegnum,   swylce he þrydlicost

ower feor oððe neah   findan meahte—,   2870

þæt he genunga   guðgewædu

wraðe forwurpe,   ða hyne wig beget.

Nealles folccyning   fyrdgesteallum

gylpan þorfte;   hwæðre him God uðe,

sigora Waldend,   þæt he hyne sylfne gewræc   2875

ana mid ecge,   þa him wæs elnes þearf.

Ic him lifwraðe   lytle meahte

ætgifan æt guðe,   ond ongan swa þeah

ofer min gemet   mæges helpan;

symle wæs þy sæmra,   þonne ic sweorde drep   2880

ferhðgeniðlan,   fyr unswiðor

weoll of gewitte.   Wergendra to lyt

þrong ymbe þeoden,   þa hyne sio þrag becwom.

Nu* sceal sincþego   ond swyrdgifu,

eall eðelwyn   eowrum cynne,   2885

lufen alicgean;   londrihtes mot

þære mægburge   monna æghwylc

idel hweorfan,   syððan æðelingas

feorran gefricgean   fleam eowerne,

domleasan dæd.   Deað bið sella   2890

eorla gehwylcum   þonne edwitlif!"

(XL) Heht ða þæt heaðoweorc   to hagan biodan

up ofer ecgclif,   þær þæt eorlweorod

"Alas, he who will speak truth can say that
Our liege lord, who gave you the rings,   2865
The battle-gears that you there stand wearing,
When he at the ale-bench often bestowed on
Those sitting in the hall helmets and battle-shirts—
A prince to his thanes, such as he could find
Anywhere, far or near, the most splendid ones—   2870
That he had utterly wasted all the battle-gear,
To his vexation, when war came upon him.
The people's king had no cause to boast of
His comrades in arms; however, God granted him,
The Ruler of victories did, to avenge himself alone   2875
With his own sword, when his bravery was needed.
I could give him little aid at battle
To save his life, but nevertheless undertook to
Help my kinsman, though beyond my power.
When I struck the deadly foe with my sword,   2880
He grew ever the weaker: the fire pouring out from
His head grew less powerful. Few of the defenders
Rushed to where the prince was, when hardship befell him.
Now treasure-receiving and sword giving,
Indeed all the home-joy and comfort, shall cease   2885
For your people; each one of the men
Of your clan must move about deprived
Of land-right, when the noblemen happen to
Hear from afar of your flight, and of your
Inglorious behavior; for any man at arms,   2890
Death is to be preferred over life in disgrace!"
(XL) Then he bade that the martial feat be announced
Within the walls, up over the sea-cliff, where the warriors

morgenlongne dæg   modgiomor sæt,   *all morning*   *sad in heart*

bordhæbbende,   bega on wenum,   2895

endedogores   ond eftcymes   *coming again*

leofes monnes.   Lyt swigode

niwra spella   se ðe næs gerad,

ac he soðlice   sægde ofer ealle:

"Nu is wilgeofa   Wedra leoda,   2900

dryhten Geata   deaðbedde fæst,   *laid on deathbed*

wunað wælreste   wyrmes dædum.

Him on efn ligeð   ealdorgewinna   *deadly enemy*

sexbennum* seoc;   sweorde ne meahte

on ðam aglæcean   ænige þinga   *monster*   2905

wunde gewyrcean.   Wiglaf siteð

ofer Biowulfe,   byre Wihstanes,   *son / descendant*

eorl ofer oðrum   unlifigendum,   *no longer alive*

healdeð higemæðum   heafodwearde   *chief guardian*

leofes ond laðes.   Nu ys leodum wen   2910

orleghwile,   syððan underne

Froncum ond Frysum   fyll cyninges

wide weorðeð.   Wæs sio wroht scepen

heard wið Hugas,   syððan Higelac cwom

faran flotherge   on Fresna land,   *a naval force*   2915

þær hyne Hetware   hilde genægdon,   *battle*

elne geeodon   mid ofermægene,   *overwhelmed*

þæt se byrnwiga   bugan sceolde,   *leader in war-gear*

feoll on feðan;   nalles frætwe geaf

ealdor dugoðe.   Us wæs a syððan   2920

Merewioningas   milts ungyfeðe.   *denied us kindness*

    "Ne ic te Sweoðeode   sibbe oððe treowe   *good faith*

wihte ne wene,   ac wæs wide cuð,

Sat in band, sad in heart, all the morning-tide,

Those shield-bearers, ready to hear one or the other—   2895

That it was their dear lord's last day, or that

He was returning. He who rode up to the headland

Told new tidings without sparing his voice.

He truthfully said for all to hear:

"Now the giver of joy to the people of the Weathers,   2900

The lord of the Geats, is fast bound to his death-bed;

He occupies a death-couch, quelled by the dragon.

Beside him lies his deadly opponent for life,

Stricken by dagger-wounds; he could not inflict

Any injury with his sword in any way   2905

Upon the ferocious fiend. Wiglaf sits,

Son of Weohstan, and guards over Beowulf,

One warrior over another no longer alive;

Wearied in heart, he holds watch over the heads

Of his beloved and the loathed. Now the people   2910

May look forward to a time of war, for the fall

Of our king will be widely known to the Franks

And to the Frisians. A fierce feud was fostered

Against the Hugas* when Hygelac went, faring

With his ship-borne force, to the land of the Frisians;   2915

There the Hetware* made an assault on him in battle,

Swiftly brought it about with a stronger force

That the warrior* in battle-gear had to bow down,

And fell in the foot-band; the prince could not bestow

Treasures on his retainers.* Since that time   2920

The Merovingian* has denied goodwill to us.*

     "Nor do I expect from the people of Sweden

Either peace or good faith at all, for it's widely known

þætte Ongenðio   ealdre besnyðede

Hæðcen Hreþling   wið Hrefnawudu,   *(Ravenswood)*   2925

þa for onmedlan   ærest gesohton

Geata leode   Guð-Scilfingas.

Sona him se froda   fæder Ohtheres,   *(old / wise)*

eald ond egesfull,   ondslyht ageaf,   *(old + terrible)*

abreot brimwisan,   bryd ahredde,   *killed the sea-king   rescued the bride*   2930

gomela iomeowlan   golde berofene,   *bereft of gold*

Onelan modor   ond Ohtheres;

ond ða folgode   feorhgeniðlan,

oð ðæt hi oðeodon   earfoðlice

in Hrefnesholt   hlafordlease.   *to Ravensholt   leaderless*   2935

Besæt ða sinherge   sweorda lafe

wundum werge;   wean oft gehet   *weary with wounds*

earmre teohhe   ondlonge niht,

cwæð, he on mergenne   meces ecgum

getan wolde,   sum[e] on galgtreowum   2940

[fuglum] to gamene.   Frofor eft gelamp   *comfort*

sarigmodum   somod ærdæge,   *sad-hearted   at first light*

syððan hie Hygelaces   horn ond byman,   *horn + trumpet*

gealdor ongeaton,   þa se goda com   *incantation   perceived*

leoda dugoðe   on last faran.   2945

(XLI) Wæs sio swatswaðu   Sweona ond Geata,

wælræs weora   wide gesyne,

hu ða folc mid him   fæhðe towehton.

Gewat him ða se goda   mid his gædelingum,

frod felageomor   fæsten secean,   *old + sad*   2950

eorl Ongenþio   ufor oncirde;

hæfde Higelaces   hilde gefrunen,

wlonces wigcræft;   wiðres ne truwode,   *adorned w/ gold*

That Ongentheow deprived Hæthcyn,* son of Hrethel,

Of his life near the Wood of the Ravens, when   2925

The people of the Geats, owing to their arrogance,

First made an assault on the War-Scylfings.

Soon the aged and wise father of Ohthere,*

Old and formidable, gave a counter-blow in return,

Cut down the sea-king,* rescued his wife,   2930

An old woman of bygone days, deprived of gold,

Mother of Onela and of Ohthere;

And then he pursued his life-enemies

Till they escaped, barely saving their lives, to

The Holt of the Ravens, runaways deprived of their lord.   2935

Then with his massive force he beset those still alive,

Weary with wounds; he often vowed woe

To the wretched band till dawn dispersed the dark:

He said he would in the morning crush them

With swords' edges, hang some on gallows   2940

For the fowls to feast on. Comfort came again

To those sad in heart together with dawning,

When they heard Hygelac's horn and trumpet,

His sound, as the good man* came leading

A band of battle-ready men on the track they had left.   2945

(XLI) The trail of blood of the Swedes and the Geats,

The murderous meeting of men was clearly visible—

How the peoples stirred up feud between them.

Then the good man* went with his kinsmen,

Silver-haired and sad, to seek his stronghold;   2950

The earl Ongentheow moved higher up.

He had heard of the battle-force of Hygelac,

The proud man's power; he didn't count on counter-stroke,

þæt he sæmannum onsacan mihte,

heaðoliðendum hord forstandan, 2955

bearn ond bryde; beah eft þonan

eald under eorðweall. Þa wæs æht boden

Sweona leodum, segn Higelace[s]

freoðowong þone forð ofereodon,

syððan Hreðlingas to hagan þrungon. 2960

Þær wearð Ongenðiow ecgum sweorda,

blondenfexa, on bid wrecen,

þæt se þeodcyning ðafian sceolde

Eafores anne dom. Hyne yrringa

Wulf Wonreding wæpne geræhte, 2965

þæt him for swenge swat ædrum sprong

forð under fexe. Næs he forht swa ðeh,

gomela Scilfing, ac forgeald hraðe

wyrsan wrixle wælhlem þone,

syððan ðeodcyning þyder oncirde. 2970

Ne meahte se snella sunu Wonredes

ealdum ceorle ondslyht giofan,

ac he him on heafde helm ær gescer,

þæt he blode fah bugan sceolde,

feoll on foldan; næs he fæge þa git, 2975

ac he hyne gewyrpte, þeah ðe him wund hrine.

Let se hearda Higelaces þegn

bradne mece, þa his broðor læg,

ealdsweord eotonisc entiscne helm

brecan ofer bordweal; ða gebeah cyning, 2980

folces hyrde, wæs in feorh dropen.

Ða wæron monige, þe his mæg wriðon,

ricone arærdon, ða him gerymed wearð,

Believe that he could withstand the seamen,
Defend his hoard, children, and women against   2955
The sailing fighters; the old man turned back from there
To hide behind an earth-wall. Pursuit was then
Pushed on to the people of the Swedes, the banners of
Hygelac swept forth over the stronghold for refuge, as
Hrethel's force* pressed forward to the fortress.   2960
There Ongentheow, a gray-haired man,
Became driven to a halt at swords' edges,
That the people's king had to yield to the doom
Eofor alone assigned.* Wonred's son Wulf*
Struck him with his weapon without restraint,   2965
That blood spurted forth from veins after each stroke
To soak his hair. A Scylfing, though old, he was
Not afraid, nonetheless, but paid back quickly
With worse exchange for the deadly blow,
When, as king of a people, he turned thereto.   2970
The brave son of Wonred* could not give
A return blow to the old man, for the latter
Had earlier cut through the helmet on his head,
That he had to bow down, besmeared in blood,
Fall on the earth; he* was not fated to die yet,   2975
And he recovered, though his wound was deep.
The hardy thane of Hygelac,* when his brother fell,
Let his broad blade, the old sword forged by giants,
Break the helmet hardened by giants' hammers
Over the shield; then the king bowed down,   2980
Protector of a people, having his life struck to the core.
Then there were many, who bound his brother's* wounds,
Raised him up rapidly, when it turned out that

þæt hie wælstowe   wealdan moston.

Þenden reafode   rinc ōðerne,   2985

nam on Ongenðio   irenbyrnan,

heard swyrd hilted,   ond his helm somod;

hares hyrste   Higelace bær.

He ðam frætwum feng,   ond him fægre gehet

leana [mid] leodum,   ond gelæste swa;   2990

geald þone guðræs   Geata dryhten,

Hreðles eafora,   þa he to ham becom,

Iofore ond Wulfe   mid ofermaðmum,

sealde hiora gehwæðrum   hund þusenda

landes ond locenra beaga;   ne ðorfte him ða lean oðwitan   2995

mon on middangearde,   syððan hie ða mærða geslogon;

ond ða Iofore forgeaf   angan dohtor,

hamweorðunge,   hyldo to wedde.

Þæt ys sio fæhðo   ond se feondscipe,

wælnið wera,   ðæs ðe ic wen hafo,   3000

þe us seceað to   Sweona leoda,

syððan hie gefricgeað   frean userne

ealdorleasne,   þone ðe ær geheold

wið hettendum   hord ond rice,

æfter hæleða hryre,   hwate scildwigan,   3005

folcred fremede,   oððe furður gen

eorlscipe efnde.   Nu is ofost betost,

þæt we þeodcyning   þær sceawian,

ond þone gebringan,   þe us beagas geaf,

on adfære.   Ne scel anes hwæt   3010

meltan mid þam modigan,   ac þær is maðma hord,

gold unrime   grimme gecea[po]d,

ond nu æt siðestan   sylfes feore

They could now take charge of the battlefield.

Then the fighting man forfeited from the other,   2985

Stripped off Ongentheow his steel-woven gear,

His hard-hilted sword, and his helmet, as well;

He bore the battle-gear of the hoary man to Hygelac.

He took the treasure and solemnly promised him

Rewards among the people, and kept his word: 2990

The lord of the Geats, son of Hrethel,

When he returned home, rewarded the battle-feat

Of Eofor and Wulf with sumptuous gifts,

And gave each of them a hundred-thousand [measurement]

Of land and linked rings—no cause to complain on the reward   2995

For any man on the earth, for they had attained the glory by merit.

And then to Eofor he gave his only daughter,

As a pledge of good will—honor to any family.

That is the malevolence and the mutual malice,

The deadly hate between men, for which I expect   3000

That the people of the Swedes will assault us,

When they learn that our lord is lifeless,

The man who has been a bulwark heretofore

Of our treasure and of our kingdom against enemies

After the fall of our heroes, the valiant shield-warriors,*   3005

And performed for people's benefit till further yet he

Fulfilled heroic deeds. Now what is best for us is haste,

That we may look at the people's king there

And bring him, who has given us rings, on the way

To his funeral pyre. Nor is a little portion to melt   3010

With the man of courage, but a mass of treasure is there,

Gold immeasurable, grimly gained,

And the rings bought now in the end

beagas gebohte;   þa sceall brond fretan,   *flanes shall devour them*

æled þeccean,   nalles eorl wegan   3015

maððum to gemyndum,)   ne mægð scyne   *commoration*

habban on healse)   hringweorðunge,   *on neck*   *torque*

ac sceal geomormod,   golde bereafod,

oft nalles æne   elland tredan,

nu se herewisa   hleahtor alegde,   *army leader*   *laughter silenced*   3020

gamen ond gleodream.   Forðon sceall gar wesan   *merriment + 'glee-joy'*

monig morgenceald   mundum bewunden,

hæfen on handa, |nalles hearpan sweg

wigend weccean,   ac se wonna hrefn

fus ofer fægum   fela reordian,   3025

earne secgan,   hu him æt æte speow,

þenden he wið wulf   wæl reafode."

    Swa se secg hwata   secggende wæs   *warrior*

laðra spella;   he ne leag fela   *story*

wyrda ne worda.   Weorod eall aras;   3030

eodon unbliðe)   under Earnanæs,   *sorrowful*

wollenteare   wundur sceawian.)   *look at the strange scene with hot tears*

Fundon ða on sande   sawulleasne

hlimbed healdan   þone þe him hringas geaf

ærran mælum; |þa wæs endedæg   3035

godum gegongen,   þæt se guðcyning,

Wedra þeoden   wundordeaðe sweolt.   *a marvellous death*

    Ær hi þær gesegan   syllicran wiht,

wyrm on wonge   wiðerræhtes þær

laðne licgean;   wæs se legdraca   3040

grimlic gryrefah)   gledum beswæled;   *terrible in its colours (SH)*

se wæs fiftiges   fotgemearces

lang on legere;   lyftwynne heold   *joy of the air*

With his own life. Flame shall swallow these,
Fire enfold—never a man shall wear 3015
A ring in remembrance, nor a fair maiden
Have round her neck a ring-adornment,
But shall, sad in heart, bereft of gold,
Tread on foreign land often, not just once,
Now our army-leader has laid aside his mirth, 3020
Joy, and merriment. Therefore, many a spear,
Cold in the morning, shall be gripped in palms,
Heaved by hands; never the sound of the harp
Will waken up the warriors, but a dark raven,
Ready to devour the doomed, will croak loudly, 3025
And report to the eagle how it has fared at the feast
While feeding upon the flesh with the wolf."
    Thus the valiant man took the pain of telling
The grievous tidings, nor did he say much falsely about
What would happen or what had happened. The whole band arose; 3030
They went, full of sorrow, under the Eagle's Bluff,*
To look on the wonder, with tears welling in their eyes.
Then they found him on the sand, soulless,
Reposing as if on a bed, who had given them rings
In bygone days; then the last day had come 3035
For the brave man, that the battle-king,
Prince of the Weathers, died a wondrous death.
    First they beheld there the creature more than strange,
The serpent lying loathsome at the site, side by side,
Facing him there. It was the fire-dragon, 3040
Terrifying in its varying colors, scorched by flame.
It was fifty-foot mark in full length as it lay
All stretched out; it had held the joy of

nihtes hwilum,   nyðer eft gewat

dennes niosian;   wæs ða deaðe fæst,   3045

hæfde eorðscrafa   ende genyttod. *earth-gallery (SH) enjoyment ended*

Him big stodan   bunan ond orcas,

discas lagon   ond dyre swyrd,

omige þurhetone,   swa hie wið eorðan fæðm *rusty*

þusend wintra   þær eardodon; *settled there*   3050

þonne wæs þæt yrfe   eacencræftig, *inheritance (?)*

iumonna gold   galdre bewunden, *wrapped in a spell*

þæt ðam hringsele   hrinan ne moste *ring-hall to reach*

gumena ænig,   nefne God sylfa, *no men except*

sigora Soðcyning   sealde þam ðe he wolde   3055

—he is manna gehyld—   hord openian, *mankind's keeper*

efne swa hwylcum manna,   swa him gemet ðuhte.

(XLII) Þa wæs gesyne,   þæt se sið ne ðah *plain*

þam ðe unrihte   inne gehydde *wrong/wickedness*

wræte under wealle.   Weard ær ofsloh   3060

feara sumne;   þa sio fæhð gewearð

gewrecen wraðlice.   Wundur hwar þonne *avenged*

eorl ellenrof   ende gefere *powerful*

lifgesceafta,   þonne leng ne mæg *life allotted*

mon mid his magum   meduseld buan. *dwell in mead hall* 3065

Swa wæs Biowulfe,   þa he biorges weard *mound guard (SH)*

sohte searoniðas;   seolfa ne cuðe,

þurh hwæt his worulde gedal   weorðan sceolde. *departure from world*

Swa hit oð domes dæg   diope benemdon *declared awful curse*

þeodnas mære,   þa ðæt þær dydon,   3070

þæt se secg wære   synnum scildig, *prisoner of own sins*

hergum geheaðerod,   hellbendum fæst, *fixed in bonds of hell*

wommum gewitnad,   se ðone wong strude, *evil/wicked*

Flight in the air at night, was wont to go down to
Nestle in its den. Then it was held fast by death,   3045
Had for the last time enjoyed its earth-caverns.
Beside it stood bowls and cups,
There lay plates and precious swords,
Eaten through by rust, the way they had remained
There in the earth's bosom for a thousand winters.   3050
Then that heritage immensely huge, gold of
The men of old, had been wound up by spell,
That any of men would not be allowed to
Reach the ring-hall, unless God himself,
The Truly-victorious King, as men's protection,   3055
Should grant him that He wished to open the hoard,
Even whoever of men as it seemed fit to Him.
(XLII) Then it was clear that the practice did not
Benefit him that had unjustly hidden the ornate works
Under the wall. The keeper at the outset had slain   3060
One, of the few he killed. Then the hostile act came
To be severely punished. It is a wonder where
A warrior excelling in bravery should reach the end
Of life allotted to him, when he may no longer
Dwell in the mead-hall, a man with his kinsfolk.   3065
So it was to Beowulf, when he sought strife with
The barrow's ward: he himself did not know
On what occasion his parting from the world should occur.
So the renowned princes, when they placed the treasure there,
Laid a deep curse on it to last till the day of doom—   3070
That he who plunders the place, would be guilty of sins,
Confined in heathen temples, fixed with the bonds of hell,
And tormented grievously—

næfne* goldhwæte   gearwor hæfde

Agendes est   ær gesceawod.   3075

    Wiglaf maðelode,   Wihstanes sunu:

"Oft sceall eorl monig   anes willan

wræc adreogan,   swa us geworden is.   *(all)*

Ne meahton we gelæran   leofne þeoden,

rices hyrde,   ræd ænigne,   3080

þæt he ne grette   goldweard þone,   *gold keeper*

lete hyne licgean,   þær he longe wæs,

wicum wunian   oð woruldende.

Heold on heahgesceap;   hord ys gesceawod,   *high destiny*

grimme gegongen;   wæs þæt gifeðe to swið,   3085

þe ðone þeodcyning   þyder ontyhte.   *urged / incited*

Ic wæs þær inne   ond þæt eall geondseh,

recedes geatwa,   þa me gerymed wæs,

nealles swæslice   sið alyfed

inn under eorðweall.   Ic on ofoste gefeng   3090

micle mid mundum   mægenbyrðenne

hordgestreona,   hider ut ætbær   *treasure hoard*

cyninge minum.   Cwico wæs þa gena,   *alive*

wis ond gewittig;   worn eall gespræc   *conscious*

gomol on gehðo,   ond eowic gretan het,   3095

bæd þæt ge geworhton   æfter wines dædum

in bælstede   beorh þone hêan,

micelne ond mærne,   swa he manna wæs

wigend weorðfullost   wide geond eorðan,   *worthiest warrior*

þenden he burhwelan   brucan moste.   3100

Uton nu efstan   oðre siðe,   *hurry*

seon ond secean   searogimma geþræc,   *precious gems*

wundur under wealle,   ic eow wisige,

Unless he, desirous of the gold, had readily perceived

The good grace that the Owner had bestowed on him.*   3075

   Wiglaf spoke, son of Weohstan:

"Often due to one man's will many a man must

Endure misery, as it has happened to us.

We could not persuade our beloved prince,

Our kingdom's bulwark, by any counsel,   3080

That he not attack the keeper of gold,

Let it lie where it had long been,

Remain at its dwelling-place till the world's end.

He held on to his high destiny. The hoard has been seen,

Grimly begotten; the fate was too powerful   3085

That pushed the people's prince thereto.

I was in there and saw it all thoroughly,

The treasures in the hall, when I was granted access—

Far from being pleasant was the passage permitted

In under the earth-wall. In haste I grabbed   3090

In my hands a massive mighty load of

Hoarded treasures, and took them out to here

To my king. He was then still alive,

His mind and senses all alert. He spoke many things,

Grand old man in grief, and bade me to greet you—   3095

Ordered that you build at the site of the pyre

A mound mounting high in memory of your lord's deeds,

A monument big and well known, as he was of men

The worthiest warrior all throughout the world,

So long while he could enjoy the riches of his citadel.   3100

Let us now hasten for a second time to

Visit and view the pile of the precious ornate gems,

A wonder under the walls; I will guide you,

þæt ge genoge   neon sceawiað
beagas ond brad gold.   Sie sio bær gearo,   3105
ædre geæfned,   þonne we ut cymen,
ond þonne geferian   frean userne,
leofne mannan   þær he longe sceal
on ðæs Waldendes   wære geþolian."

    Het ða gebeodan   byre Wihstanes,   3110
hæle hildedior   hæleða monegum,
boldagendra,   þæt hie bælwudu
feorran feredon,   folcagende,   *ruling*
godum togenes: "Nu sceal gled fretan
—weaxan wonna leg—   wigena strengel,   *chief of warriors*   3115
þone ðe oft gebad   isernscure,
þonne stræla storm   strengum gebæded   *arrow storm*
scoc ofer scildweall,   sceft nytte heold,   *quiver/flutter*
feðergearwum fus   flane fulleode."   *feather-fleced*
    Huru se snotra   sunu Wihstanes   *wise*   3120
acigde of corðre   cyni[n]ges þegnas
syfone [æt]somne,*   þa selestan,
eode eahta sum   under inwithrof   *god-cursed/evil roof*
hilderinca;   sum on handa bær
æledleoman,   se ðe on orde geong.   3125
Næs ða on hlytme,   hwa þæt hord strude,   *cast of lots*   *loot*
syððan orwearde   ænigne dæl   *unguarded*
secgas gesegon   on sele wunian,
læne licgan;   lyt ænig mearn,
þæt hi ofostlic[e]   ut geferedon   3130
dyre maðmas;   dracan ec scufun,
wyrm ofer weallclif,   leton weg niman,   *take/seize*
flod fæðmian   frætwa hyrde.   *treasure minder* (SH)

That you may look on the rings and broad gold,

Plenty of them, right there. Let the palanquin be ready,   3105

Prepared speedily, by the time we come out,

And then let us carry our lord,

Our beloved man, to where he shall long

Repose in the Ruler's protection."

  Then the son of Weohstan, man brave in battle,   3110

Bade to give orders to many of the warriors,

Of those who owned halls, that they, leaders of people,

Bring wood for the funeral pyre from far off,

For the brave man: "Now shall the fire swallow—

As flame grows dark—the chief of the warriors,   3115

Who has lived through the shower of iron, when

The storm of arrows impelled by bowstrings

Swished over the shield-wall, shaft fulfilling its task,

Busy with its feather-gear, an aid to the arrowhead."

  Indeed, the wise son of Weohstan   3120

Called forth from the troop thanes of the king,

Seven of them altogether,* the very best of them.

One of the eight warriors, he went under

Their enemy's roof; one of them bore in his hand

A torch—he who walked ahead of the others.   3125

Then who should plunder the hoard

Didn't need lot drawing, for men saw

Every part of it remain unwatched in the hall

And lie neglected. Little did any one grieve

That they had carried out in haste   3130

The precious treasures. They also pushed the dragon,

The serpent, over the wall-cliff, let the wave take it,

Let the flood engulf the keeper of the fair treasures.

Þa wæs wunden gold   on wæn hladen,   *loaded*

æghwæs unrim,   æþeling boren,   *countless*   3135

har hilderinc   to Hronesnæsse.   *grey-haired warrior*

(XLIII) Him ða gegiredan   Geata leode   *Geat peoples*

ad on eorðan   unwaclicne,   *splendid*

helmum behongen,   hildebordum,   *war-shields*

beorhtum byrnum,   swa he bena wæs;   *bright battleshirts*   3140

alegdon ða tomiddes   mærne þeoden   *in the middle*

hæleð hiofende,   hlaford leofne.   *beloved lord*

Ongunnon þa on beorge   bælfyra mæst   *on mound*

wigend weccan;   wud[u]rec astah

sweart ofer swioðole,   swogende leg   3145

wope bewunden   —windblond gelæg—,

oð þæt he ða banhus   gebrocen hæfde   *body!*

hat on hreðre.   Higum unrote   *became sad*

modceare mændon,   mondryhtnes cwealm;   *grief*   *Lord's demise*

swylce giomorgyd   [Ge]at[isc] meowle*   3150

æfter Biowulfe   bundenheorde

song sorgcearig   sæde* geneahhe,   *mournful song*

þæt hio hyre hearmdagas   hearde ondrede,   *scared*

wælfylla worn,   wigendes* egesan,

hynðo ond hæftnyd.   Heofon rece swealg.   3155

    Geworhton ða   Wedra leode

hlæw on hliðe,   se wæs heah ond brad,

wægliðendum   wide gesyne,

ond betimbredon   on tyn dagum

beadurofes becn,   bronda lafe   *strong in battle's beacon*   3160

wealle beworhton,   swa hyt weorðlicost   *most worthy*

foresnotre men   findan mihton.

Hi on beorg dydon   beg ond siglu,   *torques + jewels*

Then was loaded on a wagon the twisted gold,

Countless things of all sorts; and the prince, 3135

The hoary warrior, was borne to the Whale's Headland.*

(XLIII) Then the people of the Geats made ready

A funeral pyre for him, a splendid one on the earth,

Hung round with helmets, battle-shields,

Bright battle-shirts, as he had bidden. 3140

Then they laid down in the middle their renowned prince,

Their beloved lord; the men did so, mourning.

Then the warriors began to kindle on the hill

The greatest of funeral fires. Wood-smoke arose,

Black over the fire; the roaring flame bellowed, 3145

Mingling with the weeping—the twirling wind died out—

Till it had burnt down the bone-wrapping body-flesh,

Hot in its heart. With their souls soaked in sadness,

They mourned the death of their lord, deep in their hearts.

So, grief-stricken, an old Geatish woman* sang 3150

A mournful song after Beowulf, with her tangled

Hair bound up, and said over and over again

That she dreaded the evil days ahead sorely,

Plenty of slaughters, terror of the invading troop, being

Demeaned and enslaved. Heaven swallowed the smoke. 3155

Then the people of the Weather-Geats built

A mound on the headland, which was high and broad,

To be seen by the seafarers far and wide;

And they built in ten days a monument to

The battle-brave one, and surrounded the ashes 3160

With a wall, the way the men most prudent

Would find it to be in a way most worthy.

They placed in the barrow rings and jewels,

BEOWULF IN PARALLEL TEXTS

eall swylce hyrsta,   swylce on horde ær
niðhedige men   genumen hæfdon;   3165
forleton eorla gestreon   eorðan healdan,
gold on greote,   þær hit nu gen lifað
eldum swa unnyt,   swa hit æror wæs.   *as useless to man*
   Þa ymbe hlæw riodan   hildedeore,   *champion in battle*
æþelinga bearn,   ealra twelfe,*   3170
woldon [ceare]* cwiðan,   ond kyning mænan,
wordgyd wrecan,   ond ymb wer sprecan;
eahtodan eorlscipe   ond his ellenweorc   *heroic deeds*
duguðum demdon,   swa hit gedefe bið,   *as is fitting*
þæt mon his winedryhten   wordum herge,   *dear lord*   3175
ferhðum freoge,   þonne he forð scile
of lichaman   læded weorðan.   *(soul)*
Swa begnornodon   Geata leode
hlafordes hryre,   heorðgeneatas;   *doubtfull*
cwædon þæt he wære   wyruldcyninga*   *of all kings upon earth*   3180
manna mildust   ond monðwærust,   *fair-minded (SH)*
leodum liðost   ond lofgeornost.   *keenest to win fame*

THE END

214

All such ornaments as from the hoard before
The men who were hostile-minded had taken.   3165
They let the earth hold the wealth of warriors,
Gold in the earth, where it now still stays,
As useless to men, the way it was before.
  Then the battle-brave ones rode round the mound—
Inheritors of noble blood, twelve all told—   3170
Uttering words of grief over loss of their lord
In a mournful dirge to commemorate their king.
They lauded his manliness, and spoke highly of
His brave deeds—as it befits a man
To praise his dear lord in words,   3175
While longing springs in his heart, when he
Is finally freed from the confinement of flesh.   (soul)
So the people of Geatland mourned the death
Of their lord, recalling the warmth of his hearth.
They said that, of all earthly kings, he was   3180
The gentlest of men, the most warm-hearted,
Kindest to his people, and most eager for fame.

Textual and Explanatory Notes

Lines 6–8: Fr. Klaeber's reading shows the following punctuation:

egsode eorl[as],   syððan ærest wearð

fēasceaft funden;   hē þæs frōfre gebād,

wēox under wolcnum   weorðmyndum þāh, (Klaeber, ll. 6–8)

Elliot Van Kirk Dobbie provides a different reading:

egsode eorlas.   Syððan ærest wearð

feasceaft funden,   he þæs frofre gebad,

weox under wolcnum,   weorðmyndum þah, (Dobbie, ll. 6–8)

My translation follows Dobbie's reading, in which a period/full stop follows the word "eorlas," thus making the ensuing word "Syððan" the beginning of a new sentence. This way, the emphasis is given to the fact that a helpless, deserted infant, a foundling, eventually became a mighty ruler. The sweeping breath felt in reading the phrases describing the rapid growth of Scyld Scefing justifies Dobbie's reading.

Line 15: "þæt" (Wyatt and Chambers); "þe" (Dobbie; also Klaeber).

Line 18: Here and in line 53 the name "Beowulf" appears in the manuscript; so does it in Klaeber's and Dobbie's editions. In this translation, however, I used the name "Beow" in referring to Scyld's son, to avoid confusion with Beowulf the Geat, the hero of the epic. Scholars explain the appearance of the name "Beowulf" at this early stage of the poem as the consequence of scribal mistake.

Line 63: Heatho-Scilfing ("War-Scilfing") refers to Onela, king of the Swedes, son of Ongentheow.

Line 84b: "āþum-swerian" (Wyatt and Chambers); "āþumswēoran" (Klaeber); "aþumsweorum" (Dobbie); "aþum swerian" (Zupitza).

Lines 82–85: The eventual destruction of Heorot in fire mentioned here has no relevance to the events covered in the poem. However, allusion to the feud between Ingeld the Heatho-Bard—husband of Freawaru, Hrothgar's daughter—and Hrothgar, which led to the burning down of the mead-hall, seems to denote the futility of all human aspirations and attainments— a unifying theme of Old English poetry. Beowulf, upon returning to his homeland after defeating Grendel at Heorot, mentions the role Freawaru would play as a possible peacemaker by getting married to Ingeld, in his report to Hygelac (ll. 2020–69).

Line 149b: "forðām [secgum] wearð," (Klaeber); "Forðam secgum wearð," (Dobbie); "forðam [syðþan] wearð" (Wyatt and Chambers).

Line 159a: "(ac se) æglǣca" (Klaeber); "[ac se] æglæca" (Dobbie); "[Atol] ǣlǣca" (Wyatt and Chambers).

Line 177: The "soul-slayer" refers to the devil, the antithesis of God. It is ironic that the Danes offered sacrifices at heathen temples, rather than at Christian churches, to be rid of Grendel, a descendant of Cain. The emphasis here is that the Danes were pagans, whose souls were not yet redeemed by belief in God. It is, however, an interesting anachronism that, throughout the poem, Hrothgar's words are filled with Christian thoughts.

Line 306a: "gūþmōd grimmon." (Klaeber); "guþmod grimmon." (Dobbie); "gūþmōdgum men." (Wyatt and Chambers).

Line 348: Wulfgar is an official at Hrothgar's court; the Wendlas (or Wendle) are inhabitants of Vendel in Uppland, Sweden, or inhabitants of Vendill in North Jutland.

Lines 373–75a: Hrethel's daughter married Ecgtheow and gave birth to Beowulf, which means that Hygelac, the third son of Hrethel and monarch of the Geats, is Beowulf's maternal uncle, as well as his liege-lord.

Lines 389b–90a: To fill in this obviously missing part in the MS, Klaeber supplemented the words within brackets: "[Þā tō dura ēode/ wīdcūð hæleð,]," which are put between "leodum" and "word"—the two words appearing in the MS consecutively, without any intervening words in between (cf. Zupitza). Wyatt and Chambers put the words within brackets: "[Þā wið duru healle / Wulfgār ēode,]." Dobbie simply left the space for the two hypothetical hemistiches blank, putting three asterisks to fill the gap. A translator will naturally feel inclined to honor Klaeber's supplementation in his translation, as I have done here.

Line 403b: "[heaþorinc ēode,]" (Klaeber); "[hyge-rōf ēode,]" (Wyatt and Chambers); Dobbie simply marked the illegible part with three asterisks. I follow Klaeber's reading.

Line 455: Weland is the blacksmith of the Norse gods. The name appears also in the opening line of *Deor* and in the second line of the fragmentary poem *Waldere.*

Lines 460–61: Heatholaf was a man of the Wylfings whom Ecgtheow slew; the Wylfings were a Germanic tribe.

Line 466b: "gi*nne* rīce," (Klaeber); "ginne rice," (Dobbie); "gimme-rīce" (Wyatt and Chambers). The reading by Klaeber and Dobbie means: "a spacious kingdom." The reading by Wyatt and Chambers means: "gem-rich," or "rich in jewels." What to choose is up to the reader.

Line 472: "he" refers to Ecgtheow, whose feud with the Wylfings Hrothgar settled by paying them *wergild.*

Line 506: Breca was the chief of the Brondings.

Line 516: "wylmum." (Dobbie); "wylm[um]." (Klaeber); "wylm[e]." (Wyatt and Chambers).

Line 519: The Heatho-Ræmas was a people in southern Norway.

Line 521: The Brondings is a tribal name.

Line 524: Breca was son of Beanstan.

Line 586: "[fela]" (Klaeber); "fela" (Dobbie); "[*geflites*]" (Wyatt and Chambers)

Line 590: Ecglaf ("Sword-leaving") was the father of Unferth.

Line 620: The Helmings were the clan to which Wealhtheow belonged.

Lines 718–19: The MS reads:

nǣfre hē on aldordagum   ǣr nē siþðan

heardran hæle,   healðegnas fand! (Klaeber, 718–19)

Both "hæle" and "healðegnas" are in the accusative form, the former in singular, and the latter in plural, in number. I prefer to take "healðegnas" as the direct object of the verb "fand," and "hæle" as the complement modifying "healðegnas." The two lines literally mean: "Never in [his] days of life, [neither] before nor since, he found the hall-thanes [to be] a harder luck." I wonder why some of the translators felt the need of adding the conjunction, "or" or "nor," which is not implied in the MS anyway.

Line 747: "ongean" (Dobbie); "ongēan" (Klaeber); "*tōgēan*[*es*]" (Wyatt and Chambers). Wyatt and Chambers note that "the change is metrically essential," but I still prefer to follow Zupitza's reading.

Line 758a: "se goda," (Dobbie); "se gōda," (Klaeber); "se mōd[g]a" (Wyatt and Chambers). The textual emendation by Wyatt and Chambers is for the sake of the [m]-alliteration.

Line 875: Sigemund ("Victory-hand") was the son of Wæls (l. 877), and uncle and father of Fitela (l. 879).

Line 901: Heremod ("Army-courage") was a king of the Danes.

Line 913: "He" refers to Beowulf.

Lines 874b–915: The life-story of Sigemund and that of Heremod, as narrated here, are quite contrasting: the former was a triumphant winner of his goal, and the latter was one whose career turned out disastrous, quite disillusioning for those who had harbored much hope for him. Why did the Beowulf-poet feel the urge to insert this digression? Surely, there must have been some motive lying behind this insertion of a digression in the course of telling Beowulf's triumphant achievement as an epic hero.

As retold by the Beowulf-poet, Sigemund, a hero in the Northern saga, Wæls, attained the height of his martial glory by slaying a dragon that had been the warden of a treasure-hoard. His loyal companion throughout his martial adventures had been Fitela, his nephew (or son, since he was given birth by Sigemund's twin-sister, who had coaxed him to sleep with her); but in achieving the zenith of his martial feat, the slaying of the dragon, he was not aided by his young kin. In regard to this episode Bruce Mitchell and Fred C. Robinson make the following observation:

> A major discrepancy between Beowulf and other tellings of the story is that Sigemund seems to slay the dragon in *Beowulf*, whereas in all other versions his son Siegfried is the dragon-slayer. But if we take *wīges heard* (l. 886) and *æþelinges bearn* (l. 888) as referring to Sigemund's (unnamed) son, then there is no discrepancy. (Mitchell and Robinson, eds. *Beowulf*, 77, note)

Mitchell and Robinson overlook that l. 889, which immediately follows, contains the clause: "ne wæs him Fitela mid" ("nor was Fitela with him"). The Old English name "Fitela" corresponds to "Sinfjotli," the name of the son of "Sigmundur" (Sigemund) given birth by his twin-sister, in the Old Norse Volsunga-saga (Jack, ed. *Beowulf*, 78, note). The emphasis here is that not even Fitela, who had been Sigemund's lifelong companion in all battles, was nearby, when the latter was slaying the dragon. Moreover, contextually speaking, there is no point in emphasizing that, not Sigemund, but his son (or nephew) did the dragon slaying, in a passage glorifying the martial feat of the former. In any case, Sigemund's slaying the dragon guarding a treasure-hoard foreshadows Beowulf's slaying the fire-spewing dragon toward the end of the epic.

The life-story of Heremod, taken to be a Danish king by the poet, is that of a total failure as the leader of a nation, one who had to refuge among his enemies, and finally got killed by them, despite the great expectations his people had harbored about him. The failure of Heremod as the leader of a nation, as briefly summed up in the passage, is to cast a contrast with that of Sigemund, and ultimately with that of Beowulf. Heremod is mentioned again later in the poem, in Hrothgar's speech to Beowulf (1709b–22a).

Line 947a: Wyatt and Chambers think that, for metrical reasons, "secg" should be altered to "secga."

Line 949b: "[n]ænigra" (Wyatt and Chambers); "nænigra" (Dobbie); "[n]ænigre" (Klaeber).

Line 954a: "dǣdum gefremed," (Klaeber); "dǣdum gefremed" (Dobbie); "[mid] dǣdum gefremed," (Wyatt and Chambers). Wyatt and Chambers think that the meter demands "[mid]" before "dǣdum."

Line 976a: "in nyd-gripe" (Wyatt and Chambers); "in nīdgripe" (Klaeber); "mid nydgripe" (Dobbie).

Line 980: "the son of Ecglaf" is Unferth.

Line 985: "stīð[r]a" (Klaeber); "stiðra" (Dobbie); "steda" (Wyatt and Chambers).

Line 1009: "Healfdene's son" is Hrothgar.

Line 1015b: "māgas þāra" (Klaeber); "magas þara" (Dobbie); "māgas wāra[n]" (Wyatt and Chambers).

Line 1015: Hrothulf is the son of Halga, Hrothgar's younger brother.

Line 1022a: "hroden hildecumbor," (Klaeber); "hroden hildecumbor," (Dobbie); "hroden hilte-cumbor," (Wyatt and Chambers).

Line 1031b: "wala" (Klaeber; Wyatt and Chambers); "walu" (Dobbie).

Line 1043: Ing was a legendary king of Denmark; hence "Ing's kinsmen"— "Ingwina" (l. 1044)—means "the Danes."

Line 1055: "he" refers to Grendel.

Line 1064: "Healfdene's battle-leader" refers to Hrothgar.

Lines 1063–70: The transcriptions by Fr. Klaeber and by Elliott Van Kirk Dobbie are more or less identical:

Þær wæs sang ond swēg   samod ætgædere

fore Healfdenes   hildewīsan,

gomenwudu grēted,   gid oft wrecen,

ðonne healgamen   Hrōþgāres scop

æfter medobence   mænan scolde,

[be] Finnes eaferum,   ðā hīe se fær begeat,

hæleð Healf-Dena,   Hnæf Scyldinga

in Frēswæle   feallan scolde. (Klaeber)

Þær wæs sang ond sweg   samod ætgædere

fore Healfdenes   hildewisan,

gomenwudu greted,   gid oft wrecen,

ðonne healgamen   Hroþgares scop

æfter medobence   mænan scolde

be Finnes eaferum,   ða hie se fær begeat,

hæleð Healfdena,   Hnæf Scyldinga,

in Freswæle   feallan scolde. (Dobbie)

Dobbie's departure from Klaeber's text, besides his non-use of macrons, is minimal: omission of the comma after "scolde" (l. 1067), eliminating the brackets for the word "be" (l. 1068), changing the orthography of "Healf-Dena" to "Healfdena" (l. 1069), and adding a comma after "Scyldinga" (l. 1069). Despite the weight that the two authorities' readings carry with them, later scholars have expressed some doubts about the clarity of meaning in the transition from l. 1067 to l. 1068. Bruce Mitchell and Fred C. Robinson, for instance, read the two lines:

æfter medobence   mænan scolde:

Finnes eaferum   ðā hīe se fær begeat

(Mitchell and Robinson, *Beowulf: An Edition*, 83)

And they add in the footnote: "The syntax of [the half-line 'Finnes eaferum'] is dubious and something may be missing between ll. 1067 and 1068" (Mitchell and Robinson, *Beowulf: An Edition*, 83n).

George Jack's *Beowulf: A Student Edition* provides the following reading:

æfter medobence   mænan scolde

[be] Finnes eaferum.   Ðā hīe se fær begeat,

(Jack, *Beowulf: A Student Edition*, 90)

The numerous interpretations and surmises on what may have happened in the textual transmission notwithstanding, the most reasonable solution would be turning to the extant manuscript in hopes of making the most out of it. As a matter of fact, there is no need to seek any clue for connection between l. 1067 and l. 1068. Lines 1063–67 tell the listeners how a minstrel started reciting a tale; and the tale is told from l. 1068 to end with l. 1159a. Only a few words preceding what appears on l. 1068 are missing; and, as George Jack did, I believe a new sentence starts with "Ðā" (l. 1068).

Lines 1071–72: As the narrator's sympathy is with the Danish side, the Jutes are being blamed for the outbreak of the fray.

Line 1076: Hnæf, king of the Danes, visited his sister Hildeburh, who was queen of Finn the Jute. Hoc, former king of the Danes, was father of Hnæf and Hildeburh.

Line 1079: "heo" (Dobbie); "hē[o]" (Klaeber); "hē" (Wyatt and Chambers). The personal pronoun should allude to Hildeburh; therefore, Klaeber's emendation is justified.

Line 1083: Hengest led Hnæf's army after the latter's death.

Line 1085a: "þēodnes ðegne;" (Klaeber, Wyatt and Chambers); "þeodnes ðegna;" (Dobbie).

Line 1085: It is not clear which side first proffered truce; but in view of the predicament Finn was in, after losing most of his thanes, we can surmise that the Jutes were the ones who wanted a peace treaty. The phrase "the prince's thane" refers to Hengest.

Line 1089: "Folcwalda's son" refers to Finn.

Line 1106b: "seðan" (Klaeber); "seðan" (Dobbie); "syððan" (Wyatt and Chambers).

Line 1107: "Ad" (Dobbie); "Āð" (Klaeber); "Āð" (Wyatt and Chambers).

Lines 1108-9: "The best of the warriors of the Scyldings" refers to Hnæf.

Lines 1117: "ēame" (Klaeber); "eame" (Dobbie); "earme" (Wyatt and Chambers).

Line 1118: "The warrior" should refer to Hildeburh's son, rather than Hnæf. The word "ascended" ("āstāg" in OE) carries with it the connotation of ascending a throne. Although the word may simply mean being lifted up to be put on the pyre, Hildeburh's mourning cannot be only for bereavement: she also laments the death of one who could have become a king in time.

Line 1129a: "[ea]l unhlitme;" (Klaeber); "eal unhlitme." (Dobbie); "[e]l[ne] unhlitme;" (Wyatt and Chambers).

Line 1130a: "þēah þe hē [ne] meahte" (Wyatt and Chambers); "þeah þe he ne meahte" (Dobbie); "þēah þe ne meahte" (Klaeber).

Line 1141b: "īrne" (Klaeber); "inne" (Dobbie; Wyatt and Chambers). I follow Klaeber's reading.

Line 1142: There are two different readings of the off-verse:

(a) Swā hē ne forwyrnde   w[e]orodrædende, (Klaeber)

(b) Swa he ne forwyrnde   woroldrædenne, (Dobbie, Wyatt and Chambers)

If we follow Klaeber's reading, the line means: "So he did not refuse the ruler of the host." If we follow Dobbie's and Wyatt and Chambers', the line literally means: "So he did not refuse the world-law." Which one should we take? The most reasonable solution would be to turn to the MS. Julius Zupitza's transliteration of the line ("Swa he ne for-/wyrnde worold-rædenne") supports Dobbie's text. "The way of the world" can mean "the common practice," that is, revenging a kinsman's death.

Line 1143: The proper noun "Hūnlāfing" literally means "Hunlaf's son." From the context in which the word appears, one can surmise that Hunlaf was a Danish thane killed in the fight against the Jutes; and that his son, as a ceremonial gesture, placed his father's sword on Hengest's lap—either to pledge loyalty to the latter or to demand him to avenge his father's death. The word "his" refers to Hengest.

Line 1148: Guthlaf and Oslaf were probably thanes who had accompanied Hnæf in his voyage to Finnsburh.

Lines 1068–1159a: The recounting of the feud between the Danes and the Jutes, which is made here in a highly allusive manner, can be supplemented by the Old English poetic fragment, The Fight at Finnsburg, and be reconstructed as containing the following incidents:

Hnæf, ruler of the Danes and son of their former king Hoc, visited his sister Hildeburh, who was married to Finn of the Jutes, at Finnsburg, homestead of the Frisian (Jutish) royal family. Though the visit was meant to be a friendly one, an unhappy incident flared up a confrontation between the Danes and the Jutes that developed into bloodshed; and both Hnæf and his nephew—son of Finn and Hildeburh—were killed in the fray.

Having lost most of his retainers, Finn offered truce to Hengest, leader of the Danish band after Hnæf's death, promising to yield a hall for the Danes' use, and to treat them as benevolently as the Frisians on any occasion of ring-giving. Though it was hard for the Danes to be in friendly terms with the slayer of their own king, the Danes agreed on this precarious peace treaty. At the funeral of her brother Hnæf, Hildeburh ordered that her son's body be laid on the same pyre, and the cremation of the two kinsmen-turned-enemies was solemnized. Hengest and his band stayed with Finn through the wintry season, maintaining ostensible mutual affability, simply because the ferocious storms would not allow them to embark on a voyage homeward.

When spring came round, Hengest was ready for homeward journey, but ardor for vengeance for his slaughtered liege-lord Hnæf was boiling in his heart. Upon the instigation of his followers, Hengest finally slew Finn at his own dwelling, and took many of his treasures and his queen Hildeburh on their journey back to their homeland.

Line 1164: "nephew and uncle" allude to Hrothulf and Hrothgar, respectively.

The ensuing words—"then their friendship was still fair, Each true to the other"—make the reader recall a previous passage: "Heorot was within Filled with friends: in those days the Danes were Not prone to practice perfidy at all" (ll. 1017b–19). The implication is that Hrothulf, son of Hrothgar's younger brother Halga, later acted with disloyalty toward his uncle and liege-lord Hrothgar.

Lines 1167b–68a: What is said here reminds the reader of Beowulf's former accusation of Unferth as a killer of close kinsmen: "Though you became the killer of your own brothers, Your close kinsmen; for that you will in hell endure damnation, though your brain may be bright" (ll. 587–89).

Line 1187: "For the sake of [our] pleasure and [his] honor."

Lines 1197–1201: Both Hama and Eormenric are names mentioned a few times in Widsith, and the latter appears again in Deor. But the contexts in which they appear in these shorter poems are too obscure to throw light on what these few lines are about. Probably the Anglo-Saxon audience was familiar with the tale of Hama and Eormenric, about whom a matching tale may be found in a Northern saga:

Heimir [Hama] was a retainer of Thithrekr [Theodoric], nephew to Erminrekr [Eormenric], to whom also he had alleged loyalty. When Erminrekr banished Thithrekr, Heimir rebelled against the former, and led the life of an outlaw, intent on harassing him by stealing his treasures and killing his followers. Having spent two full decades as a drifter, Heimir, aggrieved of his wasted life, entered a monastery, bequeathing all he had to the sanctuary for his future refuge. (Cf. Jack, *Beowulf: A Student Edition*, 100, note.)

The "necklace of the Brosings" is known to have been worn by the goddess Freya (or Freyja), and been stolen by Loki, according to a Northern saga. The Beowulf-poet makes Hama the one who took the necklace from Eormenric's hoard. (Cf. Jack, *Beowulf: A Student Edition*, 101, note.)

The phrase "an eternal benefit" (l. 1201) may allude to Hama's retreat into a sanctuary for his soul's rest.

Line 1202: The word "nefa" (l. 1203 in MS) can mean either "nephew" or a "grandson."

Lines 1202–10: Later in the poem (ll. 2172–76) Beowulf presents the necklace to Hygd, Hygelac's queen, after his return to his homeland. Here it is said that Hygelac was wearing it during his assault on the Frisians; and upon his death it fell into the possession of the Franks.

Lines 1282b–87: As the poem progresses, we realize that Grendel's mother was a much more fearsome opponent for Beowulf than Grendel. By saying that those sleeping at Heorot, though terrorized by the sudden assault of Grendel's mother, underestimated her ferocity as a formidable assailant on account of her sex, the poet makes the horror they had to face later even greater. A touch of twisted understatement!

Line 1285: "geþrūen," (Klaeber); "geþrūen" (Wyatt and Chambers); "geþuren," (Ms., Dobbie).

Line 1303: "The well-known hand" is that of Grendel.

Line 1319: "the friends of Ing" are the Danes.

Line 1320: "nēodlaðu[m]" (Klaeber); "neodlaðum" (Dobbie); "nēod-laðu" (Wyatt and Chamers).

Lines 1343b–44: The MS reads: "nū sēo hand ligeð/ sē þe ēow wēlhwylcra wilna dohte" ("now the hand lies [low]/ That treated you well with all the good things").

Scholars have taken "the hand" as that of Æschere—under the supposition that Hrothgar laments that, now that Æschere is dead, the latter can no longer provide the help he used to while alive. Thus, Donaldson's prose translation reads: "Now the hand lies lifeless that was strong in support of all your desires." And George Jack, in his note, remarks: "Although the antecedent of sē þe 'which' is the feminine noun hand (1343), the reference is to Æschere; this is probably why the masculine pronoun sē has been used" (Jack, *Beowulf: A Student Edition*, 108, note).

I strongly object to the above reading. The preceding lines read: "As it may appear to many a thane,/ Who weeps in his heart for his treasure-giver,/ A hard heart-bale;" ("þæs þe þincean mæg   þegne monegum,/ sē þe æfter sincgyfan   on sefan grēoteþ,— / hreþerbealo hearde;") (ll. 1341–43a). The point is that Hrothgar's thanes feel at a loss in the presence of his inability to find a solution. "The hand [that] lies low," which used to treat the thanes well, is not Æschere's but *Hrothgar's;* Hrothgar is lamenting his being helpless in spite of his favorite thane Æschere's death.

Line 1351: "onlicnes" in Klaeber, and Wyatt and Chambers; "onlicnæs" in Dobbie.

Lines 1371b–72a: The MS reads: "ær he in wille hafelan:" (Zupitza's transliteration). Klaeber read the two hemistichs: "ær hē in wille, hafelan [beorgan];" Dobbie emended them: "ær he in wille hafelan hydan." There is not much difference in meaning between "preserving one's head" (Klaeber) and "hiding one's head" (Dobbie). So we might provide the eclectic translation: "than plunge his head into the pool to save his life," as I have done.

Line 1379a: "fela sinnigne secg" (Zupitza); "<fela>-sinnigne secg;" (Wyatt and Chambers); "felasinnigne secg;" (Dobbie); "sinnigne secg;" (Klaeber).

Line 1382: "wundnum" in Klaeber and Dobbie; "wundini" in Wyatt and Chambers.

Line 1404b: "þær heo gegnum for" (Dobbie); "[*þær heo*] gegnum for" (Wyatt and Chambers); "[swa] gegnum for" (Klaeber). I followed Dobbie's reading.

Line 1408: "the offspring of noble princes" refers to Hrothgar.

Line 1456: "Hrothgar's court speaker" is Unferth.

Line 1465: "the son of Ecglaf" is Unferth.

Line 1508: "swā hē ne mihte   —nō hē þæs mōdig wæs—" (Klaeber)
"swa he ne mihte,   no he þæs modig wæs," (Dobbie)
"swā hē ne mihte nō   (hē þēah mōdig wæs)" (Wyatt and Chambers)

I prefer the reading by Wyatt and Chambers, though I would consider "nō" as the first word of the second hemistich.

Line 1660: "Hrunting" is the sword Unferth offered to Beowulf upon his venture into Grendel's mere. See line 1457.

Line 1682b: "ondsaca," (Dobbie, Wyatt and Chambers); "andsaca," (Klaeber).

Lines 1709b–10: Cf. ll. 898–915. See also the note on ll. 874b–915 above. Ecgwela must have been a forbear in the Danish royalty, probably even before Scyld Scefing, for Heremod is known to have been a predecessor of Scyld.

Line 1803a: "[scīma ofer sceadwa]" (Klaeber); "*[scīma æfter sceadwe]*" (Wyatt and Chambers); 3 asterisks (Dobbie).

Line 1808: "the son of Ecglaf" is Unferth.

Lines 1807–12: Hrunting was not of much help in his fight with Grendel's mother. (See ll. 1518–28.)

Line 1847: "the son of Hrethel" refers to Hygelac.

Line 1917: "He" refers to Beowulf.

Line 1926a: "hēa[h on] healle," (Klaeber); "heah in healle," (Dobbie); "hêa healle," (Zupitza, Wyatt and Chambers).

Line 1926: Hygd, daughter of Hæreth, is queen of Hygelac. The sudden introduction here of Hygd, followed by the long passage on a shrew-turned-good-wife, even as a digression, is rather out of place. For that reason, some scholars think that a possible scribal error may be an explanation: e.g., "The suddenness of her [Hygd's] introduction here is perhaps due to a faulty text" (Donaldson, *Beowulf*, 33, note). However, one must not forget that one of the characteristics of the poetic sub-genre "epic" is that the poet is at liberty to start telling anything that comes to his mind at any given moment. The preceding sentence was: "The building was imposing, the king majestic, Seated high in the hall." It is only natural for the minstrel to say a few words about the queen sitting next to Hygelac. So the minstrel utters a few words in the vein of complimenting her virtues—which leads to mentioning a case that can function as a foil to enhance the effect of what he has just said: the shrewish and virago-like behavior of another woman who also happened to be a queen-to-be.

Lines 1931b–32: A student will have to choose among the following readings of the MS done by the Beowulf-scholars:
  i) "Mōdþryðo wæg,/ fremu folces cwēn, firen' ondrysne;" (Klaeber, Jack)
  ii) "Mod Þryðo wæg,/ fremu folces cwen, firen ondrysne." (Dobbie)
  iii) "Mōd Þryðe [ne] wæg,/ fremu folces cwēn, firen ondrysne;" (Wyatt and Chambers)
  iv) "Mōd Þryðo wæg/ fremu folces cwēn, firen' ondrysne;" (Mitchell and Robinson)

The editors' rendering of the above into Modern English:
  i) "Modthrytho, an imperious queen of a people, committed terrible evil." (Jack, *Beowulf: A Student Edition*, 140, note)
  ii) "Thryth, the proud (?) queen of the people, showed arrogance, carried on terrible crime." (Dobbie, *Beowulf*, 215)
  iii) "She [Hygd], brave queen of the folk, had not the mood, the pride of Thryth. . . ." (Wyatt and Chambers, *Beowulf*, 94, note)
  iv) "The excellent queen of the people (Hygd) weighed the arrogance of Thryth. . . ." (Mitchell and Robinson, *Beowulf: An Edition*, 112, note)

The interpretation by Mitchell and Robinson is similar to Kemp Malone's:

> The good folk-queen [i.e., Hygd] had weighed the arrogance and terrible wickedness of Thryth. (*Modern Language Notes* 56.2 [1941] 356.)

It seems to me that the most feasible reading can be deduced from the context, after all. The preceding passage, in my translation, is:

Hygd was very young,

Wise and well-accomplished, though she, Hæreth's

Daughter, had spent few winters in the enclosure of

The fortress; she was not niggardly, though,

> Nor too sparing of gifts, of treasures, for the people
>
> Of the Geats. (1926b–31a)

The tenor of the above passage is praising Hygd as a magnanimous person, "fremu folces cwēn"—"good queen of the people"—(1932a), which is a phrase not applicable to a shrew that was to become the queen of Offa. I feel inclined to follow Malone's interpretation, as Mitchell and Robinson did, and my rendition of ll. 1931b–32 is:

> A good queen of the people,
>
> She kept in mind the temper of Thryth, her cruel deed:

Line 1934: "her lord" refers to her father, not her husband, because her shrewish behavior manifested itself only until she was married off to Offa as a peace-weaver.

Lines 1940b–43: These lines do not mean that Thryth persisted with her atrocity of punishing the guiltless even after becoming a queen. What is meant here is that her previous behavior was no longer compatible with her status as a queen after her marriage.

Line 1944: "Hemming's kinsman" refers to Offa, king of the Angles. Hemming was a forebear of Offa and his son Eomer.

Line 1954: "the prince of warriors" refers to Offa, to whom Thryth was married.

Lines 1944–62: A case of "the taming of the shrew": Thryth was married to Offa as a peace-maker; she was completely transformed after marrying Offa; she gave birth to Eomer, who was son of Offa and grandson of Garmund—all descending from Hemming.

Line 1968: Ongentheow was a Swedish king, whose story is told in Fitts XL and XLI (ll. 2922–98). Hygelac is called the slayer of Ongentheow, for the former led an expedition against the Scylfings (the Swedes), which resulted in the latter's death.

Line 1980: "Hæreth's daughter" is Hygd, queen of Hygelac.

Line 2001a: "(micel) gemēting," (Klaeber); "[micel] gemeting," (Dobbie); "[mære] gemēting," (Wyatt and Chambers).

Line 2025: "son of Froda" is Ingeld the Heatho-Bard, to whom Freawaru, daughter of Hrothgar, is betrothed.

Lines 2032–38: i.e., "When the Scyldings, at the wedding of Freawaru and Ingeld, carry the heirlooms that used to belong to the Heatho-Bards, the latter will feel indignant."

Line 2052: Withergyld was probably a leader of the Heatho-Bards in their confrontation with the Scyldings.

Line 2072: "heaven's jewel" is an allusion to the sun.

Line 2076: Hondscio: Grendel's first victim on the night of Beowulf's vigil at Heorot; since Beowulf readily mentions his name, he was probably a Geat, one of Beowulf's companions in the venture.

Line 2105: "gomela Scilding" (2105b) can mean either "the old Dane" or "an old Dane," depending on the context. If we choose the former, it refers to Hrothgar; if the latter, someone other than Hrothgar. But since the phrase "the great-hearted king" ("rūmheort cyning") appears soon (2110b), we may as well take it as alluding to Hrothgar. For that reason, I take "hildedēor" ("the battle-brave one") on l. 2107 as alluding to Hrothgar also.

Line 2158: Heorogar was Hrothgar's elder brother and the first son of Healfdene.

Line 2160: "he" stands for Heorogar.

Line 2161: Heoroweard was son of Heorogar, therefore, Hrothgar's nephew.

Lines 2179b–80a: "nealles druncne slōg heorðgenēatas" means: "[he] never slew drunken hearth-companions," rather than "Drunk, he slew no hearth-companions" (E. Talbot Donaldson's prose translation, *Beowulf*, 38), for "druncne" is a word in accusative-plural form.

Line 2191: Hrethel was Hygelac's father.

Line 2203: Heardred was Hygelac's son, who succeeded his father as king of the Geats. The occasion of his death is narrated later, in Fitt XXXIII (ll. 2379b–90).

Line 2206: Hereric was Hygd's brother, hence Heardred's maternal uncle.

Line 2212a: "heaum hofe" (Dobbie); "hēa(um) h(ǣþ)e" (Klaeber); "hēa[um hǣþe]" (Wyatt and Chambers).

Lines 2214b–20: The MS is in such a state of ruin that scholars have given diverse readings:

   i) Þær on innan gīong

nið[ð]a nāthwylc, (sē þe nē)h gefe(al)g

hæðnum horde, hond (wæge nam),

(sīd,) since fāh; nē hē þæt syððan (bemāð),

þ(ēah) ð(e hē) slæpende besyre(d wur)de

þēofes cræfte; þæt sīe ðīod (onfand),

b(ig)folc beorna, þæt hē gebolge(n) wæs. (Klaeber)

   ii) Þær on innan giong

niða nathwylc, se [ðe] n[e]h gefeng

hæðnum horde, hond [. . .],

since fahne. He þæt syððan [. . .],

þ[eah] ð[e he] slæpende besyre[d] wu[r]de

þeofes cræfte; þæt sie ðiod onf[and],

b[u]folc beorna, þæt he gebolge[n] wæs. (Dobbie)

   iii) Þær on innan gīong

niða nāt-hwylc : : : : : : h gefēng

hæðnum horde   hond :::::::::::

since fáhne   hē þæt syððan :::::

þ[ēah] ð[e hē] slæpende   besyre[d wur]de

þēofes cræfte;   þæt sīo ðīod [onfand]

[bū-]folc beorna   þæt hē gebolge[n] wæs. (Wyatt and Chambers)

       iv) Þær on innan gīong

niððā náthwylc   se þe nīde gefēng

hæðnum horde,   hond wæge nam,

smæte, since fáh;   ne hē syððan þáh

þēah ðe hē slæpende   besyred wurde

þēofes cræfte;   þæt sīe ðīod onfand

būfolc beorna   þæt hē gebolgen wæs. (Mitchell and Robinson)

       v) Þær on innan gīong

niða náthwylc,   sē [ðe] nēh gefēng

hæðnum horde,   hond [. . .]

since fáhne;   hē þæt syððan [. . .]

þ[ēa]h ð[e] h[ē] slæpende   besyre[d] wu[r]de

þēofes cræfte;   þæt sīe ðīod onf[an]d,

būfolc beorna,   þæt hē gebolgen wæs. (Jack)

Of these diverse readings, I feel inclined to follow Klaeber's, for it conveys a meaning clear and appropriate to the context. To put the passage piecemeal into modern English:

> Thereon went in a certain one of men, he who made his way near the heathen hoard; his hand took a large cup, a shining treasure. He could not keep it [the treasure] hidden afterwards, though he [the dragon], while sleeping, happened to be tricked by the thief's treachery. The people found out, the neighboring people did, that he [the dragon] was enraged.

The interpretation of 2217b by Wyatt and Chambers seems to be wrong: "nor did he [the dragon] afterwards conceal it," i.e., "he showed evident tokens of his anger" (Wyatt and Chambers, *Beowulf*, 110, note).

Mitchell and Robinson provide a slightly different reading for 2217b: "ne hē syððan þāh" ("nor did he prosper thereafter"), i.e., the thief did not gain much from his acquisition. Though slightly different from Klaeber's reading, it rings with a similar note.

Lines 2226b–31a: Since the MS is in such a state of ruin, I did not intend to put the lines into something that makes any sense.

Line 2252b: "[Ic] nāh hwā" (Wyatt and Chambers); "[Ic] nah hwa" (Dobbie); "Nāh, hwā" (Klaeber).

Line 2288: "he" refers to the dragon.

Line 2289: "he" refers to the thief.

Lines 2361–62: Cf. George Jack's comment on the lines:

> The lines have often been taken to mean that Beowulf swam from Frisia to the land of the Geats carrying thirty suits of armour; but *hildegeatwa* "battle-gear" is a general term which need not indicate armour specifically, and . . . the lines state simply that he possessed the battle-gear when he went towards the sea, not that he was carrying it when he plunged into the sea. The point of the lines is that Beowulf had defeated thirty adversaries before he left the battlefield on which his own lord, Hygelac, was slain. (Jack, *Beowulf: A Student Edition*, 165, note)

Line 2362b: "þā hē tō holme [st]āg." (Klaeber; Wyatt and Chambers); "þa he to holme [be]ag." (Dobbie). I prefer the former reading.

Line 2363: The Hetware was a Frankish tribe allied to the Frisians in their fight against the Geats.

Line 2367: The word "oferswam" literally means "swam over"; it can also figuratively mean "sailed across," not by physical swimming, but on a vessel.

Lines 2373–76: i.e., The Geats could not persuade Beowulf to be their king after Hygelac's death, for he would not bypass Heardred, son of Hygelac and legitimate heir to the throne.

Line 2380: "the sons of Ohthere" is an allusion to Eanmund and Eadgilds, whose right to the Swedish throne, after their father's death, was taken away by their usurping uncle, Onela, Ohthere's bother.

Line 2381: "the protector of the Scylfings" refers to Onela.

Line 2387: "the son of Ongentheow" refers to Onela.

Line 2394: "the son of Ohthere" refers to Eadgils.

Lines 2379b–96: The brief digression on the occasion of Heardred's death and Beowulf's revenge for his death follows this story line:

Ohthere succeeded his father Ongentheow as king of the Scylfings. Upon Ohthere's death his brother Onela seized the throne, thereby forcing Ohthere's sons, Eanmund and Eadgils, to take refuge at the court of Heardred. On account of the favor Heardred bestowed on the two princes put in exile, Onela attacked him; and in the ensuing battle both Heardred and Eanmund were killed. When his intended chastisement on Heardred for protecting Ohthere's sons was fulfilled, Onela returned to Sweden, leaving Geatland to be in the care of Beowulf. Beowulf looked after Eadgils, the surviving son of Ohthere, and helped him reclaim kingship of Sweden after slaying the usurper Onela.

Lines 2460b–61a: The MS reads: "sorhlēoð gæleð/ ān æfter ānum." George Jack (*Beowulf: A Student Edition*, 171, note) gave the following interpretation: "'he chants one song of grief after another' (rather than 'one man chants a song of grief for the other')." Singing one song after another? Hrethel's agony is that he has lost his firstborn, whom he hoped would succeed him in time as king of the Geats. Here we must detect why the poet repeats the same word, "ān" and "ānum": the mourner identifies himself with the one he mourns for.

Line 2466: "the warrior" refers to Hæthcyn, who accidentally killed his older brother Herebeald.

Line 2468b: "þē him *tō* sār belamp," (Klaeber); "þē him sīo sār belamp," (Wyatt and Chambers); "þe him swa sar belamp," (Dobbie). I prefer the first reading.

Line 2475: "the sons of Ongentheow" are Ohthere, who succeeded Ongentheow as king of the Scylfings, and Onela, who usurped the throne after Ohthere's death. See ll. 2379b–96 and the above note relevant to the lines.

Line 2477: Hreosnabeorh is a hill in Geatland.

Line 2483: Hæthcyn, Hrethel's second son, succeeded his father as king of the Geats, for Herebeald, Hrethel's firstborn, had been killed by an accident. Upon Hæthcyn's death in the battle with the Swedes, Hygelac, his younger brother, became the next king, who, as the ensuing passage indicates, avenged Hæthcyn's death by slaying Ongentheow. Ongentheow's death is narrated in Fitts XL and XLI (ll. 2922–98).

Line 2484: "one kinsman" refers to Hygelac.

Line 2485: "the other" refers to Hæthcyn.

Line 2486: Eofor was a Geatish man who slew Ongentheow.

Line 2488a: "hrēas [heoro]blāc" (Klaeber); "hreas hildeblac" (Dobbie); "hrēas [*hilde*-]blāc" (Wyatt and Chambers). So we must choose between "heoroblac" and "hildeblac." In either case, however, the word means "battle-pale" or "pale from battle."

Line 2488: "his" stands for "Eofor's."

Line 2491: "he" refers to Hygelac.

Line 2495: The Gifthas ("Gifðas") were an East Germanic tribe.

Line 2502: Dæghrefn ("Day-raven") was a warrior of the Hugas (the Franks), who slew Hygelac and came to be slain by Beowulf.

Line 2525a: "oferflēon" (Klaeber, Wyatt and Chambers); "forfleon" (Dobbie). I prefer the former reading.

Line 2604: Nothing is known about Ælfhere besides that he was Wiglaf's kinsman; but as Weohstan is introduced as being of Swedish stock (ll. 2602–3), he was probably one of the Scylfings who fought, as Weohstan did, for Onela in his assault on the Geats—an episode narrated previously (ll. 2379b–96) and in the passage that follows later (ll. 2611–19).

Line 2607: "The Wægmundings" is the appellation for the family to which Beowulf belonged. Later in the poem, Beowulf calls Wiglaf the last of the Wægmundings (ll. 2813–14); but it is not fully explained how Weohstan and Wiglaf, who had Swedish origin, could be of the Wægmundings of the Geats.

Lines 2611–19: Weohstan, fighting for Onela in the latter's assault on the Geats for protecting the two sons of Ohthere, his older brother, happened to slay Eanmund, Ohthere's older son, during the battle. Eanmund's battlegear, including his sword, was presented to Onela as the booty of Weohstan's victory over Eanmund. Onela, knowing that Weohstan had killed his own brother's son, bestowed the heirloom on Weohstan. (Cf. ll. 2379b–96 and the note on those lines above.)

Line 2620a: "[ðā]" appears in Klaeber, but not in Dobbie or Wyatt and Chambers.

Line 2680: Nægling is Beowulf's sword.

Line 2687a: The MS reads: "wæpen wundum heard" (Julius Zupitza's transliteration of the MS). Klaeber emended "wundum" to "wund[r]um"; Dobbie also read "wundrum" for "wundum"; but Mitchell and Robinson retained "wundum" (*Beowulf: An Edition*, 142). I also prefer to stay with "wundum": the idea is "a weapon hardened by the wounds it has inflicted in battle." Somehow "a weapon wonderfully hard" (to adopt "wundrum") sounds insipid.

Line 2792b: Klaeber supplemented within brackets the two words, "[Biorcyning spræc]," between "þurhbræc" (followed by a full stop) and "gomel"—the two words appearing with no intervening words in the MS. Wyatt and Chambers supplemented within brackets the two words, "[*Bīowulf reordode*,]." Dobbie's transcription shows three asterisks between "þurhbræc" (followed by a full stop) and "gomel." I follow Klaeber's textual emendation in my translation.

Line 2829a: "hearde heaðoscear*pe*" (Klaeber); "hearde, heaðoscearde" (Dobbie); "hearde, heaðo-scearde," (Wyatt and Chambers). Many editors follow Klaeber's reading, as I do.

Line 2884: "Nu" (Dobbie); "Nū" (Klaeber); "Hū" (Wyatt and Chambers). I prefer the reading by Dobbie and Klaeber.

Line 2904: "sexbennum" (Dobbie, Klaeber); "siex-bennum" (Wyatt and Chambers).

Line 2914: "The Hugas" is a name applied to the Franks.

Line 2916: "The Hetware" was a Frankish people on the lower Rhine.

Line 2918: "The warrior" refers to Hygelac.

Lines 2919b–20a: The MS reads: "nalles frætwe geaf ealdor dugoðe." Mitchell and Robinson think that the word "frætwe" specifically refers to "the golden torque which Wealhtheow gave to Beowulf . . . and which the poet says Hygelac lost to the Franks on this expedition . . ." (Mitchell and Robinson, *Beowulf: An Edition*, 150, note). To me, the clause—"the prince gave no treasure to his retainers"—simply means that Hygelac, on account of his untimely death, did not even have a chance to reward his retainers after the battle.

Line 2921: "The Merovingian" refers to a king of the Franks.

Lines 2910b–21: Hygelac's raid on the Franks and the Frisians and his subsequent death in the battle have already been narrated earlier in the poem (ll. 1202–14a and ll. 2354b–66).

Line 2924: Hæthcyn, who succeeded Hrethel as king of the Geats, upon invading Swedish territory, was defeated and killed by Ongentheow. After his death, his brother Hygelac arrived with reinforcements, and made successful counter-attack on Ongentheow, who lost his life in the battle. Hygelac succeeded Hæthcyn as king of the Geats.

Line 2928: Ohthere and Onela were sons of Ongentheow.

Line 2930: "the sea-king" refers to Hæthcyn, then king of the Geats.

Line 2930: "ahredde," (Dobbie); "āhredde," (Klaeber); "āheorde," (Wyatt and Chambers).

Line 2944: "the good man" refers to Hygelac.

Line 2949: "the good man" refers to Ongentheow.

Line 2960: "Hrethel's force" refers to the army led by Hygelac.

Lines 2963–64a: i.e., Ongentheow's fate was in the hand of Eofor.

Line 2964: Eofor and Wulf, Geatish warriors, were sons of Wonred. Hygelac made Eofor his son-in-law as a reward for slaying the Swedish king Ongentheow. (See ll. 2472–89 and ll. 2991–98.)

Line 2971: "son of Wonred" refers to Wulf.

Line 2975: "he" stands for Wulf.

Line 2977: "the hardy thane of Hygelac" refers to Eofor.

Line 2982: i.e., Wulf's

Line 2985: "the fighting man" refers to Eofor; "the other" refers to Ongentheow.

Line 3005: "scild*wigan*," (Klaeber); "Scildingas," (Dobbie; Wyatt and Chambers). I prefer the former reading, though the latter is what the manuscript bears. Here "the shield-warriors" are the Geats, not the Danes.

Line 3031: "the Eagle's Bluff" ("Earna-næs") is a promontory in the land of the Geats, near which Beowulf fought the dragon.

Line 3074a: "næ*f*ne goldhwæte" (Klaeber); "næs hē gold-hwæte" (Wyatt and Chambers); "næs ne goldhwæte" (Dobbie).

Lines 3074-75: Interpretation of the lines varies. One interpretation, to which I strongly object, is that made by Mitchell and Robinson, who explain the meaning of the lines: "Previously he [Beowulf] had not at all seen the gold-bestowing favour of God more clearly [i.e. God had never given Beowulf a greater treasure than this one]" (*Beowulf: An Edition*, 157, note). This is a wrong interpretation. What the lines emphasize is the time-honored doctrine that only those who are destined to receive God's special favor will come to possess the treasure; and, therefore, the injunction proclaimed by the princes who buried the treasure does not apply to one to whom God's grace has already been granted. This thought is in line with the Anglo-Saxons' attitude toward the issue of life and death in a battle: "Gæð a wyrd swa hio scel" (*Beowulf*, 454b).

Line 3122a: "syfone [æt]somne," (Wyatt and Chambers); "syfone [to] somne," (Klaeber; Dobbie). The latter reading is in accordance with Julius Zupitza's transliteration; but I somehow prefer the former, if for no other reason than that it rings better to my ears.

Line 3136: "The Whale's Headland" is a literal translation of "Hronesnæsse" in the original text.

Line 3150b: "(s)i*o* g(eō)mēowle" (Klaeber); "[s]īa g[eō-]mēowle" (Wyatt and Chambers); "[Ge]at[isc] meowle" (Dobbie). Of these different readings, I choose the last one, for the word "Geatish" rings loudly in my ears.

Line 3152b: "sæ*de*" (Klaeber); "s[w]iðe" (Dobbie); "sælðe" (Wyatt and Chambers). I follow Klaeber's reading.

Line 3154b: "werudes" (Dobbie); "(wīgen)des" (Klaeber); ": : : des" (Dobbie). I chose Klaeber's reading.

Line 3170b: "ealra twelfa," (Wyatt and Chambers); "ealra twelfe," (Dobbie; Klaeber).

Line 3171a: "woldon [ceare] cwīðan," (Dobbie; Wyatt and Chambers); "woldon (care) cwīðan," (Klaeber).

Line 3180b: "wyruld-cyning," (Wyatt and Chambers); "wyruldcyninga" (Dobbie); "wyruldcyning[a]" (Klaeber).

Genealogical Charts

The Danes, or the Scyldings:

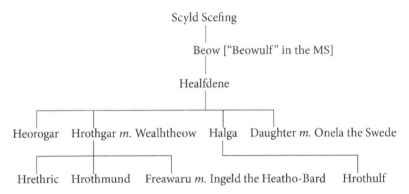

Scyld Scefing

Beow ["Beowulf" in the MS]

Healfdene

Heorogar   Hrothgar *m.* Wealhtheow   Halga   Daughter *m.* Onela the Swede

Hrethric   Hrothmund   Freawaru *m.* Ingeld the Heatho-Bard   Hrothulf

The Geats:

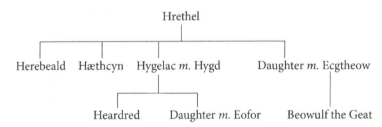

Hrethel

Herebeald   Hæthcyn   Hygelac *m.* Hygd   Daughter *m.* Ecgtheow

Heardred   Daughter *m.* Eofor   Beowulf the Geat

The Swedes:

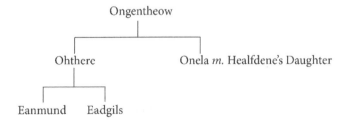

Ongentheow

Ohthere   Onela *m.* Healfdene's Daughter

Eanmund   Eadgils

Appendix

The Digressions in *Beowulf*

A reader of *Beowulf* finds it puzzling that the narrator occasionally shifts to an apparently extraneous episode that does not seem to bear much relevance to the main narrative in progress. It is an extra burden for the reader. One might ascribe it to literary convention, for interpolating digressions was a common practice in the composition of an epic. Compliance with literary convention, however, has to be justified by its contribution in intensifying the auditor's (or the reader's) absorption in the world of poetic imagination that evolves in an epic. The unexpected intrusion of passages that seem to have no direct relevance to the progress of the main narrative is thus bound to puzzle the reader, and may lead one to wonder whether it was really necessary for the poet to switch to a long digression at any given moment.

There are several digressions in *Beowulf*, and to argue that they indeed fit into the making of the poem is my task now—which is none other than trying to prove the validity of their presence. While translating *Beowulf*, I occasionally felt somewhat irritated whenever the progress of the main narrative was interrupted by the sudden switch to an apparently extraneous episode. Convincing the readers of *Beowulf* that these digressions are not irrelevant to the continuity of its epic narration, therefore, is what I undertake now. Unless each instance of digression proves to be a part contributing to effective buildup of the epic saga of Beowulf, one might conclude that, after all, it was a mere addition having no relevance to the progress of the main narrative.

To jump to my conclusion: I wish to assert that the digressions in *Beowulf* are important segments of the poem, which enhance its epic flow. To take a digression simply as manifestation of literary convention, or to regard it as mere addition, is doing injustice to this particular aspect in the artistry of *Beowulf*. By calling the reader's attention to how each digression does indeed fit into the progress of the narrative, I wish to demonstrate that it is not a redundant part we may as well do without, but an element that enriches the poem.

The first digression to appear in the poem (874b–915) is about the life-story of Sigemund, a hero in the Northern saga, and that of Heremod, a Danish king in the remote past. The two characters are mentioned, respectively representing success and failure, each as the ruler of a nation. This digression occurs in that part of the poem telling the festive occasion of celebrating Beowulf's victory over Grendel. A thane of Hrothgar, while entertaining the Danes and the Geats elated by Beowulf's triumphant success in vanquishing Grendel, recites the life-stories of Sigemund and Heremod—which do not seem to have any direct relevance to that occasion. How should we interpret the poet's intention in inserting these forty-some lines, which momentarily divert the auditor's attention to what lies outside the mainstream of the narrative?

The thane who was "endowed with eloquence . . . devised another tale with well-woven words: he in turn started to sing of the feat of Beowulf . . . and composed a tale successfully with his skills, with words set anew" (869–75a). Then the digression on the lives of Sigemund and Heremod follows. How should we relate the glory of Beowulf with the grandeur of Sigemund's life and the misery of Heremod's? The poet's intention is clear: it is to measure Beowulf's future life up against the two contrasting life-stories of Sigemund and Heremod. Heremod is mentioned again later in the poem, in Hrothgar's speech to Beowulf (1709b–22a), in which the former gives advice on becoming a successful ruler. What strikes the reader as somewhat significant in this digression is Sigemund's slaying the dragon guarding a treasure-hoard. It surely foreshadows, in retrospect, Beowulf's slaying the fire-spewing dragon toward the end of the poem. Perhaps the poet subconsciously wanted to make Beowulf's eventual death more poignant by telling the auditors of Sigemund's triumphant return with the hoard after slaying its warden.

It is quite possible that the poet inserted this digression (874b–915) and the passage (867b–74a) introducing it later, for if we skip the whole part (867b–915), the flow of the lines becomes smoother and it makes more sense in terms of the sequence of the events:

Now and again the battle-brave ones let their bay steeds

Gallop and run to compete with one another,

Where the foot-paths looked fair, not falling short of

Their fame as fine tracks. (864–67a) [Skip 867b–915]

At times, competing on horseback, they raced

On the sandy roads, when the morning light

Had approached and hastened. Many a retainer,

Firmly resolved, went to the high hall

To see the strange wonder; the king himself,

The guardian of the treasure-hoards with fame for virtues,

Also carried his steps in triumph from his conjugal quarter,

Attended by a large retinue; and his queen with him,

Followed by a train of waiting ladies, trod the path to the mead-hall.

　(916–24)

The thanes ride their horses in jubilee to Heorot to celebrate Beowulf's victory: that is the overall picture we get from reading these lines. More-over, the poetically endowed thane's recitation of a song extolling Beowulf's feat, and of other old tales, had to occur in Heorot—not during their horse riding. In the extant manuscript, Hrothgar's commendatory speech on Be-owulf's feat, and the latter's unvarnished report to the former on how he overcame Grendel, appear *after* the digression in question. It is logically appropriate, however, for any entertainment (such as a thane's recitation of old tales) to follow this formal exchange of words. For these obvious reasons, I suspect that the poet added the Sigemund-Heremod digression later, with the result that it causes confusion in the sequence of the events. Clearly, this digression was not part of the text the poet had initially com-posed, but a later addition.

The second digression (1068–1159a) is the recounting of a feud between the Danes and the Jutes, which is made here in a highly allusive manner, so much so that we need the supplementation of an Old English poetic fragment, The Fight at Finnsburg, to have a grasp of the storyline. Setting forth the story in detail may not be necessary here. Let it suffice to call to mind the backbone of the story—a friendly visit made in all good intention ending with a disastrous and tragic outcome:

> Hnæf the Dane pays a visit to his sister Hildeburh, queen of Finn the Jute. Quite unexpectedly, a fray breaks out between the Danes and the Jutes, and Hnæf and Finn's son are killed in the scuffle; thus Hideburh loses both her brother and her son. Her tragedy does not end there: her husband Finn also gets killed in time by Hnæf's thane Hengest, who, after temporary and precarious reconciliation with the Jutes, avenges his lord's death, and she herself is taken to the land of her birth as a captive on the Danes' journey back home.

The digression occurs in the middle of the passages depicting the banquet held to celebrate Beowulf's victory over Grendel. On this festive occasion, why the recitation of a gruesome tale of bloodshed between kinsfolk and breakup of a tie between two nations attained by marriage? When the digression is over, there follows Wealhtheow's addressing Hrothgar and Beowulf. In her wish-making speech to her husband (1169–87) she stresses her belief in a good bond between their sons and their nephew Hrothulf, son of Halga, in the future. And in her words of compliment to Beowulf (1216–31) she requests him to be a guardian for her sons. A few lines that precede her address to Hrothgar sound suggestive:

> Then forth came Wealhtheow,
>
> Wearing a golden diadem, to where the brave twain
>
> Sat, nephew and uncle; then their friendship was still fair,
>
> Each true to the other. (1162b–65a)

The implication is that Hrothulf, though apparently on good terms with his uncle Hrothgar now, may turn out disloyal to him. When Wealhtheow specifically mentions the love and care bestowed on Hrothulf by her and her husband, somehow it may be an indication of her concern about the possibility of Hrothulf becoming a threat to the Danish throne in time. A woman's premonition of what will happen later? It may be so. But, to get back to the question of the interpolation of the digression: the tragic outcome of Hnæf's visiting his sister Hildeburh (which he did in nothing but good intention) is proof enough that the present circumstance is no guarantee of a good turnout in the future. Thus, the digression fits into the context of the evolution of the narrative, foreshadowing Hrothulf's potential treachery, despite his present affability.

While the ring-giving to Beowulf goes on, the narrator inserts some lines (1197–1214a) that relate the transmission—which has happened before and will happen afterwards—of the precious items he receives. What is said in these eighteen lines sounds rather cryptic, but it certainly makes it clear that any treasure given to a man cannot remain his for long: the treasure exists by itself, and owning it does not mean that it belongs to its owner—for any precious item, on account of its rarity, is bound to move from hand to hand as time passes. The transitoriness of the glory of owning a treasure looms here as a thought that prevails the whole epic. Even the dragon's hoard that Beowulf comes to seize at the cost of his life cannot be his, or even the Geats': it all has to be buried along with his ashes, as being useless for men. What "the last survivor" utters (2247–66) reinforces the idea of the futility of attaching any meaning to owning a treasure. Thus, the cryptic words on the transmission—before and after—of the gifts bestowed on Beowulf take on a meaning not to be overlooked: the transience of all worldly possession or glory.

The futility of men's wish for retaining what they "own," or attaining a goal through arbitrary transaction, is repeatedly emphasized throughout the poem. Effort to rebuild good relation by creating marriage-ties between tribes or nations, for instance, will turn out futile. That is what Beowulf tells Hygelac in his report on his sojourn at Heorot (2020–69a). He predicts that Hrothgar's attempt to secure peace with Ingeld the Heatho-Bard, his hostile neighbor, by marrying off his daughter Freawaru to him, will be futile: Freawaru will not become a successful peace-weaver, as Hrothgar expects—not because of her inadequacy as a bride, but because of the inveterate hostilities in the Heatho-Bards. Though this is part of Beowulf's speech to Hygelac, it can very well be read as a digression revealing the poet's own thought on the inevitability of what *wyrd* dictates in the evolution of human affairs.

When the narration reaches the point where Beowulf, as old king of the Geats, prepares himself for his fight with the dragon, the narrator provides a retrospective account of the battles he has gone through. In this digression (2354b–96), the narrator tells the auditors a sequence of the past events that have occurred from the time when he was a loyal thane of Hygelac till he proved himself a most competent king—meting justice, even beyond his domain:

> Lines 2354b–79a: Beowulf fought in the battle against the Frisians, in which Hygelac died, and Wealhtheow's gift to Beowulf, which Hygelac was wearing, fell into the hands of the Franks. When Beowulf returned home lordless, having performed not a small martial feat in the war, Hygelac's queen Hygd asked Beowulf to take over the rule of the nation, for she didn't think her son Heardred was ready to inherit the throne; but Beowulf declined the queen's offer, and remained loyal to the young prince as his guardian till the latter grew into maturity.

The ensuing part of the digression tells us of the occasion of Heardred's death and of Beowulf's revenge of his death:

> Lines 2379b–96: When Eanmund and Eadgils, Ohthere's two sons, sought refuge at Heardred's court, fleeing from their uncle Onela, who had usurped the Swedish throne after his brother Ohthere's death, the Geats protected them well. In revenge for the favor that Heardred extended to Eanmund and Eadgils, Onela attacked the Geats, and in the battle Heardred and Eanmund died. Content with the deaths of the two men, Onela returned to Sweden, thus leaving the Geats without a ruler. Beowulf ascended the throne, took good care of Eadgils, and eventually helped the latter seize the Swedish throne after slaying Onela in revenge for the deaths of Heardred and Eanmund.

The above digression not only fits well into the progress of the narrative, but also provides strong momentum for the auditors to envision Beowulf's final fight with the dragon, in which he is to reach the end of his life. Moreover, the story of the feud between the Geats and the Swedes introduced here is carried over in other passages interpolated sparsely while the main narrative goes on, with the result that the auditors get the feeling that the intermittently appearing digressions on the feud constitute a storyline on its own, quite independent of the story of Beowulf's life—like a separate tune heard along with the main tune, creating beautiful harmony while the two crisscross each other.

In his recollection of his youthful days, Beowulf, who feels that the impending fight with the dragon will be his last battle, recounts the pain and sorrow of Hrethel over his eldest son Herebeald's accidental death from his second son Hæthcyn's bungling. According to the old law of vendetta, Hæthcyn should have been hanged for killing Hrethel's would-be heir, Herebeald; but Hrethel could not deprive another son of his life. Hrethel pined away, finally to lie on his deathbed (2435–71). What relevance does this "digression" have to the main narrative? Later, when Beowulf utters his dying words to Wiglaf, he regrets having no fleshly heir to inherit his battle-gear; but he bequeaths it to Wiglaf, the last of the Wægmundings, of which he is one. When Hrethel's grief over having lost his would-be heir Herebeald is put side by side with the absolute loneliness that Beowulf has to embrace as he encounters the dragon all by himself, the implication of the digression is clear: Beowulf stays far above the realm of the common worldlings, who attach much meaning to their fleshly ties. Nowhere in the poem do we find any mention of his conjugal life, which means that he was not meant to leave any offspring behind to succeed him, to carry on his bloodline. Beowulf's spiritual son Wiglaf would have said, "Take him for all in all, you shall not look upon his like again." Beowulf was not meant to have a biological heir; only the monument raised on the promontory to be seen from afar by the seafaring men was to make them recall that there once was a king of the Geats named Beowulf.

Having mentioned Hrethel's death, Beowulf (or, more accurately, the narrator, who is merely borrowing Beowulf's mouth in the ensuing part of the digression) tells how Hæthcyn, who succeeded Hrethel, died in a war against the Swedes (2472–83), and how Hygelac, who succeeded Hæthcyn, avenged his brother Hæthcyn's death by having Ongentheow the Swede slain in battle (2484–89). Hygelac's death in battle was mentioned earlier in the poem (2354b–79a), but in that preceding passage the narrator did not say anything about Beowulf's avenging his lord's death before returning home. Here we hear directly from Beowulf that his "fierce handgrip crushed [Dæghrefn's] pulsating heart—the flesh covering his bones" (2507–8), in revenge for his having slain Hygelac.

Why all this recounting of the deaths of the foregoing kings of the Geats? Earlier in the poem (2354b–96) the narrator told us how Beowulf declined Hygd's offer of the Geatish throne after her husband Hygelac's death, how he acted as a protégé for Hygelac's son Heardred till the latter grew into maturity, and also how he meted justice, after Heardred's death, even beyond the sea, by reinstating Eadgils as the legitimate heir of the Swedish throne. So far, all his life, Beowulf has been a bulwark of the Geats, both as a loyal thane and as a king. Now the time has come for him to conclude his life in a fight he must carry on in order to save his people. The recounting of the foregoing Geatish kings' deaths, and of what Beowulf has done so far, either as a thane or as a ruling monarch, prepares the auditors to hear his last pledge to confront the dragon all alone. Beowulf's resolution to face the dragon all by himself should not be taken as an indication of his hubris or megalomania: he knows that he will die in that battle, and also that he will somehow put an end to the devastation perpetrated by the dragon. A king caring for his hearth-companions, Beowulf does not want them to be exposed to the danger of physical harm, which they certainly will receive when they accompany him in the fight. In that sense, Beowulf, at this point of the narration, is a magnificent martyr-figure—the way Christ was.

The last digression in *Beowulf* appears in the herald's report to the Geats of Beowulf's demise and the dragon's death, toward the very end of the poem (2910b–3007a). It is about the feuds and the political entanglement that the Geats have had with their neighboring nations, and it ends with a pessimistic forecast of the fate of the Geats, now that Beowulf is gone. The long retrospective recounting of the feuds between the Geats and their neighboring nations—the Franks, the Frisians, and the Swedes—, in which the deaths of Hygelac and Ongentheow are mentioned, indeed sounds inappropriate to be part of the herald's message announcing Beowulf's death to the Geats. The whole digression reads like a later addition, rather than an outcome of the natural flow of verse-making. As a matter of fact, the herald's message would have more urgency and would be more moving, without this long recounting of the past events. If we skip the "digression" (2910b–3007a) as we read, the herald's speech sounds more natural. This digression, or insertion of past history, slackens the urgency of the herald's message, to be felt as we envision the Geats listening to the heart-breaking news of their lord's demise.

Then why does the last digression appear, which only blunts the edge of the immediate poignancy of Beowulf's death? The herald, a learned historian that he is—in view of his detailed recounting of the past history—simply does not sound like a mere bringer of the sad news of Beowulf's death while the digression continues. Surely, this last digression to appear in *Beowulf* could not have been part of the text the poet had initially composed. One might even venture to surmise that, as the poet wished to cast a bleak shadow of doom over the future fate of the Geats deprived of the protection of Beowulf as their guardian, he might have felt the urge to add this digression later, which feelingly asserts the inevitability of the impending national disaster.

So far, I have tried to re-read the "digressions" in *Beowulf* in hopes of embracing them as an integral part of the poem, which only enriches it at the cost of occasionally bewildering the auditors by their unexpected appearance in the course of the narrative. Whether they were a natural outgrowth of the verse-making the *Beowulf*-poet was engaged in while composing the poem, or later additions, is a question that cannot be answered with any certainty by posterity. These digressions should be taken as evidence of the poetic flourishes a creative artist wished to demonstrate as part of his mastery in the art of verse-making. Sometimes the digressions help to elevate the tenor of *Beowulf* as an epic; sometimes their presence leads the flow of the narrative into momentary bathos. We must remember, however, that in a work of art of grand scale, whether a landscape drawing for sweeping vision or a grand symphony encompassing the whole diapason of powerful notes, we see or hear the parts integral to its makeup, while certain parts look or sound not so much so, or occasionally out of the way, or overdone. Hence, each time the readers encounter a digression in *Beowulf*, it is up to them to decide which case it is.

𝔅𝔦𝔟𝔩𝔦𝔬𝔤𝔯𝔞𝔭𝔥𝔶

Dobbie, Elliott Van Kirk, ed. *The Anglo-Saxon Minor Poems.* The Anglo-Saxon Poetic Records, Vol. VI. New York: Columbia University Press, 1942.
———, ed. *Beowulf and Judith.* The Anglo-Saxon Poetic Records, Vol. IV. New York: Columbia University Press, 1953.
Donaldson, E. Talbot, tr. *Beowulf: A New Prose Translation.* London: Norton, 1966.
Jack, George, ed. *Beowulf: A Student Edition.* Oxford: Oxford University Press, 1995.
Klaeber, Fr., ed. *Beowulf and the Fight at Finnsburg.* 3rd ed. Lexington, MA: Heath, 1950; 4th ed. Re-edited by R. D. Fulk, Robert E. Bjork, and John D. Niles. Toronto: University of Toronto Press, 2008.
Krapp, George Philip, and Elliott Van Kirk Dobbie, eds. *The Exeter Book.* The Anglo-Saxon Poetic Records, Vol. III. New York: Columbia University Press, 1936.
Mitchell, Bruce, and Fred C. Robinson, eds. *Beowulf: An Edition with Relevant Shorter Texts.* Oxford: Blackwell, 2006.
Morgan, Edwin, tr. *Beowulf: A Verse Translation into Modern English.* Berkeley: University of California Press, 1952.
Wyatt, A. J., ed. *Beowulf with the Finnsburg Fragment.* New edition revised with Introduction and Notes by R. W. Chambers. Cambridge: Cambridge University Press, 1920.
Zupitza, Julius, ed. *Beowulf: Reproduced in Facsimile from the Unique Manuscript, British Museum MS. Cotton Vitellius A. XV with a Transliteration and Notes.* 2nd ed. Introduction and Notes by Norman Davis. Oxford: Oxford University Press, 1959.

Index of Proper Names in Beowulf

[The Arabic numerals indicate the lines where the proper nouns appear.]

2583, 2623, 2656, 2705, 2901, 2926,
2946, 2991, 3137; Sea-Geats, 1850,
1986; War-Geats, 1537; Weather-
Geat, 341; Weather-Geats, 498, 697,
1492, 1612, 2120, 2336, 2379, 2463,
2550, 2786, 3156
Geatland, 225, 362, 3178
Gifthas, 2495
Grendel, 102, 115, 127, 151, 195, 384,
409, 424, 474, 478, 483, 528, 591,
667, 678, 711, 819, 836, 927, 930,
1054, 1253, 1258, 1266, 1281, 1334,
1354, 1391, 1537, 1577, 1585, 1638,
1648, 1775, 1997, 2002, 2006, 2070,
2078, 2117, 2139, 2353, 2521
Guthlaf, 1148

Hæreth, 1927, 1980
Hæthcyn, 2434, 2437, 2483, 2924
Halga, 61, 1181
Hama, 1198
Healfdene, 57, 189, 267, 344, 467, 645,
1009, 1020, 1040, 1064, 1474, 1652,
1699, 1867, 2011, 2143, 2146
Heardred, 2203, 2203, 2375, 2377, 2380,
2384, 2388
Heatho-Bards, 2032, 2037, 2067
Heatholaf, 460
Heatho-Ræmas, 519
Heatho-Scilfing, 63
Helmings, 620
Hemming, 1944, 1961
Hengest, 1083, 1091, 1096, 1127
Heorogar, 61, 467, 2158
Heorot, 78, 166, 403, 432, 475, 497, 593,
766, 991, 1017, 1176, 1267, 1279,
1302, 1331, 1588, 1671, 1990, 2099
Heoroweard, 2161
Herebeald, 2434, 2464
Heremod, 901, 915, 1709
Hereric, 2206
Hetware, 2363, 2916
Hildeburh, 1071, 1114
Hnæf, 1069, 1114
Hoc, 1076
Hondscio, 2076
Hreosnabeorh, 2477

Hrethel, 374, 454, 1485, 1847, 1923,
2191, 2357, 2430, 2474, 2924, 2960,
2991
Hrethric, 1189, 1836
Hronesness, 2805
Hrothgar, 61, 64, 152, 234, 278, 335, 338,
356, 367, 371, 396, 407, 417, 456,
613, 653, 662, 717, 826, 863, 925,
1015, 1066, 1236, 1296, 1321, 1399,
1407, 1456, 1483, 1580, 1592, 1646,
1687, 1816, 1840, 1884, 1899, 1991,
2010, 2020, 2129, 2155, 2352
Hrothmund, 1189
Hrothulf, 1015, 1180
Hrunting, 1457, 1491, 1660, 1807
Hugas, 2914
Hunlaf, 1143
Hygd, 1926, 2174, 2369
Hygelac, 194, 261, 342, 407, 435, 452,
736, 758, 813, 914, 1202, 1483,
1529, 1574, 1820, 1830, 1923, 1971,
1983, 2000, 2151, 2169, 2201, 2355,
2372, 2386, 2434, 2914, 2943, 2952,
2959, 2977, 2988

Ing, 1043, 1319
Ingeld, 2065

Jutes, 902, 1088, 1141, 1145

Merovingian, 2921

Nægling, 2680

Offa, 1950, 1957
Ohthere, 2380, 2394, 2612, 2928, 2932
Onela, 62, 2616, 2932
Ongentheow, 1968, 2387, 2475, 2486,
2924, 2951, 2961, 2986
Oslaf, 1148

Scyld, 19, 26; Scyld Scefing, 4,
Scylding, 1791, 2105; Scyldings, 30, 351,
371, 427, 456, 500, 597, 663, 913,
1069, 1109, 1168, 1183, 1321, 1418,
1563, 1652, 1675, 1871, 2026, 2050,
2101, 2159; Honor-Scyldings, 464,
1710; Victory-Scyldings, 2004

Scylfing, 2487, 2967; Scylfings, 2203,
2381, 2603; War-Scylfings, 2204,
2927
Sigemund, 875, 884
Sweden, 2922
Swedes, 2383, 2472, 2496, 2958, 3001
Swerting, 1202

Thryth, 1932

Unferth, 499, 530, 1165, 1488

Wægmundings, 2607, 2814
Wæls, 877, 897
Wealhtheow, 612, 629, 664, 1162, 1215,
2173

Weathers, 2185, 2900, 3037
Weland, 455
Wendlas, 348
Weohstan, 2602, 2613, 2752, 2862, 2907,
3076, 3110, 3120
Wiglaf, 2602, 2631, 2745, 2852, 2862,
2906, 3076
Withergyld, 2052
Wonred, 2964, 2971
Wulf, 2964, 2993
Wulfgar, 348, 360
Wylfings, 461, 471

Yrmenlaf, 1324

About the Translator

Sung-Il Lee, born in 1943, studied English literature at Yonsei University (BA, 1967), the University of California, Davis (MA, 1973), and Texas Tech University (PhD, 1980). He taught at Yonsei University from 1981 untill he retired in 2009. While he was on leave of absence, he taught as a visiting professor at the University of Toronto (1987), the University of Washington (1994–95), and Troy State University (2002–3). He was one of the founding members of the Medieval English Studies Association of Korea (now the Medieval and Early Modern English Studies Association of Korea), and served as its president for 1996–98. He is now Professor Emeritus at Yonsei University.

He has translated Korean poetry, both modern and classical, into English, and has published six anthologies: *The Wind and the Waves: Four Modern Korean Poets* (1989), *The Moonlit Pond: Korean Classical Poems in Chinese* (1998), which was listed as an Outstanding Academic Book of 1998 by *Choice*, *The Brush and the Sword: Kasa, Korean Classical Poems in Prose* (2009), *Blue Stallion: Poems of Yu Chi-whan* (2011), *The Crane in the Clouds: Shijo, Korean Classical Poems in the Vernacular* (2013), and *The Vertex: Poems of Yi Yook-sa* (2014). His ongoing publication of Korean translations of Shakespearean and non-Shakespearean drama includes *Richard II* (2011), *Julius Caesar* (2011), *Richard III* (2012), *Othello* (2013), *Macbeth* (2014), *The Duchess of Malfi* (2012), and *Dr. Faustus* (2014). Twice a prize-winner in *The Korea Times* Modern Korean Literature Translation Contest, he received the Grand Prize in translation in the Republic of Korea Literary Awards (1990) and the Fourth Biennial Korean Literature Translation Award (1999), both given by the Korean Culture and Arts Foundation.

Printed in Great Britain
by Amazon

49110992R00170